Linda Smolkin

The Secret We Lost

A novel

Copyright © 2018 by Linda Smolkin.
All rights reserved.

Thank you for supporting the author by reading an authorized edition. No part of this book may be reproduced, scanned, or distributed in any form or uploaded and stored in any information retrieval system without written permission from the author.

ISBN 978-0-9986171-4-5 (paperback)

Cover design: AS Designs

Cover photo: Sweet Ice Cream Photography on Unsplash

Book layout: EbookLaunch.com

This is a work of fiction. Names, characters, businesses, places, organizations, events, and incidents portrayed in this novel are either a product of the author's imagination or used fictitiously, and they are not to be construed as real. Any resemblance to actual persons, living or dead, events or locales is entirely coincidental.

Chapter One

The Departure
Washington, DC: 1993

I never ate chocolate croissants for breakfast—at least not every day. But I was already working on my second one when the sticky note fell off the fridge.

Cup-a-Soup. Tampons. Woolite.

The list had to get my attention, as if there weren't already enough reminders. I hated packaged soups and no longer needed tampons. My skin never got along with Woolite, no matter how many times I tried.

I picked up the note and walked down the hall, stepping over books and winter hats lined up by my bedroom door. There, Laura stood, analyzing items covering every inch of my bed. I could sense her stress as she chewed on her lip and scrunched her eyebrows, making a crease in her forehead.

Ready to help, I put the note and croissant on the ceramic tray Laura made for me when she was seven. I'd always been the world's best packer. But this wasn't a normal trip. Or a normal day of packing. My daughter was leaving for Russia the next day and for that reason alone, I made sure to take a good, long look at her.

Wearing a striped cotton tank top and old faded jeans with holes on the knees, she still dressed like a teenager. For now, it was a look she could get away with. Sometimes I'd tell her to trade in those jeans for something nicer, and every time she'd say the same thing. *Mom, people pay an arm and a leg for new ones like these.*

I watched her gather up some sweaters and reminded myself she wasn't fifteen anymore and didn't need my advice or protection. What she needed was a change, an adventure. Or at least that's what she told me.

As Laura bent down for a pair of boots, her ponytail fell across her face. "I swear I'll never fit everything in here," she said, forcing the boot into her suitcase.

"Sure you will. Watch this," I replied and stuffed socks in every shoe and tampons into the boot.

Laura passed me a few more items, and I stopped for a moment, feeling a heavy weight come over me, one that Laura picked up on. She got up and sat next to me on the bed.

"Mom, I'll be fine."

Of course, she'd be fine. She'd always be fine. But I still worried enough for the both of us, and the thought made me reach for my chocolate croissant for a little comfort. My affair with croissants was a fairly monogamous one over the years with little competition. But as a child, I loved éclairs more. One Sunday every month, my father would take me to Marty's on 72nd Street, where the best éclairs in the world were sold and where we ate many.

Though tempted with all the cookies and cakes in the showcase, I ordered the same thing every time, devouring one, sometimes two éclairs. He'd laugh and watch me take every bite as whipped cream shot out the other end. His memory consoled and calmed me while I mentally prepared for my daughter's departure.

Laura scooped up some photos and looked through them. "So, you've changed your mind about visiting, right?"

"You're relentless," I joked. "Not until they figure out how to get rid of all that snow."

As I shivered thinking about the cold weather, my bedroom door opened slightly. A shadow appeared across my floor. The door opened farther and my mother Millie stood in full form as she held one hand on her hip and the other on the doorknob. At eighty-four, she still looked meticulous, with her hair dyed a blush wine and nails beautifully manicured with clear polish. Millie got dressed every day whether she left my apartment or not. She always wore the same button-down dresses she bought from Macy's, and on that day, she had on a perfectly pressed navy and white one with a thin leather belt that matched.

Even at just five foot even, my mother had the presence of a military leader. The kind who gave orders with ease. The kind you couldn't beat in a battle, even with reinforcement.

"*Oma,* tomorrow's the big day," Laura said as my mother stood in the doorway staring at the bed.

"What did you say?" she asked.

"Mother? Are you wearing your hearing aid?" I asked slowly, letting my frustration take over. "That's what we got it for."

She ignored my question or couldn't hear me, frustrating me even more. "I'm finished with the newspaper. Do you want it?" She paused, eyeing the mess on my bed again. "Do you need help?" she continued.

"Sure," Laura began as I interrupted and told my mother we were almost done.

Millie stared at me then hung her head and stepped back slowly. "I miss New York. *Ich will Michael sehen,*" she repeated twice before closing the door.

"Mom, she could have helped," Laura whispered.

"We're on a roll. And you don't want her messing up our piles."

"Piles?" Laura said, with her sarcasm easy to detect. "She's not gonna mess it up. You just don't want her in here."

Laura was right. I didn't want my mother in my room. It was the only place to get some peace and quiet—and privacy.

Laura picked up a sweater from the floor and began folding it. "She seemed so sad, like she wanted someone to talk to. And she mentioned her brother again. Do you think she wants to go back to New York where her friends are?"

"Friends? They're all gone. Her social activity was attending funerals."

"Mom!"

"It's true, and even if she wanted to go back, she can't live on her own anymore."

Laura didn't respond, getting distracted by a picture she found. "You and Dad made a cute couple. How old were you guys here?"

I smiled and took the photo after reaching for my glasses. "Twenty-three."

"Wow, you were young."

"Yep, young and in love," I said and tried not to think about all I'd lost.

Chapter Two

Laura put the photo of Max and me on the dresser, and we went back to packing. After making a wall out of chicken noodle soup, she sat on the bag. It took a few tries and some rearranging, but we managed to zip it up. She playfully yelled *success* and did a twist across my hardwood floor. I smiled but only for a second.

Parents were supposed to rejoice when their kids finished high school and began college, or when they moved away from home for a new, exciting job. But as proud as I was of Laura and her determination, it didn't feel all that great to be finished packing. It meant we were about to say good-bye for a long time.

She pulled the suitcase up and dragged it to the corner to share space with the other one half its size. Laura was thin for her five-foot-seven-inch frame, and she and her long legs could have been track and field stars. But instead of jumping over hurdles, she dove into books. She read during spare time, dinnertime, anytime, morning to night. When she was younger, I'd often catch her reading way past bedtime with a flashlight under the covers.

During college, she took Russian literature courses and got hooked. It was her dream, she said, to read Tolstoy and Dostoyevsky in Russian, sure that the English translation couldn't possibly compare to the richness of the original. Her fascination with Russia continued to grow. Upon graduating, Laura began meeting Russians so she could practice speaking and learn more about the culture. Soon after, she found out about a year-long teaching program in St. Petersburg. It took her two years and four tries to get accepted.

"Mom, why don't you relax, and I'll start prepping for tonight," she said and plopped down next to me on the bed.

"That's right, I almost forgot," I said and reached out to hug her close. "What are your friends going to do without you?"

"I'm going to miss them, for sure," Laura said and hugged me back.

I got up and reached for my furry slippers. "Do you think anyone will come for a visit?"

"Maybe Matt. Greg's pretty much allergic to anything colder than seventy."

"Same here. You'll stay bundled up, right?"

Laura placed her carry-on bag on top of the larger suitcase by the wall and came back over. "Not sure what's worse, you complaining about the weather, or all the worrying."

"Hello? I'm a Jewish mother. Worrying's in my blood." I looked up at her, almost staring through her, hoping to see her cautious side make an appearance. "Just be careful, okay?"

"Will you stop already?" she said with an air of independence while pacing the room. "I'm planning to travel as much as I can. And I really don't want to think about what could happen. If I did, I wouldn't be going. I'd still be working that same dead-beat job."

"Oh, you mean the job that gave you the opportunity to save money so you could go to Russia and work for peanuts?"

"You're right. Let's hear it for boredom and stability," Laura sang out as we walked to the kitchen to start prepping for her going-away party.

Laura opened the pantry and pulled out the chips and salsa then grabbed the cutting board to chop up the veggies. My galley kitchen made a tight fit, but it didn't bother me. It was a welcoming closeness on the last full day with my daughter as we slithered by each other to reach for cups, plates, and snacks.

"I'm sure a lot of people are envious about you going because they're afraid to do it themselves."

"I don't think they're afraid," Laura said. "I think they have too many responsibilities, like a mortgage and kids. In a way, it's pathetic that I don't have any of that. I guess if I did, I wouldn't have this opportunity."

"Sweetie, you're only twenty-five." I continued, "You have plenty of time to get married and have kids."

We set the food out on the table, and about an hour later, the doorbell rang. Gina, always the first to arrive, was followed by a few more friends who yelled out to hold the door as they ran down the hallway.

My mother came through the living room when she heard the commotion. She walked slowly, using her cane in one hand and holding her lower back with the other. Often when she thought I wasn't paying attention, she'd walked freely without any help. This time, Millie made her way to the kitchen slower than a driver stuck on the Beltway during a snowstorm. She poured a glass of water and passed by Laura's friends on the way to examine the dining room table. One of the pastries caught her eye. She stopped to examine the desserts and asked about it in her thick German accent.

"Try one. They're tasty," I said.

As she opened her mouth to take a bite, her original teeth made an appearance, stained by decades of coffee and tea. She'd been blessed, though, and at age eighty-four, she still had a full set with only a few fillings. "Blach. This is so dry. They should have used sour cream in the dough."

"My mother used to bake all the time. Laura, do you remember the cakes she made?"

She nodded. "I always asked for seconds."

Greg reached for a mini-éclair. "My grandma used to buy the mix and pretend she made them from scratch."

"How'd you know?" Gina asked.

"I used to hide my joints on the top shelf behind the mixes."

"Seriously?" Laura asked.

Greg smiled and wiped his mouth with a napkin. "I can't eat pound cake without thinking about it."

"Ah, the munchies. I kept our corner market in business for that reason alone," Gina said.

Everyone laughed except for my mother who still hadn't put in her hearing aid. After eyeing the food, she leaned over the table, wrapped two cookies in a napkin, and put them in her pocket.

"Mother, we have plenty of plates."

"This has dates? I love dates. They keep me regular."

I cringed out of embarrassment, for her, and looked around to see if anyone noticed the impairment that often came with aging. "Mother, here, take one."

Millie stared at me for a long time, as if she was trying to recognize a long-lost relative, before taking the plate. She passed by Laura's friends again and offered a hearty hello, working her way into the group.

"Mother, isn't *Wheel of Fortune* on?" I asked to get her to leave. A small part of me felt guilty, knowing it would be the last time in a long while before she'd see Laura again.

I took the cookies out of her pocket, unwrapped them, and put them on her empty plate. She said good-night and walked back to her room while hanging her head. *Ich mermisse Michael. Ich will Michael sehen,* she repeated several times.

"What did she say?" Matt asked.

"How she misses Michael and wants to see him," I said and bent over to pick up some crumbs that had fallen to the floor from my mother's cookies.

"Who's Michael?" Gina asked.

"It was her brother," Laura explained. "She says it when she gets upset."

"Why? What happened?"

"This isn't the time for sad stories," I said. "We'll talk about it another time."

"She's so sweet," Karen said, looking toward my mother, who waved as she turned the corner to her room.

Sweet? Maybe like a wild grape kind of sweet. Looks good on the outside, but don't expect the sweetness to last very long once you've taken a bite.

"So Laura, once you're gone, I don't think you'll miss the men in DC," Gina teased. "I've heard Russian men are hot."

"Mom, did you hear that? Maybe you'll change your mind and come for a visit?" she said and nudged me with her elbow.

"I'll pass, but if you find a rich one, bring him home, along with some amber jewelry."

Laura rolled her eyes at my failed attempt to make a joke. "Don't worry, I'll get your amber."

"One out of two's not bad," I replied and flung a napkin at her.

Greg caught it in mid-air and threw it back at me. "Yeah, and it won't leave dirty socks lying around."

"Or snore," Matt said and, after a good laugh and few more jokes, it hit me. In less than twenty-four hours, Laura would be gone and my place would be an empty space—even with my mother in it.

• • •

I began cleaning up while Laura said good-bye to Matt and Greg, the last ones to leave, the ones she'd known the longest. They were Laura's closest friends and had been together as a couple since she'd met them in college. Saying good-bye was difficult, and I'd say mine in the morning.

We took turns carrying plates into the kitchen and putting the leftovers in the fridge. Laura turned off the water with her wrist and pulled the rag off the stove's door. "If you stay really busy while I'm gone, time will fly by," she said while drying her hands.

Her words came out of nowhere. Did she notice the worry I tried to disguise all evening? "That's my plan," I said, knowing all along that staying busy would only help so much.

"I've mentioned it a thousand times," Laura added, "but thanks for letting me crash here. I know you think I'm crazy going there."

"It always takes a little craziness to follow your dreams," I said, remembering my own. Every child has one or two, as they get older.

One of mine started around age eleven. When most girls my age were playing with dolls, I was drawing. But not butterflies or flowers. I drew houses. Big brick houses. Tudor-style houses. Colonial houses, you name it. And, I drew the inside, with all the rooms, every detail, even designing wallpaper for each space. One night, my mother walked in, and I made the mistake of showing her my sketches.

She glanced at them and smiled—until I told her about my dream of becoming an architect. She snatched the pictures out of my hand and told me that would never happen, that her daughter would never become an architect because it was a man's job.

She'd already planned out my future, just as precise as the directions on a medicine bottle. I'd take typing and shorthand. I'd prepare for a secretarial career. And I'd find a husband. Right out of her mouth, in that order. Defying my mother never crossed my mind, but I still dreamed about architecture and continued drawing when she wasn't looking. My Aunt Regina, who lived with us, would pretend to be my customer, often requesting glorious estates with master suites, marble bathrooms, butlers' quarters, and guest houses.

That's why I could never tell Laura how I really felt—how I loved that she was following her dream but wished it wasn't five thousand miles away with an ocean between us. And as much as it hurt to see her move so far away, I'd never tell her it wasn't the smartest idea to quit her job and give up her steady salary. Instead, she'd have my blessing. But it didn't mean I'd stop worrying. Or stop missing her for even a second.

After we finished the dishes and said good-night, the TV kept me company with its addictive glow. It had been my bedroom companion for the longest time, pretty much since moving to DC.

"Mom, are you still awake?" Laura whispered after tapping on my door.

"Yes, sweetie, come in."

"Can I borrow your cleanser? Mine's packed in that bottomless pit called a suitcase."

"Sure, it's the one with the blue top."

Her baggy pajama pants dragged across the floor as she walked toward the bathroom. She turned on the light and fumbled in the cabinet.

As Laura washed her face, I flattened out my pillow and reached for a handful of M&M'S. A few fell on the floor. I picked them up, quickly examining for dust, or the five-second rule as we always called it, before popping them into my mouth, one after another.

"Aha! Caught you!" Laura teased when she walked out from the bathroom.

"Geez, you scared me to death. Want some?"

"Plain or peanut?"

"It's your lucky day. No need to choose," I said and opened my nightstand drawer to reveal two king-sized bags of both.

"So that's where you stash them," Laura said and glanced over at the TV. "Mom?" She paused and walked toward the door. "Never mind."

Was my daughter about to lecture me about staying busy to keep my worrying at bay?

"Never mind what? Just tell me."

"Do you want to see if there's a stupid movie on?"

I nodded and handed Laura the remote. She jumped on the bed and crawled to the other side, leaning over to grab the bag of M&M'S with one hand.

Chapter Three

Laura put the suitcases by the front door and took a good look around my apartment, not only to make sure nothing was left behind, but also to soak everything in. Even though she stayed with me for just three months, she'd be leaving her home of DC, where she'd lived since starting college.

Walking over to the window, she checked on her plants and made me promise I wouldn't kill them. That would be a hard one to keep for someone like me who could practically kill the plastic ones without even trying. She stared out on Wisconsin Avenue, as I'd done so many times. My ninth-floor corner apartment had huge wall-to-wall windows on both sides, and morning light always warmed the rooms as sun cascaded across the floor and onto my dining room table and sofa.

"Oh, I forgot to ask. Can I take this? I promise to bring it back." She held up my wedding picture, the one we looked at the day before. "Look how skinny Dad was."

"Me, too. Maybe I can build up some muscles carrying your luggage to the cab."

We tried to pick up the bags and decided pushing them to the elevator was a better idea. Between the books, boots, and endless supplies stuffed in every nook and cranny, the weight of the luggage became too much to bear.

Before we left, Laura spent a few minutes saying good-bye to my mother, who stood at her bedroom door. Millie held a tissue and dabbed her nose with the end and slipped some money in Laura's pocket. Laura bent down to give her a long hug and turned back to wave good-bye before we pushed the bags out of my apartment and down the hall. The elevators stopped twice, and we sent them on their way when each showed up full.

"You know," Laura said, "last night I was thinking about *Oma*, and why I feel sorry for her."

"Why? She's got a roof over her head, plenty of food, a warm bed. Feel sorry for me for having to put up with her," I replied.

Laura folded her arms and leaned against the elevator wall. "You're always so melodramatic. Seriously, I feel sorry for her because she's old. She's probably just living out these last days of her life, with nothing to look forward to."

The elevator door opened, and we rolled the bags to the curb. "When you're young," I said as our cab pulled up and the driver popped the trunk, "you don't know what lies ahead. When you're older, you're not afraid. You become used to the idea. Sometimes I think it's easier for people who've lived a good life."

Laura opened the door, and we slid into the back. "A good life has nothing to do with it. Either you're afraid of dying, or you're not."

"Maybe," I said and pulled on her ponytail, "but don't worry. Longevity runs in our family, so you'll have plenty of time to think about it."

We sat in silence, staring out the window. The driver took Rock Creek Parkway, a scenic route with its curved road, stone bridges, and a sea of bicyclists whizzing by between joggers. Before we knew it, we were out of the city and into Virginia, on our way to Dulles Airport.

I was so proud of Laura and all that she had accomplished at such a young age. By the time she was twenty-three, she had made a list she called *Before I Croak*, which was her bucket list with a twist. It included all the things she wanted to do by the time she turned forty. She had already crossed off half of them.

The trip to Russia was on it, but she wanted to wait until landing on Russian soil before checking it off. In her mind and on paper, she'd been planning this trip for a few years, determined to get a spot in the exchange program, even if she had to apply over and over again. She told me it wasn't meant to be yet, that she had a lot more to learn before she could appreciate the experience. To her, it wasn't just to travel around the world and say, "been there, done that." Laura wanted to come back with more than just photos. She wanted the experience. A connection to the people and country.

Laura was the adventurous type, a trait she inherited from her father. I'd never go to Russia—or anywhere outside the US, for that matter—to teach English for a year. I'd never quit my job and leave my family and friends behind for a foreign place, one so far away.

"Where ya going with such big suitcases?" our cabdriver asked.

"Russia," we responded in unison and looked at each other with a grin.

"You're brave going now. No more Soviet Union, but a lot of Mafia and crime. Everything has changed since the Curtain opened. Have fun, but be careful."

"See, I told you. Sounds like the Wild West to me," I said, thinking it should have been enough for Laura to read Russian books, watch Russian movies, and meet Russian people here instead of quitting a job and traipsing halfway around the world for peanuts.

"Mom, will you stop? Washington is practically the crime capital of the United States, so what's the difference?"

"There's no comparison. You'll be more vulnerable there. And people will take advantage of you if you're not careful."

"I'm street smart," Laura said. "And every Russian person I've met tells me that I look Slavic, so I'll just blend in with the crowd."

"What airline?" our cabbie asked as we approached the departure signs.

Laura pulled out her paperwork to double-check. "Delta, please."

"Wait a minute. I see your plane." I pointed toward the sky. "It's taking off as we speak—there it goes. What a shame."

Laura elbowed me as our driver stopped in front of the departure zone. Two attendants came to our rescue and lifted the bags onto the cart. While biting her nails, she watched them wheel the cart away. For the first time since packing, Laura had a worried look.

"I hope they don't lose my luggage."

"Everything can always be replaced," I said and rubbed her arm. "If you can't find it there, I'll send it to you."

"You never stress out over anything," Laura said, and we watched the attendant disappear as the automatic door opened and closed behind him.

"Not anymore," I added, remembering how my Aunt Regina always told me to lighten up, but it took a long time.

The terminal bustled with businessmen and their briefcases, families with their strollers, and summer groups headed back to school. Announcements of nearby cities like Chicago and faraway places of Beijing and Tokyo rang out from the intercom. As we approached security, Matt and Greg stood waiting.

"Oh my God! What the heck are you doing here?" Laura exclaimed as she threw her arms around them.

"We couldn't let you leave before one last good-bye," Matt said as he pulled her close for a long hug.

"Don't make me cry," I said.

Matt broke free and put his arm out, motioning me to join them. We huddled together like a team getting ready for their next play, the anticipation of not knowing the outcome but hoping it would all work out okay.

"Yeah, don't get too heavy on us," Laura said. "Unless you want us to shed some tears. And that won't be a pretty sight without my waterproof mascara."

I was laughing, but only on the outside, trying my best to hide my selfishness from those around me. It seemed so much easier a few months back when she made it official over the phone, when it hadn't quite sunk in yet, when I brushed her news off with a nervous giggle.

In two hours, my daughter will be gone for a year.
An entire year without seeing her.
How could I be ready for this?

With the two short hours to spare, it gave us enough time to make small talk yet not enough time to pretend I wanted her to leave. We walked to the airport café and grabbed a table. Matt brought back a tray filled with muffins and bagels. But I couldn't eat one bite.

Laura inched over to give Matt some room. She nibbled on a muffin and kept checking her watch, getting antsy and nervous at the same time.

Matt put his arm around her. "You're so lucky to have this experience. I loved Prague and always wanted to see Russia. There's something mysterious and romantic about it."

"Please," Greg blurted. "A bunch of people eating sacks of potatoes. Arctic temperatures, long lines, and that harsh language. What's so romantic about that?"

"It's cold, I'll give you that," Laura said. "But they're a lot more advanced in many ways. And they don't sit around eating potatoes all day."

"Don't worry, Greg." I winked. "I don't get it either, but she's all grown up now."

Our conversation was interrupted by the boarding announcement. We picked up our belongings and headed toward

17

the gate. Laura's first stop: Frankfurt, Germany—my father's birthplace and where he took his first steps. Soon my daughter would be there, even just for a layover, and the world felt small again.

"Well, this is it," Laura said as she went down the line to plant a kiss on everyone.

"Remember." I grabbed her hands. "Remember what I said. If you can't hack it, come home. Me and the pull-out sofa will still be here."

We hugged for a long time, and I couldn't let go. I didn't want to let go. As Laura walked away and handed her ticket to the gate attendant, she turned around and waved. Her ponytail danced from side to side as she walked down the passageway toward the plane. She always complained about her hair and how it flipped up naturally on the ends. I was glad her hair didn't lay flat and that it had a life of its own. It bounced and flipped as she left, and it made me smile.

Chapter Four

Greg darted ahead of me, only realizing it when he looked to both sides and didn't see me. Tangled between passengers rushing to their assigned luggage carousels, he turned around and stopped as I caught up. Matt had gone ahead to fetch the car and, when he pulled up by the curb, we climbed in. As they complained about the traffic backed up on the Beltway, I turned to the empty seat next to me. Laura was already on her way to escape from what she called a routine life to start a new adventure. She'd moved on and out so easily, something I couldn't relate to in my teens and early twenties.

As a Jewish girl with an Orthodox upbringing, I couldn't move out unless I found a Jewish husband. In those days, a girl couldn't just live on her own, or at least that's what my mother told me. "It's not respectable," she'd always say. The idea seemed believable at the time, but part of me thought she was more concerned about what the nosy neighbors would think.

So in a way, in a very good way, Max was my ticket out. It was a chance for a different life, one that made me feel like an adult, like a woman, and gave me a place of my own. And even though I loved my Aunt Regina, we had to share one of the two bedrooms. In our cramped apartment in Manhattan, privacy was an afterthought, a luxury we didn't have.

Before Max and I started dating seriously, the *yentas* at my parent's synagogue tried to set me up with a husband. They weren't particularly gracious with my refusals, especially when they thought they'd found me the perfect match. But I wanted to pick my own husband, or I wouldn't get married at all.

The two of us chose an apartment in the Bronx and, before moving in, we spent a few days making the apartment our own, giving it a facelift with a fresh coat of paint and a good cleaning. It was small, but cozy with two bedrooms and a galley kitchen. We'd seen a few more apartments and, while I dreamed of having a balcony off the living room, Max insisted on spending the money on an extra bedroom in hopes we'd start a family soon.

"So what do you think?" Max asked.

"You're talking about the walls, right?" I teased while looking at his freshly painted face and hair. He'd added a few extra highlights to his eyebrows and long sideburns to finish up the new look.

"Sweetheart, why don't you help me with a little touch-up?"

He moved toward me with the brush in the air and began chasing me around our apartment. While coming around the corner, I slipped on the sheet covering the carpet. Max crashed into me and down we went. He landed on top with the paintbrush sandwiched between our legs.

"I like this position," he said, catching his breath.

"When you get a chance, can you move the brush?"

"Sure! Which way? Up? Down? Sideways?" he teased and, while pretending to look for the brush, began tickling me.

I wiggled my way out and sat on top of him. "Now try getting out of this."

He lifted his shoulders off the floor and reached up to kiss me. "I don't think I want to."

"Why are you looking at me like that?" I asked.

"Like what?" he teased back.

I got up and took the compact mirror out of my purse. White paint had covered my nose and cheeks in a similar pattern as his. Instead of washing it off, I put the compact down and playfully went after him, grabbing a second brush around the turn and skidding across the tarp-covered floor to catch up.

A few weeks later, with our apartment ready and furnished, we packed up the last two suitcases from my parents' place. Max carried them out and, as we boarded the bus, I turned around to wave good-bye to my father and Aunt Regina. My father's face, disguised with a worn smile, stayed with me. He'd later tell me that he suffered from allergies, but we all knew the real reason. It was from holding back the tears. I'd miss seeing him and Aunt Regina every day but was glad to leave and get away from my mother, even just those few miles away in the Bronx. In that freshly painted apartment, I'd start my new life with Max.

Although Laura and I were very close, we didn't talk much about Max as she got older. I regretted it—and regretted not starting a family sooner. Our friends began right after they got married, and we decided to wait. Actually, I was the one who decided. Max wanted to start, but we were enjoying our time together. I didn't want to give that up, knowing once we had kids everything would change. And did it ever. But in a way nobody expected.

Soon after having Laura, Max was taken from me. From us. That small, cozy apartment with the extra bedroom, the apartment we grew to love, became a small box with belongings without him. Right after he passed, I covered the walls with his photos. I'd point at them and say *look, there's Daddy* and share memories with Laura, who was two at the time.

As she got older, the photos remained but the stories faded. Perhaps time grew more distant. Maybe life took over. The truth was I'd compartmentalized the memories and tucked them away so Laura wouldn't have to hear me blame my bloodshot eyes and red nose on allergies, like my dad had done years before.

At that time in the early '70s, life suffocated me with a strong weight on my shoulders. Max had died the year before, and I was raising Laura on my own. I tried to tackle life and be strong for her, even if it meant disguising my pain. Even if it meant working harder to provide for her. We needed more money coming in, and my job wasn't cutting it. I could only think of one solution: finding a new one. Besides, I'd wanted to get away from Mr. King, my horrible boss at the time, who thought yelling at me was part of the job description. My fear of change got the best of me, but I finally got up the courage to call Johnson Staffing, a recruiter for secretaries, to help me with my search for a new position.

A month later, they had a lead. They'd just received a call from an architectural firm looking for an assistant to one of the partners. Of course, it sounded perfect, with a dreamy location in Midtown right on Fifth Avenue. I'd always wanted to be an architect and imagined working there even before getting an interview, even without the architectural credentials behind my name or the building sketches in front of me.

We set an appointment for a few days later, and it took me about that long to decide what to wear. I settled on my navy jersey dress with its matching hat slanted to one side. Suntanned stockings outlined my legs and my three-inch black patent leather pumps pushed me to five-foot-five, the height I'd always dreamed of. I pulled on my gray wool coat, slipped my keys and gloves into my purse, and blew kisses to Laura as she sat with our babysitter.

At 2:30, the bus let me off at the corner of 62nd and Fifth and, with some time to spare, I walked over to Madison Avenue, where the IBM building and other skyscrapers towered over me. Designer clothing and jewelry stores lined the street. Glamorous women, with their fur coats and matching hats, strolled out of stores carrying bags from Bergdorf Goodman and small boutiques. I peeked into a jewelry store, tempted to go inside, just for fun, after spotting pearls, diamonds, and sapphires in the window display. Instead, I glanced at my watch and took a deep breath before crossing Madison over to Fifth and slipping through the building's circular entrance.

A "Chase and Associates" sign hung on a panel outside their nineteenth floor office. In the waiting area, two men sat on a dark-cherry sofa while flipping through architectural books. I ran my fingers over the lacquered mahogany table before walking over to the large, picture-frame window. It was hazy, but with such a view, I could still see skyscrapers and imagined the Hudson River behind them. Central Park unfolded in front of me and I dreamed of having lunch there when it warmed up while watching moms with strollers and bicyclists out on their adventures.

"Elsa, Mr. Chase is ready to see you," the receptionist said as she took my coat and led me to his office.

She knocked twice and then motioned for me to enter. A middle-aged man in a tobacco-colored suit swiveled around in his leather chair.

"You must be Mrs. Kartchner. How do you do?"

He stood up and extended his hand to greet me. His well-kept nails with their satin finish caught the light.

"Good afternoon, Mr. Chase. You have a lovely office."

"Please, call me Raymond. Would you like some coffee or tea?"

"No, thank you," I said and looked over at the orange velvet couch that sat in front of the beige wall. More architectural books, family photos, and mini architectural models lined the shelves next to the window.

We sat down and Mr. Chase described the position. He was looking for a Girl Friday: someone who could write correspondence, set up appointments, and be his assistant to keep him organized and on his toes. Within minutes, I knew I wanted the job.

"Elsa, you're very qualified," he said after we spoke for half an hour. "But I have a couple other girls to see from the agency, then I'll make a decision."

"Mr. Chase, I would love the opportunity to work here. I'd be willing to take half the salary for the first month to prove myself," I offered.

He smiled and looked down for a moment while trying to sort the phone messages on his desk. "No, no, that won't be necessary. You deserve every penny I'm offering, from day one. But out of respect for the others, I can't have an answer until tomorrow. You do understand?"

"Yes, of course," I said without showing my disappointment.

Mr. Chase took me to the reception area and held up my coat. I got one last look at the office and, after riding down in the elevator, walked a good ten blocks and onto Madison for the bus back to our Bronx apartment. I wanted my walk on Fifth to last. And not just one day for an interview. But five days a week. Luckily, my good vibes over the next few days paid off. Georgette from the agency called the following week and offered me the job.

Chapter Five

Back in the early '70s, I couldn't wait to start the job at Chase and Associates. My priority was raising Laura, but it seemed the perfect way to fill my life with something new after losing Max. I wish Max hadn't crossed so fast in the middle of the street, that he'd been more careful like me. But Max wasn't the careful type. Together, we always crossed at the light even though, on many occasions, he tried to get me to the other side faster. Sometimes he'd grab my hand and start walking across. I'd stop, pull away, and walk to the light to wait for it to turn green. Whenever that happened, he'd follow and wait with me.

I rehashed it in my head over and over again, year after year. The day he rushed out of the house and didn't look when he crossed our busy New York street. I especially thought about it when looking at Laura. They shared the same beautiful hazel eyes that changed color in the light. Sometimes brown, sometimes green, and sometimes they had a life of their own.

So many people said to me "the good always die young." They'd say it over and over, annoying me like the scratch on a favorite record. Others didn't know what to say. And then there was my mother, who told me he shouldn't have crossed in the middle of the street, in New York of all places. I knew that. My friends knew that. We all knew that even though we never dared to say it out loud. But my mother always spoke her mind, whether it hurt my feelings or not, whether it was the right thing to say.

I desperately wanted that job with Raymond Chase and thought it was a sign for a new year, a good year. Eventually, it would keep me busy and help me move on and stop thinking about the accident. I was ready to walk into that gorgeous office five days a week and escape, even if they wanted to call me Girl Friday, which seemed like a funny name to call an assistant who came in all week. Why not Girl Five Day or something that made more sense and matched the position?

For the entire bus ride on my first day, I recalled my interview—tapping my heels on the marble floor in the foyer, admiring every crystal vase, and soaking in the views from the window.

Introductions to the staff, client background, and company history took up the first few days. By the third week, it all became second nature, like I'd worked there for years and knew all the ins and outs regarding the clients and their projects.

One morning while typing away, I looked up to see Mr. Chase leaning against the wall with one hand in his pocket. He pulled out a pack of cigarettes and tapped it against his hand. I hit the return on the typewriter and handed him the client letter. We stood in silence as he read through it and, after a minute, he reached for a pen from my desk.

"This is good, just add my title at the bottom." Mr. Chase signed his name and continued. "So, when are you planning to move?" he asked and pointed to the alcove next to his office.

"I'm waiting for the desk to arrive. And the receptionist to recuperate from the flu."

"Don't get too comfortable." He smiled at me. "I need you to help me sort out my life!"

"It's fun up here. I get to answer the main lines and greet all the clients," I said and sat down to put the letter back in the typewriter.

"Oh no, we can't have you like your job too much," he joked. "Why don't you call Callahan's and double-check on the delivery date." He walked off and turned around before getting to the corner. "And while you're at it, price some credenzas. I'd like to see ones under $200."

• • •

The desk arrived the following Monday and Judy, the receptionist, returned. I moved to the back office and thought sooner or later Raymond's personality would change, thinking he was being overly nice and accommodating because I was still new. After several months, the Raymond I'd seen all along was the real deal. He never raised his voice, never once patronized me; he was always even-tempered, unlike my last boss, Mr. King.

I had a few names for him. But King wasn't one of them. "Call this person," he'd spit as he threw message slips on the floor even with my hand out to take them.

One day, King called me into his office to take shorthand and, as usual, kept me there while calling his numerous girlfriends, making me wait to complete his correspondence. He always propped his hairy feet on the desk, made snorting noises as he talked, and chewed on pen lids before spitting them out.

That particular day, his annoying and disgusting habits ate at me far too long. He slammed the phone receiver down, cleared his throat, and threw a piece of paper at me with a name and number.

"Call and make an appointment for this week," he said without looking at me.

I bent down to pick up the slip from the floor. "What time would you like to meet with him?"

He looked up at me with unsightly dark eyes, like raisins left out overnight in an open bag on the counter. "Why do you always ask me such stupid questions? You're the one with my damn calendar. Just take that smart little head of yours, look at the schedule, and set a time. Seems simple to me," he said as he threw the chewed-up pen on the desk. It ricocheted and hit my knee.

He continued talking without an apology. "And get me some more coffee; this tastes like mud."

The abuse, the yelling, the horrible habits, the pitiful belittling: it all overwhelmed me. I didn't deserve this. Nobody did. Speechless, I walked to the kitchen and heated up water for his coffee, making sure it was piping hot. My agency had already lined up the job with Mr. Chase, but they hadn't told King yet. How would I last another week, yet another day? I went to the bathroom with the cup in one hand, a spoon in the other, and closed the door with my hip. Instead of topping off his coffee with sugar, I topped it off with water from the toilet. It was foolish and far from courageous, but it was easier than telling him off. I brought him the coffee, handed over his calendar, and resigned on the spot.

"What the hell are you doing? Come back here!" Mr. King yelled.

He picked up the phone. "Martha, stop her! Don't let her leave."

Martha smiled and winked, watching me pass her desk. Yes, I was technically unemployed for a week and yes, we needed the money, but it never felt better to leave that office with no regrets, with nothing but my purse and a grin.

• • •

Raymond's business was small but successful, with two partners and fourteen employees. He expected hard work but never treated me poorly or raised his voice. Every day at noon while Judy, the receptionist, took her break, I covered for her up front. One day when she came back from lunch, she asked me to organize the magazines on the front table before heading back to my spot.

"Psst, Elsa, come here, fast," Judy whispered.

I gave her a puzzled look and rushed over. She continued with a whisper, "You started your period. Some blood got on your skirt."

I ran to the bathroom and looked in the mirror. Blood, at least the size of a quarter, had stained my outfit. I didn't want to rinse it and make it worse, so I took off my jacket, tied it around my waist, and knocked on Mr. Chase's door.

"Excuse me, Mr. Chase, I've got a small problem, and I need to leave early."

"Is everything okay?"

"Yes." I hesitated, pulling the knot tighter on my jacket. "It's just that my skirt split in the back," I lied.

"You poor thing," he said. "Why don't you take a taxi?" He pulled a twenty-dollar bill out of his pocket and handed it to me.

"Mr. Chase, it isn't necessary. Besides, that's too much for a cab."

"Just take it. But come back tomorrow. I can only live without you for a half a day," he joked and went back to the table to work on his drawings.

• • •

When I arrived the next morning, Mr. Chase asked me to come into his office right away.

"Morning, Elsa, shut the door behind you," he said.

He'd never asked me to shut the door before, and his request made me nervous. *Was he having second thoughts? Did the previous Girl Friday call and ask for her job back?* After all, my three-month probationary period ran for another week through the agency, so anything could have happened.

"I have something for you. It's by the window," he said after I walked in.

29

A beige rectangular box sat on the table. It had the Bergdorf Goodman name in dark blue printed across the top. Once during my lunch break, I'd walked over to Bergdorf's and looked through the women's handbag department. It was an exquisite, elegant store where only wealthy people could afford to shop. I opened the box and separated the white tissue paper. The whole time, I felt his eyes on me and imagined him looking out above his rectangular, tortoise-shell glasses.

"Go ahead, don't be shy."

I pulled out a sleeveless shift dress airbrushed in a vibrant apple-green. "Goodness, what have you done?"

When held up to the light, the A-line design featured beautiful stitching in cream that stylishly disappeared above two small front pockets. Underneath the dress and still packed in the box lay a cropped jacket with the same cream stitching along the shoulders and waistline.

"The sales attendant was about your size, so we went with a six. I hope it fits. If not, you can exchange it."

"Mr. Chase, I can't accept this." I folded the dress and placed it back on top of its matching jacket. My hand brushed across the fabric, a textured velvet or corduroy that reminded me of an outfit Mary Tyler Moore might have worn.

He walked toward me and reached out, putting his hand on my elbow. "Elsa, I hope I haven't offended you by buying this."

"No, not at all," I said, looking down. His touch caught me off guard, but not in an uncomfortable way. Sure, we'd worked closely together and on occasion our elbows bumped, but he'd never touched me that way before.

The sun shined through and cascaded across the dress, and it made me imagine how it would look against my favorite fire-engine-red lipstick. The green became even more vibrant against the white tissue paper. It stood out and left me breathless, like the times I watched Laura chase and catch snowflakes with her green mittens.

Mr. Chase stared at me, contemplating what he'd say next, cautious and calculated with his words in a way he'd never shown before. "I felt bad about what happened yesterday. It must be hard being a single parent and making ends meet." He paused again. "Look, I was at Bergdorf's buying a suit and saw the dress in the window."

"I don't know what to say."

"Just think about it. If you don't want it, I'll return it. Whatever you want, but at least try it on before you decide. And stop calling me Mr. Chase, will you?"

I thanked him again and walked back to my desk, taking the box with me and placing it in a bag, one that I always brought along for picking up groceries on the way home.

For the rest of the day, it was difficult to get my work done. Why did he buy me the dress? What were his intentions? Did he like me on a personal level? Or was he just being nice? He was my boss and liked my work, but worry sometimes took over—especially as a single parent with bills to pay.

After arriving home, I tried on the outfit like he suggested, standing in front of the mirror and admiring it at every angle. Once Laura went to bed, I tried it on again and kept it in my closet instead of wrapping it in the box and bringing it back with me to the office.

• • •

That beautiful outfit stayed with me for the longest time, in the far right corner of my closet, covered in a garment bag to keep it dust-free. Over the years, I'd pull it out and try it on, recalling the early days with Raymond. I couldn't imagine getting rid of it, even when its style had been replaced with decades of new fashions. As Matt pulled onto Wisconsin Avenue and led us back from the airport, I giggled thinking about the dress, trying it on, and staring at my reflection as I'd done all those years ago.

"What's so funny?" Greg asked from the passenger seat when Matt pulled up the driveway and stopped in front of my building. My daydreaming got the best of me and made me forget, just briefly, that Laura was gone and wouldn't be back for close to a year.

"Oh, nothing," I fibbed while reaching for my purse. "Just remembering a silly chat with Laura."

Thinking about her made me teary-eyed. Matt picked up on it right away, telling me not to worry about Laura, that she's street smart and would be fine. I waved good-bye and entered my lobby where the attendant greeted me, as he'd always done. After making chit-chat with a few old ladies in the elevator, I got to my quiet apartment, a place that felt empty, even with my mother there.

In the hallway on the closet door, Laura's scarf hung slightly off center with one end scrunched up. Next to it, a few books piled up with a note Laura wrote on the top for donations. I evened out the scarf, escaped to my room, and let the TV keep me company, flipping through the channels to find a show to ease the loneliness.

The latest news, no thanks. Too depressing.

Frasier, maybe, for a good laugh.

I kept flipping.

Ooh, Indiana Jones, perfect. Just what I need. Harrison Ford's the only one who looks good in all-over khaki.

"Elsa, is that you?"

"Yes, Mother. Who else would it be?" My tone wasn't the best and guilt ran through me. But the guilt only lasted a second. I turned up the volume while staring at Indiana Jones.

"Elsa, do you have any stamps?" she asked without an answer. "Elsa?" she repeated.

"I'm in the bathroom," I fibbed from my comfortable bed. "I'll get them after I'm done."

I threw off my shoes and eyed the bag of M&M'S, discovering it was empty after shoving my finger into the corner. Frantically pushing aside my checkbook, a notepad, and pens in my nightstand, I uncovered a half-eaten chocolate bar and then devoured it while watching Indiana find some lost ark, or do whatever he does so well with that whip.

Chapter Six

The hardest part about Laura being away was not being able to just pick up the phone and talk. For many reasons. It was expensive. It was for emergencies only. It was oh-so inconvenient with the time difference. That's why I was stuck to every word when her letters started to arrive after she discovered the fax machine at a hotel's business center. It was cheaper than making a call and the most convenient way to stay in touch. Besides, reading the letters more than once would somehow make up for the distance between us.

September 27, 1993

Mom!

 Previet (that's hi in Russian, in case you want to learn a little, you know, when you change your mind and come for a visit!).

 Well, let me first say I've got a lot of practicing to do. Since stepping off the plane, I haven't been able to understand 75% of what people are saying. For all I know, they're asking me if I like playing poker naked, and I'm just nodding in the affirmative. It's kind of frustrating to be clueless, but I know each day will get better and easier.

 Life is interesting, to say the least. Men push you out of the way to get on the Metro, the telephone system is horrible, and people fight while standing in line to buy bread. And that's another story—you can't just go into a store, put the stuff in your basket, and go to the checkout line. First, you have to see what they've got in the showcase, then get in another line to tell them what and how much you want. Then, you go to another line to pay for it. After that, you bring the receipt to the person at the first counter, so she can give you the items you wanted from the showcase. So it's like four different lines before you walk out with your stuff! I wonder if that's why Tolstoy wrote War and Peace and its gazillion pages. So people have something to read while standing an unbelievably long time! Oh, and you have to bring your own bags with you, or buy a bag if you don't have one. At least I know how it works, and I don't leave home without some. You never know if you'll find a great deal while out. And if I don't, I can always blow air into the bags and stick them in my bra for a cheap effect.

On a positive note, my job is great. I only teach twelve hours a week, and the rest is FREE TIME! And, my first class isn't until eleven o'clock. It's like a vacation. I can't remember the last time I had a job where I worked so few hours and didn't get up until ten. I think Tim's Takeout in high school might have been it, but at least I don't have to wear uncomfortable polyester and stand all day.

So far, I love the students. They're quiet, but very smart and appreciate that I'm here. They ask tons of questions about Americans. What type of music we like. What type of cars we drive. How many kids we have. What type of food we eat. How much money we make. If we really take two showers a day. I swear, it's like they're trying out for a Census Bureau job.

I'm meeting some interesting people and getting acclimated. St. Petersburg is absolutely breathtaking. Now I know why they call it the "Venice of the North." There are about sixty canals and lakes in and around the city. I live in a great location, right downtown in the center of everything. The Hermitage, the third largest art museum in the world, is a fifteen-minute walk from my room, door to door! So, except for adjusting to the few cultural differences, I'm loving every minute.

This weekend I'm going home with one of my students. When someone invites you home, they really pull out the red carpet. They stuff you with food and the hospitality is grand. She's from Ruza, a small town outside Moscow. It's about an eight-hour train ride from St. Petersburg, so it should be an adventure. We'll have an overnight compartment and wake up there the next morning. I'll tell you all about it in my next letter! Oh, and don't worry, I've been eating lots of potatoes. But, I haven't gained any weight...yet.

That's all for now. I hope you're staying out of trouble. And the biggest of Happiest Birthdays! I'm sorry I'm not there to celebrate with you.

Until my next letter,
Your loving dochka (daughter) Laura

Before Laura left DC, she mentioned how she'd miss the conveniences, the ease of life here, and she wasn't kidding. Her description of the shopping sounded horrible, like the worst possible version of government red tape. And all the questions her students asked had me cracking up. Why would they even care how many showers we took? I reread the letter many times and practically had it memorized when the phone rang.

"Hello, stranger," Raymond said and, in his off key but charming attempt, sang happy birthday to me. I laughed as he belted out the last line a little too high-pitched as if he were twelve again.

He called every year on my birthday, and I always looked forward to hearing his voice and reminiscing with him, often about our office antics, other times about our lives outside of work, and sometimes when these two worlds collided.

"I have some bad news," he said after singing, and my stomach dropped. "Remember that Chinese restaurant around the corner, the one with the great chicken and broccoli? They went out of business, just like that. There one minute, gone the next."

"Well, that's a relief," I sighed. "I thought you were about to tell me something dreadful."

"That is dreadful!" He said and, as he paused, I glanced over at the closet thinking about the green dress again. He continued, "At least the place lasted longer than my toupee, remember that?"

Raymond hardly brought up the toupee these days, but even so, how could I forget? We joked about it over the years, and it wasn't the actual toupee that kept me holding on to the memory.

"I have to say, I wish things had turned out differently."

"With the toupee?" Raymond joked.

"No silly, with us."

"I know. But things turned out okay in the long run, right?" Raymond asked.

I didn't know how to answer and after a pause, an almost awkward one, he filled me in on his business, the firm's new clients, and projects he'd bid on and won.

We said our good-byes after our short chat, like always during our two calls a year for each other's birthdays. I put Laura's letter in my nightstand and sat back thinking about the time the toupee, the one Raymond spoke about, made its way into our conversation the first time.

One night after working for Raymond for seven months, he asked me to stay late to help prepare for a client meeting the following day. He'd felt bad for making me work overtime and insisted on paying the extra cost for Laura's babysitter.

After checking in with the sitter, we ordered some dinner from that same Chinese restaurant on the corner, and they delivered the order twenty minutes later to a quiet office. Everyone had left early for an off-site function, while we continued to work in Raymond's office. The thought had crossed my mind that we were alone, but I just concentrated on the work. I put the food on the bar, and Raymond walked to his desk and shuffled some papers.

"You know what? Why don't we eat first? I can't work on an empty stomach." He rose from his leather chair, straightened the bottom of his charcoal double-breasted jacket, and ran his fingers across gold cuff links. "Let's see," he said while looking in the bag. "Oh, good. They remembered the chopsticks."

Raymond opened a container and put it close to his face, getting a whiff of the chicken with broccoli. After closing it back up, he piled the containers on top of one another and carried them to the coffee table. I pulled out utensils and plates from the drawer and laid them out.

"Forks? We don't need forks."

"You might not."

"Come on, let me show you," he said. "It's not that hard. Just takes some practice, that's all."

"And while I'm practicing, I'm dropping rice all over the place and starving myself to death."

He split a pair of chopsticks and, after rubbing off the splinters, placed the pair in my hand.

"I'm left-handed, remember," I said.

"Oh, that's right," he said and stood up to move around to my left side. "Now watch. You've got to place them between your thumb and index finger and move them around like so." He leaned over me to demonstrate and reached for his own pair. "Then bring the container close to your face so if you drop some, it lands back where it came from and not in your lap."

I managed to get a good grip on the broccoli, but before reaching my mouth, it fell through the chopsticks, hit the top of the container, and landed on the floor. A complete failure, except for the brown stain left on the beige carpet.

"I'll stick with utensils. I've already mastered those," I said and leaned over to dab the carpet with a napkin.

"Suit yourself, but it's not as much fun," Raymond said and every time he took a bite, the sauce hit him in the face, leaving little brown spots on his cheeks and glasses. It made me giggle and, in return, he stopped eating and put his chopsticks in the container.

"What's so funny?" he asked.

"Nothing," I smiled and looked down.

"You do know you're a really bad liar," he said playfully.

Instead of telling him, I reached for my purse and pulled out a compact mirror. He flipped it open and held the mirror up to his face.

"And I just thought I was sweating because the food is so damn spicy," he said as he took a napkin and wiped his cheeks. He held the mirror up higher and wrinkled his forehead. "Let's see if there's anything on the top, besides my shiny bald spot."

"It shouldn't bother you," I said. "You look distinguished."

"Ha, that's just another way of saying old. I started losing my hair right after college, and it has been going downhill ever since."

"Well, actually uphill, then downhill," I said, motioning above my head to the back of my neck.

He laughed and got up from the sofa, taking the mirror with him. "Stay here. I'll be back in a jiffy."

I wanted to start on our project to get home at a decent hour to see Laura before she went to bed but had to confess—I hadn't laughed this much in a long time, since being with Max. It was hard to believe I could be myself in front of my boss who insisted from day one that I call him Raymond, not Mr. Chase.

39

"Well, what do you think?"

I turned around and for a second tried to hold back my laughter.

"That bad?" he said while holding up the mirror again. He looked at his reflection and rearranged the sides of his toupee while moving the mirror around to see from all angles.

"I'm sorry." I giggled. "You caught me by surprise."

"Don't make excuses. You hate it, don't you?" he asked and came closer.

"Well..." I paused.

"Just tell me already."

I hesitated, not only out of politeness, but he really did look better without it. I called him distinguished because telling my boss he was handsome didn't feel right. "I'm not too keen on it because it doesn't look real," I finally said.

"Hey! I paid a pretty penny for this. I like it, and I'm going to start wearing it."

"Suit yourself, but you look better without the toupee."

"Bald, right? Shiny and bald."

"If it makes you feel better, you should wear it," I said trying to backtrack for being too direct. "But why are you asking me?"

"Just for an opinion, that's all," he said and sat down to finish his meal.

He looked at me as he took a bite of chicken, and we both began to laugh. And nothing could stop us. Every time we looked at each other, we giggled even more. We laughed so hard we were bent over, holding our sides from cramps that wouldn't end. After several minutes, I grabbed a napkin from the table and wiped away the mascara that had crept into the corners of my eyes.

He stared at me for a few seconds and then leaned in for a kiss. He pulled away almost immediately. "I'm sorry, that was very uncalled for," he said and walked over to the window to peek out the blinds. "Honestly, I've wanted to do that since I first saw you."

"I guess that means you don't like me for my mind?" I joked, trying to alleviate the awkwardness.

He kept looking out the window. "I apologize. That shouldn't have happened."

I got up and walked toward him, placing my hand on his arm. "I really didn't mind."

He turned to face me. "Does that mean I can try again?"

"On one condition. You get rid of the rug you're wearing."

Raymond laughed and leaned in to kiss me again. He took off his toupee and threw it across the office. It hit his desk and fell into the potted plant.

"Ah, the perfect burial," I said.

"Maybe it will help the plant grow," Raymond joked and led me to the sofa.

I never thought we'd become romantically involved. I needed to focus on my job and on Laura, who was almost four and the best little companion. Raymond looked at me sometimes, but I never thought much about it. Men always looked my way when I was young and pretty. It happened often enough to take for granted. It was when I got older, after hitting fifty to be exact, that the longed-for attention became so easy to miss—and dwell on.

Back in the day, Raymond wasn't really my type. He was handsome but looked nothing like Max who, as my friends always said, could have taken Elvis's place in a heartbeat without notice. Max's wavy brown hair, a few shades darker than the dusting of freckles across his cheeks, got wavier in the summer heat. He always wore collared shirts tucked in with a belt around his slender waist, with matching ankle boots that zipped up the side, a style so popular in the late '60s. Whenever Max had the chance, he'd stop in a terminal or department store to get his shoes polished while chatting about music.

He was slim and managed to stay that way even with his fair share of root beer floats. My friends used to call him tall and lanky. Even after all these lost years, I still remembered how I'd stand on my toes to kiss him, even in three-inch heels.

Raymond, on the other hand, stood just a few inches taller than me and had some extra pounds around the waist he could afford to shed. His formal suits, glasses, and bald spot made him look beyond his age. It didn't matter. He won me over with his even-tempered personality and humor. From that first moment we kissed, he had a special place for me. But it was never completely for sex. We became companions, friends with a good ear. I listened to him talk about the architectural business and his kids. At the same time, he filled a void in my life.

Tuesday evenings became our tradition and every Tuesday afternoon, he'd hand me a note that said where to meet him and at what time. About a year into our relationship, during Christmas 1973, his Tuesday note said, "Trader Vic's at the Plaza Hotel - 7:30."

I left the office at seven o'clock and hailed a cab. Even with my Girl Friday salary, I always dressed in the latest styles and that Tuesday's outfit was no exception. A black dress with a squared collar and white piping around the sleeves kept me fashionable. My knee-high boots, gray tweed jacket, and matching hat kept me warm.

The driver stopped in front of the Plaza and the hotel attendant opened my door. I stepped out of the cab and watched horse-drawn carriages line up across the street by Central Park.

"Welcome to the Plaza," the doorman said and extended his arm to let me pass. The largest Christmas tree I'd ever seen stood before me, at least thirty feet tall and still not touching the ceiling. The lobby, adorned and framed in gold, warmed me from the outside cold. When I reached Trader Vic's, the maître d' escorted me to a table in the back where Raymond was waiting. He stood up and helped me with my coat.

"You always know the most interesting places," I said and sat down while looking around the restaurant.

"That's because I've lived here my entire life."

"Me too, so what's my excuse?" I said and leaned closer for him to light my cigarette.

When the waiter approached, Raymond ordered for both of us and took a long drag from his cigarette before setting it on the ashtray.

The waiter came back with another round of whiskey sours and our first course. Raymond hadn't touched his food; instead he rested his hand on his chin, holding his cigarette as the smoke disappeared above him.

"What's wrong? You're not eating," I said.

He had a mischievous smile, the kind that Max had the day we painted our first apartment and he chased me with the brush.

"Why are you looking at me that way?" I asked.

"What way?"

"You're staring at me."

"I think it's obvious," he said and paused to stir his drink. "I adore you. I love everything about you."

"I knew you had good taste," I teased.

"I love your mind, the way it works. I love the way you walk when you're upset or mad about something. And your laugh. Do you know you snort when you laugh?"

"Snort? I do not!"

"Oh yes you do, my dear." He paused and reached for my hand. "I'm trying to tell you in my own way that I'm crazy about you."

Raymond let go, puffed on his cigarette, and blew smoke to the side after smashing his cigarette in the ashtray. "Well, aren't you going to say anything? You were all words a minute ago."

"I've been waiting for you to say that for the last year," I answered. "But what exactly do you mean? That you want to marry me some day?"

"Elsa, as much as I'd love to, I can't. If I divorce my wife, I don't know what kind of relationship I'd have with my kids. She might take it out on me by not letting me see them. I'd be risking too much."

The table next to us cleared, catching my attention, giving me time to push back the tears. His words tore through me—to hear one minute that you're loved and the next that your relationship is going nowhere. "What's the point in telling me all this?"

"Elsa, I can never leave my wife. For the sake of the kids. I love you, and that's why I'm being honest."

Being honest? Telling me that you love me but can't be with me, really be with me? How could I have let this happen? With my boss, of all people, at a job I love.

The waiter came by and took the rest of our order, helping to break up the uncomfortable silence. As he walked away, the rest of my whiskey sour burned on the way down.

"I thought sooner or later we'd be together. Boy, I was wrong."

"We are together. We're having a wonderful time. Let's not ruin it." Raymond reached for my hand again as I pulled away.

"Never mind. I shouldn't have assumed you'd leave your wife in the first place."

"Elsa, I don't want to hurt you. And I don't want to lose you. But I'll understand if you'd rather end it. You deserve to have someone who's committed only to you."

I pushed my food around for the rest of the evening. Raymond tried many times to reach out to me and left his hand on the table until I didn't pull away. "Let's enjoy what we have. That certainly won't change," he said as we put on our coats.

The Secret We Lost

We walked out of the Plaza and into separate cabs on our way back home, his a few blocks over on the east side and mine more than a hundred blocks up and into the Bronx.

By the time I got home, it was close to ten. I paid my sitter for the extra hours, threw my coat on the sofa, and locked up behind her. *What was wrong with me? Why did I become involved with a married man, let alone my boss?* Laura slept soundly, and after kissing her forehead, I threw off my shoes and curled up next to her before falling asleep.

Chapter Seven

Laura told me staying busy would make the time pass quickly while she was away. Sure, my job as office manager at an architectural firm in Georgetown kept me more than occupied. Making flight and hotel arrangements for busy partners. Preparing proposal packages for delivery to clients. But I quickly realized how much I depended on my daughter on an emotional level. We couldn't talk daily. Or even weekly. She had always been the center of my life, which now felt off balance.

After a long day at the office helping my boss prepare for a new client presentation, I stopped at the grocery store to grab a salad, replenish my chocolate supply, and pick up a few items for my mother.

"Hey gorgeous," a woman called out.

I knew right away, without turning around, that it was my friend Susan. The two of us initially met each other in our Tenleytown neighborhood, and finally after running into each other several times, we exchanged phone numbers. Right away, we discovered we had a few things in common. We grew up in New York City, liked reggae music, and were single and over fifty. With Laura gone for three months, hearing a warm, familiar voice made my day and filled a void.

"Looks like we're having the same thing for dinner," she said, pointing to our salads.

"I'm having chocolate as my appetizer. Want to join me?" I asked, hoping for some company.

"I'd love to," Susan sighed, "but my pajamas are calling. Long day at work. How about dinner next week?"

"Sure," I said, trying to hide my disappointment. "Next week sounds great."

Susan walked to the checkout line and loneliness worked its way through me. The kind of loneliness that lingered. The type you get when you're going solo on Thanksgiving or New Year's Eve, wondering enviously about other people's lives, their happiness, and their big extended families. I froze and watched Susan take her bags and walk out. The loneliness took me for a loop, enough that it made me walk to the side and lean against a wall. I put my groceries down and pulled out an address book from my purse.

It was small and leather-bound, with the edges curled up on the front that made a crease on the corners. Once bright red, it had turned pink from sitting on my windowsill, fading from the sun. Aunt Regina had given it to me on my fifteenth birthday, and I still carried it with me, with the names of those long gone and long forgotten fading away with time. I'd never found the courage to erase or mark through them, or the ones once—or still—loved.

I flipped through the book for my DC friends and acquaintances, working my way to *K* before realizing I'd lost touch with so many. I put the address book back in my purse and made my way to the checkout, got in line, and inched my way up and out to my Wisconsin Avenue apartment.

Having Laura crash on the sofa for several months, even with the messy dishes she left along the way, made me miss having company. The kind that made me laugh. The kind where you felt so comfortable, the kick-off-your-shoes and show-your-bare-feet, calluses-and-all comfortable.

This kind of comfortable was impossible with my own mother. Even with her with me, we rarely ate dinner or spent time together. She always ate early, about the same time I went to all my afternoon meetings. When I got home from the store, I plopped my feet on the ottoman, picked at my salad, and pulled out Laura's recent letter, the one I'd already read several times to keep me company.

November 11, 1993

Mom,

It's me again! By the time you read this, it will be almost Thanksgiving. A few of us are planning to make a feast, but it looks like we'll have to serve chicken since there are no turkeys to be found. The poor turkeys probably overheard us Americans talking about our holiday and ran for cover deep in the Russian forest. But it's the idea that counts, right? Besides, then we don't have to say it tastes like chicken because it is!

Enough about how easy my life seems, especially compared to the tough time Russians are having. Nothing seems to stay the same. Each month my stipend goes up because inflation is so bad, but it makes me wonder how they're coping, especially ones living on pensions. Every day I see more and more homeless people on the street, including children. It breaks my heart. The children live near the subway station or within the underground tunnels. Or sometimes they roam around, begging for money and approaching people who look like tourists. Sometimes the kids are with an adult and sometimes alone. Their clothes are old and torn and their faces so dirty. And now that it's cold, they're always rubbing their hands together to warm them up. Maybe things were better under Communism. Sometimes I overhear people talking about how they're going to survive or buy food with hardly any money.

People stand on the sidewalk, usually in front of a store or market, to sell items. Some items are used, some new. I've even seen babushkas selling boxes of matches and plastic bags on the street. It's very depressing. I can hardly look them in the eye as I pass, but when I do, it looks like each babushka's face is wearing the entire history of Russia on it. One woman was holding up wool socks, just standing there holding them. I wound up buying two pairs, and the look on her face told me she could eat for a month. They're handmade and they keep your daughter's toes warm!

Speaking of wool and warmth, the one thing I wasn't prepared for was the winter. It's SO COLD here! It must be about five degrees right now, right smack in the middle of the day. The first snowfall came in the middle of October, and the ground is covered with snow and ice. I've heard that it will stay this way for six months. I'm glad I found a warm coat and hat—and those wool socks!

It has been too cold to do all of my sightseeing but I've been on what I call Museum Mania. I go to the Hermitage and Russian Museum at least once a week, and have been visiting a lot of my students' homes, eating and drinking a lot of Russian champagne. I gave up on vodka after realizing that if you say you drink vodka, you'll have to drink vodka all night long. I've started using the excuse that I'm allergic to it; seems to do the trick until they reach for the champagne.

Remember how I mentioned going to Ruza? Well, I had a great time. It's a small town about an hour from Moscow with some seriously old churches, really quaint and quiet where everyone seems to know each other (that could be a good or a bad thing). Not sure how it came up, but we got to talking with some neighbors about Oma. There was an accident in Ruza exactly like Michael's, and it made me feel so bad for Oma and her parents.

But enough sad talk. I've got other news. Drumroll, please: I have a boyfriend (I know, something you probably don't want to hear). He's a sweetheart. He's gorgeous—looks *like Johnny Depp. I met him on the train going back to St. Petersburg. He's an engineering student at one of the universities here. He was visiting his family and happened to be in our compartment. I know what you're thinking. Don't worry, I'm not going to fall in love and bring him home with me in May. I promise! Last thing I need is some mail-order husband or whatever you want to call it.*

By the way, I keep hearing how Russian I look. People don't believe me when I tell them I'm American. You didn't happen to have an affair with a Russian milkman? Or a postman from St. Pete? Just kidding...but did you?

I hope you and Oma are well. Remember, I'll be home before you know it. Also, I've tried to fax some photos with the letter—I hope you'll be able to see them even in black-and-white.

I love and miss you,
Laura

On the bottom of each photo, Laura wrote the date and some details. In one of the pictures, she looked so Russian. She wore a winter coat and a mink hat that framed her face beautifully. Snow surrounded her and a church crowned with domes sat in the background. To me, it looked like a typical Russian winter scene. On the bottom, she wrote, "A day in Novgorod, four hours southeast of St. Petersburg. One of the oldest cities in Russia dating back to 892. The church is from the 11th century."

The other picture, taken indoors, showed Laura kneeling in front of about twenty students. Her hair was pulled back and she had on a sweater and jeans, the same ripped ones she wore the day we packed. "These are my students. It was our American Halloween party, but I was too lazy to dress up."

The last picture showed her room, and in it, she had long johns, underwear, socks, and towels lined up from wall to wall, hanging over her chair, desk, and radiator. On the bottom she wrote, "What a great experience! This is my room, and I'm wearing all this stiff underwear since my dryer went MIA—not really, I never had one!"

After reading Laura's letter a few more times, I pulled out my address book once again, this time going straight to *S* instead of *K* where I'd left off in the store. Seeing Laura with her students made me want to call Susan to firm up plans for dinner the following week. I always kept my contacts under their first name and skimmed through to find Susan's number, hoping she'd still want to trade in a night at home for some time with me.

Chapter Eight

Susan and I took the Metro to Dupont Circle and walked down Connecticut Avenue to Kaplan's, our favorite spot, which had a bookstore on the bottom floor and a restaurant on the top. When we got there, we stopped in front to admire the window. They always had great displays and made art pieces out of the books. This time, *The Bridges of Madison County* took up most of Kaplan's window space, and they matched it with several books about architecture and a bridge created out of other hardcovers.

The hostess took us upstairs and picked a great table for us overlooking the bookstore. While we waited for our meal, Susan told me she was having a hard time. Her husband had died the year before, and she was still grieving.

"I can't imagine life with someone else. I can't even imagine being intimate with another man," Susan confided in me over our second glass of wine.

The thought of being married to Max and how we often talked about growing old together left me longing for a relationship like Susan's. "I bet you're one of the lucky ones who had a long, wonderful marriage."

"After being married for more than twenty-five years, you love that person deeply, but the relationship changes." She paused for a moment, getting distracted by the young couple next to us. "It's the companionship I miss the most."

"You can have companionship and not do anything else, at least not right away," I said, hoping it didn't sound like a consolation prize.

Susan leaned back and took a sip of her wine. "I know. Honestly, I'm just afraid. I don't like the dating thing." She continued, almost in a whisper. "You know how long it's been?"

I snorted, remembering my non-existent dating life. "It can't be any longer than me. I haven't been on a date since the telephone was invented. You know how I know?"

Susan shrugged then wiped her mouth with the napkin.

"Because I don't get any calls from men!"

"Well, I haven't been on a first date since 1961," Susan added. "And that was with my husband. So, I'm a bit rusty, to say the least."

"I have an idea. If you're up for it, after dinner we could go out for drinks, maybe some dancing?" I asked, even surprising myself with coming up with it.

"Where? I have no clue what's hopping these days."

"Me neither. If anything, we could just find a place and people watch."

"Oh, what the hell. I haven't been out in ages," Susan agreed and pulled out her compact mirror to reapply her lipstick.

We paid our check and made our way to Wagner's on Georgetown's waterfront, a place the hostess recommended. There, Susan danced all night, enjoying numerous invitations. I spent most of the evening people watching, a hobby I picked up at a young age.

Through the cigarette smoke, women vied for attention, some using playful poses, push-up bras, and flirtatious glances. Susan, on the other hand, didn't have to try. She was exotic with her olive complexion, silky black hair, and long legs. Compared to her and the roomful of platinum blondes, I felt short and barely noticeable. When I was younger, men always stared. But now that middle age had reared its ugly head, the attention and long gazes had disappeared and self-criticism had taken over.

For many years after Max died, I found room for Raymond and held on to him for the longest time, clinging to unrealistic scenarios I dreamed up. Here it was, almost a decade later, with no one in my life. I really hadn't moved forward. That night at Trader Vic's, Raymond did the right thing by being honest with me. But I couldn't be honest with myself and break it off to find someone committed only to me. *What made me think that one day he'd have a change of heart and leave his wife? Had I relied too much on him—and my daughter—for my happiness?*

We left Wagner's at midnight and during the cab ride home, Susan thanked me for going out. In the same breath, she told me to let loose and have more fun. I had no excuse not to; my loss wasn't as recent as hers. Yet, as we said good-night, I felt so alone, more alone than ever.

After getting home, I got undressed and went to the bathroom to wash my face. The cleanser washed away my makeup and left me looking tired, with the expression lines around my mouth deeper and more defined. They were parentheses of middle age, made especially for me, smack dab in the center with no way to forget them. And they were staring back, almost smirking, with their distorted curves and their passage of time.

Aging was for the birds and maybe that's why they called them crows' feet, those other lines around my eyes that made me stop and stare. Nothing was going to help their permanence. At least nothing from a tube. Even still, I dotted my eyes with the cream that touted the most results in those commercials and walked over to my bed.

The light from the nightstand reflected on the photos Laura sent. I couldn't wait to talk to her again, to hear her voice and have her describe how she was surviving the Russian winter, all layered in wool to stay warm and cozy. Another light from the hallway swept under my door and across the floor. My mother often got up at this time to make her way to the bathroom, making me worry, hoping she wouldn't fall from becoming disoriented. Her first fall landed her a broken leg and an unwanted stay in the hospital.

Back then after her fall and before she moved in with me, she'd spent two months in a rehab center near her New York apartment. I came up from Washington every other weekend and, during my third visit, ran into her doctor.

"You know, you have to decide what you're going to do with her," he said, referring to my mother like a bulky piece of furniture too big for an already cramped studio apartment.

"What's your advice?" I asked.

"You could move her to a nursing home, or she could live with you."

He flipped through her chart and scribbled some notes. "She can't go back home by herself, at least for right now. Someone could come by, but that adds up if it's not covered."

A nursing home was out of the question. My father and Aunt Regina were long gone, but they wouldn't have approved of me putting my mother in a home, unless she needed the extra care that only a full-time nurse could provide. *We take care of our family; we take them in; we don't send them away*, I could hear them saying.

When she left the rehab center, we went back to her New York apartment. The doctor told me she couldn't live alone, so I stayed with her for a week while we made some decisions. I thought it would be difficult to convince her to move to DC, but when brought up, she didn't fight me. Was it because she missed my father and was lonely after losing so many friends? Or was it because we had coexisted and survived that week together? Whatever the reason, she seemed okay to leave, even with her air of independence.

During that week, I helped her get ready for the move. And since we didn't talk much, the packing took over in a speedy fashion. Over the years, there were so many things I wanted to talk to my mother about, but she'd never open up. Changing the subject—or ignoring me altogether—seemed to be her favorite pastime and something she did well. Conveniently for her, we only talked about the move. How many boxes she needed. What she planned to keep or throw out. What she wanted to donate.

After hours of sorting and packing dishes, I sat on the sofa, put my feet up, and flipped through the TV shows. When I was a young girl, I'd always sit in front of the window and watch the traffic go by. Looking out on Broadway, I'd always think, *Why are they walking so darn fast and where are they going?* I'd wonder who they were and how old. What they did for a living and which apartment building they lived in. The honking from the cars and taxis and squealing from the brakes—all of it invigorated me, especially when it rained.

On the last day of packing after helping my mother to bed, I looked at old photos and finished up a crossword puzzle. While digging for a pen in the dresser, I found my old sketch pad with all my drawings, the architectural ones my mother didn't get a chance to rip up. When I pulled them from the drawer, a hankie fell out with my braid tucked inside, the one hidden long ago that I should have never kept.

Chapter Nine

Right after my thirteenth birthday, I arrived home from school and went to the kitchen to grab a snack, my usual routine after sitting in a wooden chair all day, getting arithmetic drilled into me, or writing passages about my summer vacation. My father was at work and my Aunt Regina had gone out to run errands.

"Elsa, hurry up and come help in the kitchen," my mother demanded in German, the language spoken in our home.

"Yes, Mamma. I need to change first. I'll be right there."

I followed the long narrow hallway to the bedroom that my Aunt Regina shared with me. Lipstick and rouge with the same gold-flecked packaging laid next to each other on the dresser. Aunt Regina must have just bought it. She loved to wear different shades of red lipstick and sometimes left them out on the dresser. I looked closer and saw that it had been opened. Knowing my mother was expecting me in the kitchen didn't matter. I'd never worn lipstick before and desperately wanted to try. I was thirteen, a teenager, after all.

First, I studied the positioning of the case to make sure to place it back in its exact spot and then leaned over the mahogany dresser to get a closer look in the mirror. Following the exact moves of my Aunt Regina, I applied the lipstick, one with the color of the sweetest red pepper. I opened my mouth slightly and began in the middle, moving toward the right, then the left, and around the bottom. My bright lips matched my red hair ribbon perfectly and made my blue eyes stand out. As I turned around to grab a tissue from the nightstand, my mother caught my attention and made me gasp. She stood at the door with her hands on her hips but immediately walked toward me and grabbed my elbow. The tissue fell out of my hand.

"You're too grown up to help in the kitchen?" my mother said as she hurried me down our long hallway to the bathroom.

"Mamma, I'm sorry," I cried. "I was coming right away, I promise."

My mother sat me down on the stool in front of the sink. She took a tissue and firmly rubbed the lipstick off, smearing half of it across the bottom of my cheek. Then she scolded me about using Aunt Regina's lipstick and not being old enough to wear makeup. Just when I thought she was done, she opened the medicine cabinet and took out a pair of scissors, the pair she always used for trimming hair.

"Mamma, what are you doing?" I cried.

"Sit still and be quiet or the neighbors will hear."

Without another word, she leaned my head forward and cut off my braid. She put it on the edge of the sink, ribbon intact, and told me to clean up and come to the kitchen.

I couldn't lift my head. Instead, I looked at the strands that had fallen into the sink. *Was playing with my aunt's lipstick that bad? Was it wrong to want to feel older, just for a few minutes?* When I found the courage to look up and in the mirror, my blonde hair was left lifeless as it hung a couple of inches below my chin. I wept while cleaning up, rolled two tissues around my braid, and tucked it in the drawer. After joining my mother in the kitchen, I licked the tears that fell so they wouldn't make their way onto the cutting board and into the soup.

Later that night, I overheard my parents talking in the kitchen. I'd hoped my father would ask why she'd cut off my braid so carelessly. But my father never confronted my mother, never raised his voice or argued. He was calm, even-tempered, always something I wanted in a man, something both Max and Raymond had. My father tried to come to my rescue many times, in his own soft-mannered way, and I loved him for that.

"Why don't you let her have a little fun?" my father said to Millie.

I tiptoed down the hallway, holding onto the wall with my palm and onto my breath so they wouldn't hear me.

"First school, then cooking. That's what's important. Not wearing makeup. And especially not drawing houses and dreaming about architecture and wallpaper and how many bathrooms there should be. She doesn't even hold the pencil correctly. Besides, it's a man's job."

"But she enjoys it. What's the harm?"

"She needs to learn how to take care of the household. And cook. Architecture could have been—" She stopped in the middle of her thought.

"Could have been what?" my father asked.

"Never mind. What's lost is lost."

"Are you thinking about the baby?"

My mother didn't answer. The apartment stood quiet and the only sound came from the cuckoo clock over the living room door.

"Millie, it was a difficult time on the ship. But you shouldn't take it out on Elsa. It's not her fault you had a miscarriage. And it's certainly not her fault for what—"

"I'm not blaming Elsa," she interrupted. "If only we didn't have to leave Germany."

"What a beautiful life we had there," my father said solemnly. "But we are the lucky ones, the ones who left when we still could."

They both stopped talking, and the clock took over the silence again. I peeked around the corner and could see my father reaching over to hold my mother. She pulled away and put both hands on the kitchen counter.

"Gus, we've lost so many dear things along the way. *Wie könnte das passieren?* How could it happen to us, how?"

They began to put away the dishes, and it was my cue to tiptoe back to the bedroom. "*Liebshen*, what took you so long?" Aunt Regina asked.

"I saw some pimples," I lied, pretending I'd spent extra time in the bathroom trying to scrub them away. Just a few months earlier, pimples had begun their unwelcomed stay on me, so it didn't feel too much like fibbing.

Tante's face lit up, like every time she ordered an egg cream at the neighborhood soda shop. With enthusiasm, she shared the perfect acne remedy, something about mixing baking soda with vinegar and would show me after school, after getting a good night's sleep—my beauty sleep she always called it. She reached for the light as I interrupted.

"*Tante*, what was Mamma like when she was young?"

My aunt lingered to remember. Then she sat up, fixing the pillow and pulling the bottom blanket up to her chest.

"Millie was a fun-loving soul. She worked hard at school, very bright in science and mathematics, but also knew how to have fun. We used to go swimming together during the summer. It was a glorious time growing up in Germany. But things don't last."

"Not even good things?" I asked.

"Elsa, whatever you do, remember that you must adapt to change. Sometimes things don't last forever. When difficult moments happen in life, and you cannot adapt, it's easy to become sad."

"Like Anna's mamma?"

"No, like Millie."

I sat up even more, surprised at how *Tante* had described my mother. "Mamma isn't sad. She's mean."

"No, my darling, Millie is sad. Now go to sleep. You have school tomorrow." My aunt reached across the bed again and turned off the light on her nightstand.

"*Tante*, why didn't you ever get married?" I asked as my eyes adjusted to the darkness. The light from the street dashed across several family photos that hung on the wall above my dresser.

"Oh, I don't know. I couldn't find my cup of tea."

"What does that mean?"

"I couldn't find someone I liked enough to spend the rest of my life with."

Her answer surprised me. "You've never been in love?" I asked and pulled the covers up over my shoulders and rubbed my feet together to warm them up.

"Oh sure, once or twice. But it didn't last. Love needs to last longer than a week to get married."

"Maybe you'll still get married," I said, imagining my *Tante* walking down the aisle with a beaded white dress and on the arm of a tall man with slicked-back hair and a mustache.

"Or I'll just wait and go to your wedding one day."

"Maybe I won't get married either. Especially with these pimples," I said and lifted my hand across my chin to feel the bumps.

"Elsa, don't worry. Those pimples will be gone as soon as you say good-night *Tante*."

"Good-night *Tante*."

Chapter Ten

Instant gratification: my first cup of coffee on a Saturday morning. Within a few seconds, the machine growled like an empty stomach and coffee dripped into the pot. The aroma of hazelnut-flavored coffee boosted me, and its warmth was my antidote for tired eyes. As the coffee trickled, I lifted the blinds and looked outside. *Ah—what a great day to stay in bed to beat back the cold, rainy winter that brewed outside.*

I took the half-and-half from the fridge and on the door saw my note to call Laura in Ruza at midnight, my time. It had been one month since we'd spoken and five since she'd left. This time would be the first time on my dime. We could talk for more than a few minutes. We could talk for hours, if we really wanted. I set my alarm for 11:45 and put a list of questions to ask on my nightstand.

Are you staying warm?
Are you eating enough?
Are you going out with a group at night and not alone?
Are you having fun?

• • •

Later that afternoon, Matt and Greg called to check on me and get me out of the house. It wasn't the first time they'd tried. This time, they suggested bowling, but it was a great day to stay home with the TV as my companion.

"Seriously?" I said. "It's nasty out, seems better to stay in bed all day and watch old movies," I told them.

"You can't stay in bed. You have to get that blood circulating. Wait, what?" Matt yelled. "Greg said he agrees with me, and my impressive attempt to sound like a doctor. We'll pick you up in an hour," he said before hanging up.

• • •

We walked into the alley and made our way between kids sliding around in their socks and colorful birthday balloons attached to chairs. After the attendant gave us our scorecards, Matt shoved them in his pocket, and we took over the lane at the far end as a league packed up to leave.

I never figured out why bowling and smoking went together, I thought on our way to our lane, even though I was tempted to take out one of my own. But, it wasn't part of the plan. I'd cut back after Laura got on my case—not for smoking too much, but for smoking in general.

It was way too hard to quit, though. I'd been smoking since my early twenties and couldn't imagine giving it up altogether. So, over the summer, mostly because Laura kept nagging me, I went from my five-a-day habit to two: one in the morning and at night. Being in the alley with all the smokers made me crave one, but instead, I grabbed some gum and handed the pack to Matt.

"Why on earth would they allow smoking with all these kids?" Matt wound up saying, practically reading my mind.

"The stench from these is way worse," Greg said as he sprayed his rental shoes with Lysol he brought from home.

Matt picked out a ball and rubbed chalk on his hand. "He'll complain until he gets his first strike, then, all of a sudden, nothing else matters."

"At least they're playing good '70s music. I always loved Blondie," Greg yelled out and sang "Call Me" by the lane.

"Can you sing over there while I take my turn? And by the way, it was 1980."

Greg stopped singing and stood by the chair. "No way, it was like 1976. Are you sure?"

Matt stared at Greg with raised eyebrows. "I forgot," Greg added, "he's like a walking encyclopedia when it comes to music."

"Not the best skill to have, would've been better to remember all those formulas in geometry."

Matt picked up the ball and concentrated on his aim. As we watched him prepare for a hopeful strike, Greg put his arm around me. "How you holding up with Laura being away? You know we're here for you, right?"

His question took me by surprise, and I found myself biting the inner part of my lip to hold back my emotions, a trick I'd learned many years ago when Max passed. "Can I ask you something, and you'll be totally honest?" I blurted out.

Greg nodded.

"Did Laura ask you to check on me while she was away?"

"Maybe. But we would have done it anyways."

"What if I'd said no to bowling?"

"Then we would've come over with a bottle of wine or three," Greg said matter-of-factly and got up to take his turn, doing a little twist when he got a strike for the first time and, for the rest of the afternoon, wound up winning every match.

Instead of taking me back to my apartment, the boys dropped me off at Cafe Upton, my favorite coffee shop by the Metro. I wasn't ready to go home, to stare at the walls or the TV, or to pretend my mother wasn't there. The barista poured my usual, a vanilla-hazelnut blend with plenty of room for cream, and we chatted in between his customers. It was hard to focus with Laura on my mind and, while thinking about the questions I'd prepared for our call at midnight, I watched people pass by as they went on their way drenched by the city's rain.

• • •

The caffeine did the trick and when midnight rolled around, I dialed the number in Ruza and heard two long rings.

"Mom?" she asked, and when I heard her voice, it breathed life into me.

The notepad with my questions sat on the nightstand. I picked up the pen, marked through the first question, and started doodling on the side. "Are you staying warm, sweetie?"

"Yep, spending lots of time inside. Last night we drank a lot of champagne and stuffed our faces!"

"Oh yeah? With who?" I asked.

"My boyfriend, Yuri, and some of his friends."

I put the pen down, caught off guard and surprised that he'd gone with her. "Laura, don't get too attached."

"What's that supposed to mean?"

"Simple. It means you're American; he's Russian. It'll never work."

"Mom, if you called to lecture me about international love, which you know nothing about, you're wasting your money. We're miles apart and rarely speak. Why would you even bring that up?"

"Sweetie, I just don't want you to get hurt."

"I'm old enough to take care of myself, remember?" Laura huffed.

I quickly changed the subject, knowing that we'd argue and nobody would win. "How's everything otherwise?"

"Everything's great. It's crazy, but I love it here. There's something magical about this place."

"How's your Russian coming along?"

"Not that great. Actually, a few days ago the program manager told us that if we want to teach again next year, we need to tell her by March."

"Wait a minute. You're going back?" I burst out in surprise.

"I've thought about it. Maybe for one more year if my Russian isn't up to par."

"Are you trying to give your mother a heart attack? First the Russian boyfriend and now this? If I have to get on a plane and pull you home by your hair, I will," I said without thinking, regretting the words that were too late to take back.

"Mom!" she screamed. "It's my life. You're treating me like a child."

There was a long pause. I closed my eyes, knowing I'd made a big mistake turning the talk into something negative. I didn't want to fight with her or have it become distant and cold like the relationship between my mother and me.

Before we said our good-byes, I got distracted and didn't tell her how much I missed her. Meddling became my favorite pastime and everything else took a backseat, including all the questions on my list. *Was Laura really thinking the relationship through? Did she really believe something good would come out of it? Maybe he did like her. Or maybe not, and he was seeing her to get a free ride to the United States.*

Of course, she was old enough to take care of herself, but I still worried. Would he take advantage of her, of the situation? Especially since she said her Russian wasn't all that great. She probably spoke Russian beautifully, though, but didn't admit it. Laura had always been modest about her knowledge and abilities, the traits that got her accepted to top-notch colleges without much of a try.

When Laura told me she wanted to go to college in DC rather than an in-state one in New York, it didn't seem like a good idea at first because of the expense. But after she got a scholarship, we agreed to give it a shot and she started at American University. I'd thought about moving as well to put some distance between Raymond and me. But not right away. What if it didn't work out? What if she wanted to come home? But that day never came.

When Laura began her junior year, I decided it was time to move. Raymond helped me find a job at an architectural firm in Silver Spring, Maryland, about forty-five minutes from Laura, so it worked out well. We weren't on top of each other; we respected each other's privacy and always called before visiting.

On one hand, I was ready to move away from Raymond. By then, we'd been seeing each other for sixteen years. But it was hard to get over him. His voice, his laughter, his even temper, they all consumed me. After the move, I rarely saw him, maybe two or three times a year when visiting my mother. By then, we'd moved on from being lovers to friends. It was a pleasure to call him a friend, just a friend, after all those years together.

But even after the move, I always compared other men to Max, my sweet Max, and then to Raymond. Maybe it was the energy I gave off, but I hardly went out. Just a dinner here and there. Other than the comparisons to Max and Raymond, nothing ever lasted.

When Laura graduated, she began working for a local publisher and moved to Dupont Circle. A few months earlier, I'd started a new job and moved into Washington's Tenleytown neighborhood after falling in love with my ninth-floor apartment and its wall-to-wall windows. But I could enjoy my apartment for only a short time. Before long, my mother moved in.

At first, I had an open mind, trying to put aside all our differences and the disappointment we'd held onto. She was my mother, after all. Of course, if she had it her way, she would have gone back to her roach-infested apartment in New York where she lived alone for many years—where the early memories of her family remained, not like the bits and pieces scattered about in my apartment.

I ripped up the note with the questions I'd neglected to ask Laura during our call and searched for some chocolate in my nightstand, thinking about the heated conversation we had about her new Russian boyfriend. The chocolate wrapper stayed open and empty, with little shavings of chocolate spread about like splinters, annoying me like the sand in a pair of shoes you can't quite shake out.

I hurried down the hall to the kitchen and found a chocolate bar my mother had partially devoured. After shoving the last piece in my mouth, I snapped my fingers and pulled the stool into the pantry, remembering Greg's story about hiding his joints. Wobbling as I stepped up, willing to break an arm or leg in the process from a fall, I lifted the unopened bars to their new home on the highest shelf. If anyone was going to succumb to death by chocolate, it was going to be me.

Chapter Eleven

February crept upon me, and I couldn't believe six months had passed since Laura left. I spoke to her at the end of January and decided not to bring up the Russian boyfriend again. Sure, I knew his name but didn't want to get accustomed to saying it. Instead, we talked about the weather, her students, the museums, and some goodies she asked me to send in a care package.

The necessities from her list came first and were an easy find: Woolite, multivitamins, and ponytail holders. Then, special requests for new music took me to Foggy Bottom's Tower Records, where I handed over her list to a guy behind the counter who pushed his long hair aside to read the names while air-drumming with one hand. *Cool*, he said, then told me to stay put and, within minutes, brought back cassettes by Depeche Mode, Pearl Jam, and Nirvana, ones I'd never heard of before but now knew how to pronounce. He threw them in a yellow plastic bag along with some postcards and bumper stickers.

While fixing Laura's package, I realized how much we took for granted, being able to waltz into any store, at any time, and buy all these goodies. Sure, we were warned that packages wouldn't make it to her in one piece or that they'd arrive open and rummaged through. It was a chance we took and something I didn't try to understand, even as crazy as it sounded. It was the slice of life, not the conveniences that enticed her. But at the same time, like she'd said more than once, being an American made it easier. It made it fleeting, in a positive way. Laura had people she could count on and could leave whenever she wanted. She could fly away at any given moment and take the memories with her, leaving any worry or hardship behind.

I had fun preparing the package and got up earlier for work to put it together, filling it up with the goodies and letters from her friends as a surprise. Matt and Gina wrote feverishly to get them to me the next day. The package included three letters including mine, some essentials, the cassettes, and her favorite butterscotch candies and bubblegum, enough to last a good month.

While I reached for the tape, my mother began screaming from her room. I ran over and found her sitting on the floor with her hand on the side of the bed, trying to pull herself up.

"I fell again," she moaned and began crying.

She had a cut on her forehead and was bleeding from it. I sat her on the bed and went to get some washcloths. As I cleaned her up, she told me how she tried to get out of bed and slipped from the mattress to the floor.

"Maybe you got dizzy again."

"I'm a bother," she cried. "You don't want me here. I'm just in the way."

After two years with me, she finally spoke the truth. And I wanted to agree with her. To tell her it was terrible we couldn't talk about our issues. How it felt when she cut my braid. Or when she ripped up my drawings. How, even once, it would have been nice to hear that she loved me, even if she didn't mean it, just to say it out of obligation or, better yet, out of habit. I wanted to tell her all of this when she mentioned being a burden. But instead, I lied.

"No, Mother, you're not any trouble. These things happen. Even I fell the other day in front of the building. You'll be fine.

Here, take this," I said and gave her a second washcloth. "Hold it over the cut a little while longer."

This wasn't the first time my mother had fallen, but the wound made it more serious. Would it be better if she went to a nursing home? A place where she could get more care, more help? Working full-time hadn't allowed me to give her the extra attention she needed, even if we could stand being around each other that often.

I grabbed some coffee, sat on my bed, and tried to keep my eyes open, checking on my mother every few minutes. I pulled out Laura's letters and reread them. Her letters always made me laugh. They gave me energy, along with the coffee, to get ready for work. But sometimes all I wanted was to get into bed. With its four fluffy pillows, it looked more enticing each day especially this winter, which had turned out to be just as cold as the Russian one. If Laura had to suffer through a bitter winter, we would as well, my coworkers joked. Spring couldn't come soon enough, here or in Russia. Before taping up the box, I threw in a pair of wool socks, even though she didn't ask for them, and prayed the package would make its way to Laura in one piece.

Chapter Twelve

A few weeks later, a letter and photographs from Laura arrived in the mail. I pictured her sitting on the floor of her room, as she had in high school, listening to music while writing in her journal. Or sitting on her bed in St. Petersburg, looking across the room as she thought about what to write while listening to the tapes from Tower Records.

March 2, 1994

Momitchka,

Thanks so much for the supplies! Not sure if I should tell you, but when I got the package, it had already been opened. All the supplies were in there, but I don't know if anything was taken. I know you mentioned you were planning to buy a few cassettes. Absolutely no big deal if you forgot. But if you did, somebody else is listening to them, and I'm sorry you went through all that trouble. Anyways, I devoured the candy and gum within the first few days, although I'm glad to say that I can find those here. They've even got Milky Way and Twix bars. But it must be pronounced "Meelkee Vay" and "Tveex" or the salespeople won't understand you. Once I asked for a Twix and after asking a gazillion times, the guy finally said, "Oh, you vant a Tveex" as if I had a speech impediment.

You'll be happy to hear, although you'll deny it, that Yuri and I are no longer seeing each other. All of a sudden, he stopped coming to visit me. No visits, no phone calls, no

Yuri. I was worried at first, so I went to his dorm. His roommate came to the door and pretended that Yuri wasn't there. C'est la vie, as they say in Russian, I mean French, or whatever the hell language you choose. It's no big deal, except there's a better way of doing it. Do you think it was the cultural difference? Or maybe he was tired of playing charades when we were just trying to communicate. I need to find a nice American guy, one who understands me, my life, my humor, and my damn language skills.

I started my second semester a few weeks ago, and it's still only two days a week of teaching. What a job! I'm getting used to working so little and having so much fun. I've started taking Russian lessons twice a week now to help thaw my brain. It seems that living in the foreign dorm has its downside: most people speak English. My teacher really pushes me on the hard stuff and gives me lots of homework (yuck), so I'm hoping things will start moving along.

They've got a great exhibit at the Hermitage—Impressionist paintings by Monet, Picasso, Degas, etc. It's here only until the end of April. Maybe you'll change your mind and come over, even if it's just to see the exhibit?

By the way, Happy International Women's Day! It's on March 8. All women get to celebrate, not just sweethearts like on Valentine's Day. I really like the idea. Maybe someone will have an urge to buy me some flowers. I'd even settle for a Milky Way or Twix, I mean Tveex.

Overall, everything is great. I'm looking forward to some warmer weather, which won't be for another couple of months. I fell on my butt the other day when I turned to check out some cute guy, and I didn't see the ice patch. Lesson learned—don't check out hot guys on cold days.

I think about you all the time and miss our Sunday morning chats over coffee and bagels. Oh, I read that your *winter has been brutal! I guess you're suffering like me—suppose we'll have our winter war stories to share. Hope you're well and staying warm.*

Love,
Dochka

Laura knew me all too well. I was relieved that Yuri hadn't called or shown up. She needed to focus on her job and the experience, what she was really after. I considered giving her another reason to dislike Russia by telling her about the tapes that didn't make it but decided to keep it to myself in the next letter, especially after Yuri dropping her like that.

The TV blared from my mother's room, a telltale sign she wasn't wearing her hearing aid. She always made it loud, and if she couldn't find the remote, she'd call for me to turn it up. Watching the news or game shows became her favorite pastime. And for the last two weeks since her fall, it seemed like every channel showcased nursing homes, saying how poorly they were run, how the patients weren't receiving enough attention, and how the staff didn't seem all that concerned. I hadn't seriously considered a nursing home, but what if she kept falling? What if she needed more care? Or what if I stopped caring?

All these years, I'd tried to understand what she'd gone through, her miscarriage, leaving Germany, all she and my father left behind. Did she—or did we—have too much baggage to care for each other? Was having her with me just to make myself feel better? Or a responsibility and nothing more than a nod to my father and Aunt Regina? To take my mind off it, I read Laura's letter over and over again, only getting even more angry about the tapes being snatched and enjoyed by someone else, until my mother called out for me from her room.

"Did you see this program? It's about a nursing home and how terrible it is." She lifted her arm and pointed at the television. "That man sitting there drooling. And the screaming was coming from every direction. Nobody paid no attention."

"Mother, not every place is like that. Those news programs need to report on something when it's a slow news day. They want to show their humanitarian side. That they're exposing something to the community."

"Ach, it's terrible," she said. "That's where you want to send me. To the crazy home," she added with a nervous laugh.

"Who said I was sending you there? Or anywhere? Besides, a crazy home is for crazy people. You're not crazy. You know exactly what you're doing every second of the day."

I left her room and went to the kitchen to prepare dinner. My eighty-four-year old mother would be with me until one of us died, a thought I had to get used to, one that made me take it out on the poor vegetables as the knife attacked them, leaving stains of vegetable flesh wounds in the wooden cutting board.

Growing up, I'd always help my mother chop vegetables and prepare the table, but it was done with a lot more care and control. That's how I earned my allowance. It was only ten cents a week, but I was diligent and saved every penny for two years for a bicycle.

"Mamma, guess what?" I said after counting my money that day, all excited to go shopping. "I have enough money to get my bicycle!"

"Elsa, I've thought about it and decided it's not a good idea to get one."

"Mamma, you said I could."

"I know what I said. But there's no place to put it, or ride."

"Mamma, you promised," I cried.

"Elsa," my father called from the hall. "The éclairs are waiting for us."

As I ran down the hall to meet my father, he whispered, "I will talk to your mother later about the bicycle, okay?"

75

My father never yelled. He never wanted to upset my mother, so even when he discussed the bike with her, the answer was still no. All my girlfriends had them and they would go to the park on weekends with their family and friends. I never learned how to ride until I turned twenty-three when Max taught me on our honeymoon. He was determined, running beside the bike all sweaty to make sure it didn't fall. He said the best place to learn was on the grass with a slight slope. I was nervous and, of course, thought he was crazy.

After an hour of trying with Max running alongside me, I got the hang of it and we rode every day during our honeymoon. We couldn't get enough. When we got back to New York, we bought bikes and always rode when the weather agreed. Many weekends in the summer, we'd pack a picnic and stop to have lunch along the way.

"Let's find a shady spot," I said as we hopped off our bikes one day at the park.

"You could use a little sun. It's good for you," Max said and put his bike down.

"But I'm already shvitzing like crazy," I whined fanning myself with my hand while he spread out a blanket for us.

He walked over and wrapped his arms around my waist. "It's good to sweat, gets rid of the bad stuff."

"Tell that to my hair. It probably looks like I stuck my finger in a socket."

"You look beautiful no matter what, but I have a solution." Max took a cloth napkin from the picnic basket and tied it around my hair like a scarf. "See, problem solved."

"Can we just stay here all day and not go to my parents' place?" I asked but knew Max would convince me to go. It was Aunt Regina's birthday after all, and we always celebrated with her.

Max reached into the basket for our sandwiches and apples. He placed them on top of a cloth napkin after smoothing it out.

"It's your mom, isn't it?" he asked, reading my mind. "Let me talk to her, tell her she's being too hard on you."

"Oh God, please don't," I said, sitting up and leaning on my elbows. "We just don't see eye to eye."

He came closer and smelled strands of hair that had fallen out of my makeshift scarf before tucking them back in their place.

"Max, promise."

"Okay, okay. I promise," he said and started to kiss my neck. He pulled me down to the grass and tried to put his hand under my shirt.

I giggled. "People will see."

"Nobody's watching. Well, maybe those two squirrels over there. They're trying to get some pointers."

"I think they're just eyeing our sandwiches."

"They can have my lunch. I'd rather nibble on something else," Max said before we kissed like two teenagers lost in our own world.

• • •

"So when are you going to start a family?" Aunt Regina asked later that evening as Max cut her birthday cake and passed pieces around the table.

"*Tante*, we've hardly been married a year," I answered.

"Why wait? Before you know it, you'll be sixty-five like me, with one foot in the grave," Regina said.

"You love being dramatic, don't you?" my father teased. "I think you missed your calling to become an actress."

Max handed me a piece of chocolate cake. "She has a point, sweetheart. Why wait?"

"Ah, our Max is ready," my father said with a grin. "Usually it's the other way around."

Max stared at me with the most beautiful, innocent smile anyone could give, his big hazel eyes having their way with me. "I'd be lying if I said I wasn't ready," he added.

"Forget the cake, go home now, and start working on your baby."

"*Tante!*" I screamed, embarrassed that she'd say that in front of my parents.

"Don't rush her," my mother interrupted. "She needs to grow up more."

"What's that supposed to mean?" I said defensively. Max put his hand on mine and started rubbing it.

My mother didn't answer and, instead, took a bite of her cake.

"Mother, what did you mean by that?"

"Parenting is a huge responsibility. You need to be ready to look after children and give them the care they need."

"You don't think I'm ready?" I asked.

Again, my mother didn't answer, choosing to ignore me or pretending not to hear.

Aunt Regina walked over to fix my scarf and rested her hands on my shoulders. "Of course she's ready. She's a very responsible young lady."

Anger overcame me after my mother's comment sank in. She never thought I was ready for anything. Never ready for makeup. Never ready for a bike. Never ready to become an architect. I was never ready for anything, in her book. I pushed the chair back and stormed off to the kitchen.

Max followed me. "Sweetheart, come back to the table." He stood behind me and wrapped his arms around my waist as I started washing the dishes.

"I'm letting my mother get to me again. On *Tante*'s birthday, no less."

"Elsa, put those dishes down, right now," Aunt Regina said by the kitchen doorway.

"I'm sorry, *Tante*, for ruining your birthday. It's the same old thing, over and over again."

"You didn't ruin it, *leibshen*," she whispered and came closer to take the sponge out of my hand. "Don't let Millie get to you. She's a sad soul."

"You're always saying that."

"Come now, really, don't let it eat at you. We all think you'd make a wonderful mother," she said before walking back to the living room.

Max kissed the back of my neck and leaned over to turn off the water. In spite of my mother, I wanted to go home right away and start working on our family, like *Tante* teased, proving my mother wrong. But I wasn't ready. Not because I had to grow up, but because I was selfish. I loved Max, loved being married to him, spending time with him, just the two of us. Becoming parents would have changed our relationship, and I didn't want that to happen yet.

"Elsa, Max, come sing with me. It's my new favorite song," Aunt Regina yelled from the living room as she put on her favorite tune, "Georgy Girl."

We left the dishes in the sink and joined in, even though Regina sounded much better solo. Max grabbed our hands and took turns spinning us around the living room and several more times when she replayed the song. My father joined us in his own special way, by clapping along. When Max bumped into the table, the record skipped a few beats and Aunt Regina playfully hit him over the head with the newspaper for being so clumsy. We all roared with laughter except for my mother, who stared across the room, deep in thought and so far away.

Chapter Thirteen

Right before Passover, I began cleaning house, truly cleaning. I was never known to be a neat freak, but it had always been a tradition to get ready and organized for Passover—and even more so now that my mother lived with me. Before changing the dishes and cleaning bread crumbs from the cabinets, I went through three closets and made piles of clothing not worn since the year before Laura left for Russia. *Maybe one day it will come back in style*, I'd often say before moving the hanger aside in the closet.

Not this time. This time I indulged in spring cleaning and filled ten bags with clothing, piled high by the front door for the Salvation Army. The refrigerator was next and then the pantry, where I climbed the stepladder and pulled down the Passover dishes to replace my everyday ones.

After that, I plopped on the sofa like a used mop and rested for an hour before getting ready to meet Susan at Pasquale's in Woodley Park. Their hearth-cooked pizzas were the best in town and my favorite came topped with pesto, artichokes, and red peppers, a perfect treat before shunning bread during Passover. We got our favorite table and ordered some Chianti.

"Just think," Susan said while filling up my glass with more wine. "No pizza for eight days, that's if you're planning to follow Passover."

"I rarely crave pizza, but just because I'm not supposed to have it, I'll want it every day."

"Kind of like sex."

I laughed. "I've never heard anyone put pizza and sex in the same category."

"What I meant was," Susan added, "if you're not having sex, you kind of forget about it, then you have it once, and you want it all the time. But with me, it's not the sex that's the problem, it's the dates."

Normally, she'd fidget with her wedding band when explaining her thoughts. But her finger was bare, with a decades-long tan line taking the place of her ring. It was the first time she'd left the house without it since her husband died and, to me, it felt sudden and complete all at once.

"Really? I can't imagine you having a problem getting dates. You're gorgeous."

"They're either married or messing around on the side, and who needs that?" she said.

Susan looked down at her hand and, after realizing her ring wasn't there, she played with the edge of her napkin. "How are we supposed to meet men? What about—"

"No way," I interrupted. "Not one of those Jewish singles dances. What do you call them, matzo mixers?"

"What's wrong with that? You have to meet them somehow," she said.

"I'd rather watch reruns of bad talk shows than go to one of those."

"How many have you been to?" Susan asked, holding her gaze on me.

"None, but I've heard horror stories."

"Then," she said, raising her glass and grinning, "how do you know without trying?"

I wanted to say *touché*, but instead I shrugged and waited to answer after the waiter left. "Can't imagine standing around the room with other single women looking for the same thing. Seems so desperate."

She pushed her long hair back and behind her shoulder. "With that kind of attitude, you're never going to meet anyone."

"I don't know. On one hand, I want to meet someone, but on the other, I'm trying to accept that I'm over fifty, and it's just gonna be that much harder."

"Maybe, but it's worth a try," she said and signaled for the check.

Was Susan turning a new leaf? Was she finally ready to open up and meet someone?

After dinner, we strolled along Connecticut Avenue. I stopped to light a cigarette and put the pack back in my purse. Washington had just gotten over its out-of-the-ordinary cold spell with more people out and about, leaving their scarves, heavy coats, and gloves behind. Some waited outside restaurants for tables to open up and others rushed toward the Metro with their backpacks and computer bags strapped across their shoulders.

We walked for a short while, with some window-shopping in between, then parted ways on the corner of our street. Susan crossed and I waited for the light to turn green, fumbling in my purse for a mint to fight the garlic that had overstayed its welcome.

"Laura, wait up," a woman yelled.

Hearing the name startled me and made me turn around fast, out of habit, even though it wasn't my Laura she called out for, with her Southern accent so unfamiliar. Two girls, in their late teens and looking alike, approached. They held bags from the Gap and Banana Republic, twirling them around and then letting them spin.

Two adults about my age joined them a moment later. The woman held on tightly to her purse, making me think it was a family of tourists who'd come to DC for spring break. The man rubbed the woman's arm and accidentally knocked off the sweater resting on her shoulders. He bent down to pick it up and gave her a kiss before tying it around her waist. One of the daughters caught me looking over and smiled.

I smiled back and immediately my heart ached, thinking of Max, our time together when we were young, his desire to add to the family, something we never got the chance to do. If he hadn't been taken from us, how would our lives have ended up? Would we still be living in New York? Picnicking in Central Park? Going on our very own spring break vacations? Would Laura have a brother or sister? I was living vicariously through this family on the corner of Wisconsin Avenue, a family of strangers who obviously still loved one another deeply, which made me dream of the same for me, for us.

Chapter Fourteen

It took me a few weeks to escape from the spell that perfect family on the corner put me under, with their two beautiful daughters and loving parents. I'd often fall asleep thinking about them and wake up doing the same. One morning, I finally snapped out of it, got up without hitting the snooze button, and made my way to the kitchen after picking up the newspaper that sat outside on the mat by my front door. My mother usually beat me to it, but on occasion she'd sleep in. As I waited for my coffee to brew, I sank into the sofa to read the paper, usually skipping right to the style section, but the front page news shocked me.

"CEO's Son Kills Two Women on Dupont Circle."

The headline said everything but I read further, skimming the words to get to the bottom. *Son of local CEO. Driving 80 mph. Doesn't stop at red light. Hits two women in their twenties. Both women die at the scene.* The first thought that came to mind was Laura and how that could have been her. She used to live on Dupont Circle, just one block from the accident. That moment was the first—and only—time in all these months I was glad she wasn't here, living in DC, out and about in her old neighborhood. I drank my coffee while reading the style section but couldn't concentrate. Picturing the accident brought me back to losing Max. I imagined the look on the parents' faces when the police came to their door to break the news.

After rereading the article, I took the newspaper to the hall table and left it for my mother. A light glowed from her room, so instead of putting the newspaper on the table, I laid it on her bed and noticed my mother in her chair. She sometimes napped like that after getting up and dressed for the day. Usually when she fell asleep in her chair in the morning, I'd leave her alone. But this time, something felt off. It was the littlest thing that nobody would have noticed: She was still in her nightgown, as if she'd slept in the chair all night. My mother hardly went out but, no matter what, she always put on a dress and stockings after waking up.

"Mother, are you feeling okay? Why don't you go lie down," I repeated twice, but she didn't respond.

I walked closer, picking up her watch from the floor by her bed, and noticed that although her head was bent over and resting on her chin as if she were sleeping, her eyes were open. I shook her hard, screaming for her to wake up. She sat there, lifeless and slumped over. Her brown eyes, which still sparkled at her age, were glassy and lacked luster. I rushed to the phone and dialed 911.

"What the hell took you so long?" I screamed at the two paramedics who arrived ten minutes later.

"Ma'am, please calm down. We got here as quick as we could."

They wouldn't tell me if she was dead, but I already knew. I already knew they wouldn't be bringing her back. After asking a few questions, they told me to give them some room.

I watched as they felt for a pulse. How they lifted her out of the chair and laid her down on her side before picking her up. How they put her on the stretcher. How they finally told me there were no vital signs and covered her face.

When we arrived at the hospital, the doctor was ready and waiting for what had to be done—and for what had been done so many times before. Why did it seem so simple? People die.

Hospitals pronounce them dead. They write out a death certificate and move onward. On with the next one, like an assembly line called life but instead of pieces being put together, they're pulled apart.

There were many details to take care of, but where to start? My mother led a long life, longer than anyone in my family. She died in my home, in her room, and not in some strange place or in a nursing home where she thought she'd end up one day.

I sat in the emergency room and stared at the floor, counting the checkered pattern that reminded me of the linoleum floor in my kitchen growing up. So many memories, so many lost and regretful, took place in our New York apartment. But there, in the ER, I couldn't get myself to cry over the loss of my mother. No matter what, the tears wouldn't come. Was it because nobody was with me, to console me, to allow me to break down against? Why wasn't I crying for the loss of my parent? Now that both of them were gone, I had become an orphan and being an orphan, at any age, changed people, making them stronger and more vulnerable at the same time.

A nurse stopped by and offered to order me a cab. When I got home, I immediately called the rabbi from her synagogue. They'd coordinate with the hospital to transfer my mother so she could be buried the following day. It was late morning and my next call was to Russia to break the news.

Since Laura didn't have a phone in her room, I called her advisor who lived in the same dorm. We could only use this number for emergencies, although I often wanted to take advantage of it many times and pretend my calls were urgent, just to hear her voice. He answered and called back to ease the cost.

"Mom, what's wrong? Did something happen?" Laura asked, skipping her usual greeting.

"I didn't want to tell you over the phone." I paused.

"Now you're scaring me. Tell me what?"

"*Oma* had a stroke this morning."

"Is she okay?"

I could hardly get the words out. "She didn't make it," I whispered.

The line became silent, long enough to hear the static and crackling from a bad connection. Laura cried while trying to continue. "I can't believe it. I told her I'd be back, and we'd spend time together."

"Laura, don't be hard on yourself. You spent plenty of time together."

"I should have sat with her more." She paused again, longer this time. "It makes me sad that we can't say good-bye to our loved ones."

"Sweetie, she didn't suffer, and I'm glad for that. But I know how you feel about saying good-bye. There were so many things I wanted to say."

"Like what?"

"Oh, I don't know." I thought for a moment. "To talk about our relationship and how it could have been better."

"Mom, I don't want you to be alone right now. I'm coming home."

"No, don't. I'll be fine," I said and thought through all the details to get ready. "It's all happening so fast. I'm leaving in the morning for New York to bury her."

"Can you wait an extra day? I'd have to call the airlines, but I think I can be there by tomorrow evening."

"Wish I could, but she needs to be buried tomorrow. You know, it's Orthodox tradition and something that can't wait."

"Okay," she said. "Why don't you come here afterwards?"

I let out a nervous laugh. "That's crazy."

"I can keep you company. And it might be good to have a little distraction."

"How many times have I said I never wanted to go there, don't you remember?"

"Come on, please," Laura pleaded, with her positive energy trying to make its way through the long-distance connection. "It'll take your mind off things. And the weather is warming up. I'll take care of everything. Well, except for the plane ticket."

"I don't know. The only thing that's of any interest is Red Square. But you're not in Moscow."

"That's easy. It's just an overnight ride on the train."

"Let me think about it, and before I leave for New York, I'll let you know. I love you, kid," I said after Laura kept asking me to make the trip.

Visiting Laura was the last thing on my mind. The cold weather. The snow and ice more than half of the year. The long lines. The robberies and violence. The packages being opened and rummaged through by thugs. Bleak seemed like an understatement.

But the sound of my daughter's voice, when she begged me to come more than once, pulled at me. It made me give the trip a second thought. It made me want to see her and not have to wait two months.

Throughout the evening, I went back and forth until deciding to go. It would only be for a week and since my coworker Donna knew the ins and outs of foreign travel, I didn't sweat over the details of getting prepared. I'd leave in two weeks, at the beginning of May. That would give me a chance to settle my mother's affairs, work another week, and mentally prepare for the trip to a place my daughter called her second home.

I phoned my boss after lighting my fifth cigarette, three over my daily limit, then made all the arrangements for my mother's burial, which was within the Orthodox Jewish tradition—to be buried simply and within one day. She'd be buried next to my father. And next to Michael. For all these years, only my parents, Max, and Aunt Regina knew what happened to Michael. Nobody else. Not Raymond. Not even my daughter. For Laura's whole life, I lied about Michael, the Michael she thought was my mother's brother who died as a teenager. The Michael my mother used to mumble about in German whenever she was sad or wanted to go back to New York.

For my entire life, my mother told me not to talk about it or ignored me when I tried. She never wanted to hear a word. She could hardly say his name. Now that she was gone, would I be able to open up to the person I loved the most? Would I be able to tell my darkest secret about the darkest day of my life?

But one day, with or without me, Laura would visit my parents' gravesite. When my father passed, Laura came with me to the cemetery, but she was so young, too young to put two and two together. Eventually, the day would come, the day she'd notice something that didn't make sense when she looked at the dates on Michael's grave. And that was the reason why I had to go to Russia, the one place I never dreamed of going.

To confess after all these years.

Chapter Fifteen

It was September 28, 1952. A Sunday. I remembered the exact day so well. I was ten years old and my brother Michael was four. Yes, I had a brother named Michael. I loved that boy. Even though he was much younger, I loved playing with him more than anything.

It was the day before Yom Kippur and my mother was hard at work in the kitchen preparing our evening meal. She'd always make a big fuss out of it, spending hours in there since we'd have to fast the next day. She made a big pot roast, potato salad, vegetables, and an apple crumble for dessert.

It was always a busy time, and I always helped her in the kitchen until Michael started to walk. On that day, my mother asked me to do a simple task: to watch my brother for a short time while she and my Aunt Regina finished up the apple crumble.

I should have been watching my brother. And I was. Except for that one, very brief moment I left him to use the bathroom.

I should have called out to my mother, just to let her know that Michael would be alone for a minute. It was one of those days in September, a smoldering day inside and, with all the cooking, we needed some fresh air. It hadn't dawned on me that she'd left the window open in the living room.

My mother had opened it to let in some air. But never told me. Or maybe she did, but it didn't register. After washing my hands, I could hear my mother's footsteps pound the floor as she stomped up and down the hallway, as if she were in combat boots marching to keep up with soldiers in her battalion.

"Where is Michael?" she called out. "Michael? *Wo ist sie?*"

"In the living room, Mamma," I responded after opening the bathroom door and following her.

"He is not there," she said and started pacing the hall and walking back and forth.

"Michael?" she repeated over and over, each time her voice getting louder and more strained.

My heart started to pound like the rapidly firing sounds from my mother's frantic footsteps. As soon as I was about to say *that's where I left him,* my mother bent over and looked out our living room window. The curtains swept against the side of a chair, one that wasn't in front of the window a few minutes before.

My stomach dropped. I felt nauseous. And at that very moment, my mother screamed and ran down our long hallway to the front door. Then Aunt Regina screamed and wailed with an intensity that paralyzed me. I tried to go toward the chair, finally finding the courage to walk into the living room and look out the window from our apartment.

That was the last time I saw Michael. Several people surrounded him as Aunt Regina pushed them back. My mother leaned over his body and then looked up toward the window. Her mascara ran down her face like dirty train tracks.

I looked away and sunk onto the floor in front of the chair, covering my ears as the sirens blasted out and got louder as they approached our building.

No matter how many times I relived it, I couldn't remember what happened next. I couldn't remember what, if anything, Aunt Regina said to me. I couldn't remember what, if anything, my parents said. They wouldn't allow me to go to the cemetery because I was too young, or that's what they told me that evening. On the day they buried Michael, before they left our

91

apartment, my father held onto my weeping mother, but not out of comfort. He held her up because she couldn't walk, her grief so strong it pulled her down.

All those childhood years and into adulthood, Michael should have been right by my side, growing up with me. Chasing me. Playing hide-and-seek. Asking for advice. Telling me about his crushes. Sharing secrets he'd kept from our parents. After that day in September, I never sat by the window again to watch the traffic on Broadway. And I never remembered my mother opening another one.

• • •

My mother's bedroom in my DC apartment stayed empty and cold, and I could picture her last days there. Sitting in her chair, watching TV or tweezing the few long hairs that had grown on her chin. It didn't seem like much of a life, like Laura said, growing old with nothing to do or look forward to. The closet door was open and on the shelf sat her burial garment. In the Jewish religion, the funeral was simple. No open or fancy caskets to etch in our memory. I pulled her garment from the shelf then looked in the closet and around her room, deciding what else to bring with me.

I took out her photographs stacked in a shoebox beside her bed. In it, pictures of her father and mother, scenes from Germany, and one of Michael when he was two years old, made up her family. Not one photograph of me. I looked through them and wept, remembering my loving father before putting them back and packing for the short trip to bury my mother.

• • •

The following day, we held the ceremony at the funeral home in New York. Not many people came, mainly congregants from her synagogue. Most of my mother's friends and relatives had died years before. She outlived just about everyone: my father, Aunt Regina, Michael—at least anyone who mattered to her.

For the first time in many years, I saw my father's grave and Michael's right beside his. After the rabbi said a few prayers, he handed me the shovel, and I began covering my mother's casket with dirt, over her and the bitter memories we'd felt for so many years. How I wished we could have talked about Michael out in the open. But she never let me mention his name and, if I brought it up, she always changed the subject or ignored me. Maybe blocking it was the only way she could handle the tragedy. Maybe blaming me for it made life a little less devastating. I handed the shovel back to the rabbi and he took over, adding more dirt on the casket before passing the shovel around so he could say a few more prayers and finish the service.

After everyone left, I went back to my hotel room to lie down. It had been an exhausting day, but thoughts about Michael kept distracting me. I reached for the phone to call Raymond, to speak to someone who knew me well. I needed a friend, a familiar voice, even one from the past. It had been three years since we'd seen each other, and it made me wonder what he looked like. Did he still wear his tailored suits, the ones in tweed or seersucker that came complete with a matching pocket hanky? Or a fedora to cover his shiny bald head he often made fun of?

On the first ring, his assistant answered to screen his calls. It was always strange to hear her voice and reminded me of having that wonderful job so many years ago.

"Hello, Elsa, what a nice surprise," Raymond said. His scratchy, distinct voice lifted my mood.

"Hi," I said. "I know, it's not your birthday yet."

"Let's not hurry it up. Last year was hard enough when I hit sixty. Is everything okay? Where are you?"

"In your neck of the woods."

"Really? For work?"

"No, it's not that kind of trip." I sighed. "My mother died yesterday. We had the funeral this morning."

"I'm so sorry. Why didn't you call me? I would have gone."

"It happened so fast. I'm doing okay, considering. I'm leaving first thing in the morning but wanted to see how you're doing."

"Why don't we meet for a drink before you leave?" Raymond offered. "At the Hilton like old times? I'll clear my schedule."

Would seeing him after all these years be good for me? Would it make me miss him again? But after the day I'd had, having someone to lift my spirits was a better idea than sitting in my hotel room staring at the TV. "Sure," I finally answered. "They do make the best Bloody Marys in the city, and I could use a drink."

• • •

I freshened up and hailed a cab to Midtown, 53rd Street to be exact, and my old stomping grounds with a great job and a wonderful boss. The city was dirtier than ever, with trash overflowing from the garbage cans and cigarette butts squashed repeatedly by pedestrians. I'd forgotten how honking was a constant way of life here that never bothered me before but now grated on my nerves. I tried to overlook the bad parts about the city, an ignored reality, the kind I brushed away in hopes for a beautiful life with Raymond.

The bar in the Hilton was crowded, and I rushed to grab the last table by the window like a city driver scoring an unrestricted parking space on a busy street. I craved my Bloody Mary but decided to wait until Raymond arrived. A moment later, he walked toward me wearing a big smile and a beige hat that matched his suit and tie. As I'd remembered and as always, he was still a classy dresser.

"Is this seat taken?"

I got up and planted a kiss on his cheek.

"I'm so sorry to hear about Millie. How's everything else? Your job in Washington?"

"Everything else is fine. The only other news, other than my mother passing, is that I'm going to Russia to visit Laura."

He flicked his ashes in the tray and blew smoke to the side. "Russia? I never imagined!"

"That makes two of us," I grinned and motioned for him to pass me a cigarette.

"You hate cold weather. You'd complain every time we had to walk more than a few feet in the cold. As if you were going to die," he teased as the waitress approached. Raymond ordered two Bloody Marys, extra spicy the way we liked them.

After we reminisced for a little while, it was as if we had nothing else to talk about so we stared at each other before he looked away. We missed one another, certainly not for the sex, which was over many years ago. We missed having conversations, the jokes, the companionship.

Even though my relationship with Raymond never panned out, I never regretted the years we spent together. He made so many of them bearable after losing Max, and though he would never leave his wife, he never abandoned me. That was one reason dating in Washington became difficult. I always blamed it on getting older or being stuck in my ways, but it was more than that. I constantly compared men to Max and then to Raymond.

On the train back to Washington, I thought about the years that had passed and the time spent in New York when I was younger, Laura's age now. Then I started to prepare myself mentally and physically to travel halfway around the world to see my daughter and, in her words, visit the most magical place. But the real reason for my visit would be to confess my darkest secret. How would the words come out? How would I find the courage? Since my mother never talked about it, how could I possibly know how Laura would react? To help with my confession, I jotted down some notes on the train ride back home.

Laura, I have some bad news.

No, scratch that. She'll get scared that something serious happened, and she'll worry.

Laura, I've been hiding something from you all these years.

No, scratch that, too. That starts in such a negative way that she'll have no choice but to be mad at me.

Laura, I've been living with so much guilt that I couldn't find the courage to tell you all these years.

Okay, that's really bad because it sounds like I want her to feel sorry for me.

Laura, I had a brother once.

That's it. Be direct.

I used to feed him. He hated sweet potatoes and would spit them at the wall. I used to play with him all the time. He loved peek-a-boo. But, instead of covering my eyes and yelling peek-a-boo, we'd close our eyes together and yell it at the same time. I always had a funny look on my face when he'd open his eyes, and boy, he would let out the most hysterical, contagious laugh. He was so ticklish, more ticklish than anyone I'd ever known. I didn't even have to touch him, and he'd giggle. I would put my hand really close to his belly and start moving my fingers in the air, pretending to tickle him. I used to make him laugh. A lot.

When he was a baby, I'd push on his nose and make funny noises. So whenever he hurt himself, I'd come to the rescue, push on his nose, make funny noises, and make him forget about the pain.

We often went to the park and on the way back, without my mother knowing, we'd go to the corner market and sneak a chocolate bar. My father always gave me pocket change, and I bought little goodies for us. I always told Michael not to tell Mamma. He loved that it was our little secret.

He loved when I would draw funny pictures. When I brushed his teeth while singing funny songs. When I tucked him in and sang "Itsy Bitsy Spider." He always asked me to stay, so I would lie down next to him. It seemed that as soon as his head hit the pillow, he'd be fast asleep. And, I knew that about five minutes in, I could tiptoe out of the room because his cute snoring would be my cue to leave.

In the mornings, he'd often cry when I left for school. He didn't want to be without me. To cheer him up, I'd do a chicken dance, flap my arms, and move my legs in and out. Even to this day, I still remembered the look on his face when he stopped crying and, while laughing, he'd lick the tears that fell down his cheek and onto his lip.

Chapter Sixteen

My apartment felt empty even though I'd been waiting for this moment for such a long time. This moment of privacy. The moment all to myself. The moment I could breathe.

My mother had been with me for years. Now, if I wanted, I was able to walk naked through my apartment. I could dance in my underwear from room to room. But being alone without anyone around took an adjustment and so did getting my mind wrapped around going to Russia.

Donna took care of everything for the trip. She ordered my visa and plane ticket. Everything seemed to be falling into place. Except a lot distracted me—my mother's death, my confession to Laura. Many years ago, I promised myself to tell her when she was old enough, but it never happened, and many times at the last moment, I'd chicken out. Then the years flew by and, with the years, so did my courage to open up. I pushed it off, like a messy linen closet that needed organizing. For the longest time, for more than forty years, my mother lived in denial. So why not me?

But I couldn't hold the secret anymore. Millie wasn't around to make me wonder about opening up a wound that, no matter what, wouldn't heal. But when would I tell Laura? And where? Somewhere alone or out in public? The long flight to St. Petersburg would give me time to decide. The week and a half flew by and before leaving for the airport, I got one last letter from Laura.

The Secret We Lost

April 27, 1994

Mom,

 I can't wait to see you! I still feel so bad that I wasn't there. It must have been so hard to handle that all on your own.

 I've arranged for you to stay with me. The two hotels down the block cost a gazillion bucks, so what's not to love about saving money?! I also bought tickets for the theatre, and the train tickets for our short excursion to Moscow. You mentioned you wanted to see Red Square, so I'm excited to show you. You're going to have a great time, I promise!

 Another piece of good news: the weather has warmed up, but it's still only in the upper 40s, so bring some warm clothes and comfortable shoes you don't mind getting dirty. Or even bring winter boots, since you won't be used to the weather. Everything will be great, so don't worry. If you need to reach me, call Andrew's number. I'll see you at the airport!

Da skorava (until soon)
Laura

Her one line made me snicker.

Everything will be great, so don't worry.

Easy for her to say, without a care in the world. I was pretty sure everything wouldn't be great, if she couldn't forgive me.

• • •

Matt and Greg offered to take me to the airport, setting a tradition since they'd become so used to coming and going to Dulles. They shoved my suitcase in their hatchback, and off we went, making great time, especially with the DC traffic being so unpredictable.

As we walked to the gate, I looked away when they asked about checking on Millie. Shame on me for not mentioning my mother earlier. They were leaving for vacation the day she passed, and I didn't want to ruin their trip. It broke my heart to break it to them like this, but it couldn't wait another two weeks.

"Guys, I'm sorry. I was about to tell you," I said.

"Tell us what?"

I stopped walking and waited for them to turn around. "My mother died a few weeks ago."

"What! What happened?" both Matt and Greg yelled at the same time. Matt stopped and put his hand on my arm.

"She had a stroke," I said.

"Why didn't you tell us?" Greg asked and hugged me.

"I'm sorry. I didn't want to spoil your vacation. And you just got back and, I don't know, I decided to tell you in person."

"You should have called," Matt said as he looked straight ahead, avoiding eye contact with me. "So what if we were leaving for vacation. It was important."

I couldn't handle someone else being angry, especially not knowing how Laura would react to the news. The twelve-hour flight would give me plenty of time to think it through, something I'd thought about since childhood, in a different way but with the same amount of guilt. "Please, don't be mad. It's the last thing I need right now."

"Come on, what makes you even think that?" Greg added, "We could never be mad at you."

"You guys are too good to me. What would we do without you?" I said and hugged them good-bye, promising to have a fun time.

"So sorry about Millie," Matt said as I walked off and to my gate.

"*Dosveedonyah!*" Greg yelled and waved good-bye.

• • •

On the plane, a young woman sat next to me. She reminded me so much of Laura, with her dirty-blonde hair pulled back in a ponytail, ripped jeans, and an oversized, v-neck sweater. She'd been to Russia a few times before and was on her way to spend the summer in Moscow to develop her language skills.

As she munched on pretzels, she shared stories about her visits there, flying the Russian airline where passengers passed around bottles of vodka to their neighbors on the flight. When I told her this was my first visit, she divulged some insider tips. Her eyes widened when she spoke about Russia, and I imagined Laura doing the same while writing her letters.

When we reached Frankfurt, the two of us went our separate ways, she on a plane to Moscow instead of St. Petersburg. There wasn't much of a layover, so I went directly to the next gate. A few familiar faces from my first flight gathered in the waiting area, along with some new ones. Young couples holding hands. Kids sitting on the floor, playing with their cars and dolls. Businessmen in suits, reading their newspapers or talking about their recent meetings.

I boarded the plane and took my seat, hoping the one next to mine would stay empty. Before long, a man with light-brown hair around mid-forties stopped in the aisle next to me. He placed his black leather jacket in the overhead compartment, looked at his ticket, and compared it to the number on the overhead. He squeezed by and, after organizing his briefcase, took out a book with an unrecognizable alphabet. I glanced at his well-defined arm as he turned the pages and, out of habit, noticed he wasn't wearing a wedding ring.

After we took off and got settled, the stewardess came by and asked what we'd like to drink. My neighbor waited for me to order then asked for straight vodka with soda on the side. He reached over to take his drink and stared for a few long seconds.

Why was he staring at me?
Did I have something in my teeth?
Or stuck in my hair?

"*Guten tag,*" he said after putting his drink on the tray.

"*Guten tag,*" I answered back, hoping the quick response would hide my nerves.

"*Besuchen Sie Russland zum ersten Mal?*"

I smiled without answering, not because I didn't understand but because my brain had to work harder to speak it. He quickly switched to English.

"I'm sorry, you look very German. Is this your first visit to Russia?"

I nodded. "I'm visiting my daughter. She's teaching English there. And what about you?" I asked. "Do you live in St. Petersburg?"

"I used to. Now I live in London and just go for business." He paused to stir his drink. "I love London, but Russia is my home, and my family is there."

"I hear you. It's hard to leave family behind," I said, watching him flip the plastic stirrer on his napkin.

"You know," he said, "growing up, they would always tell us it's a horrible place, a land of evil." He looked down and a grin appeared, making small wrinkles more prominent around the corner of his eye. He continued to grin and looked my way, as if he were about to relive a story that involved the two of us. "But now, after the collapse, everyone tells us how wonderful it is. Since I've never been, what's it really like?"

I wanted to go into all sorts of detail, to pretend I was well-traveled like him, to answer his question and talk about all the places I'd been. But when Laura was growing up, we didn't go on vacations or at least ones outside of Atlantic City. We lived on one salary and travel was the last thing on my mind. I'd been to Niagara Falls with Max and California with Raymond once, and recalling those memories helped me answer. "California is very different from the East Coast, where I'm from," I said. "There are many good things, but like any place, we've got our problems."

His book fell off the seat, and he bent down carefully to pick it up, making sure not to tip over the drink on his tray table. "I'm glad I was a contortionist in my previous life," he joked and placed the book in the seat pocket in front of him.

"They say it looks good on a résumé."

He laughed and continued to ask questions about the United States: how many cars people had, how much people made, questions that an American would never ask, the kind Laura mentioned in one of her letters. I still hadn't caught his name, but imagined he was a Rudolf like the famous Russian dancer, although his deep-set eyes, medium complexion, and golden brown hair reminded me of Harrison Ford.

After about an hour, I closed my eyes and rested for a short while but couldn't sleep. His aftershave with a crisp, fresh-cut grass scent, like the one I once smelled at Bloomingdale's, kept me awake and made me think of his accent and faraway romantic places I'd seen in movies. But I couldn't get distracted about a chance encounter. I was going to Russia for one reason—to tell Laura about Michael. I had to tell her during this trip, or I'd never do it, and was ready to accept the responsibility and weight of it, even through my fear.

I opened my eyes and as an announcement rang out that we would be landing in less than an hour, my excitement quickly turned to nervousness.

"I'm sorry, what a fool for not introducing myself. I'm Alexei," he said and put his hand out to shake mine. His grip was firm, and my pulse quickened when the sleeve of his sweater brushed against my wrist.

"I'm Elsa," I said, finally letting go of his hand.

"So, Elsa, what are your plans during your stay in St. Petersburg?"

I shrugged, thinking about how many details to share. "Not sure. My daughter is taking care of everything. I know we're going to Moscow for a couple of days."

"Ach, Moscow," he said and waved his hand, dismissing the thought. "It's big and dirty with absolutely no charm. You will enjoy St. Petersburg much better. It's a beautiful city."

"Maybe," I said, taking in his comment about the city, "but might as well see Red Square after coming all this way."

Alexei reached down to his briefcase, opened it, and pulled out a card. "I would like to invite you to a Russian restaurant during your stay and show you our way of dining. Seven or eight o'clock in the evening? I will be in Russia for five days. Call me as soon as you know your plans, yes?"

He handed me his business card, and I put it in my purse. *Was he just being nice by showing me around his hometown? Or was he asking me out on a date?* His eyes were still on me when I looked over. With a smile, he turned away first and picked up his book, flipping to find the page to begin again.

I'd never been out with a European man. Or even attempted a long conversation with one. Alexei seemed very different from the men I'd met. He was charming, but assertive and confident, something I wasn't used to. But then again, it had been forever since I'd been on a date.

The plane landed and passengers gathered their belongings. Alexei leaned forward to look out the window while waiting for the plane to start clearing. We stood up and after everyone moved up and out, Alexei lifted the overhead compartment and handed me my bag and coat.

"You'll need to go through customs first, so it will be a little time before you get to see your daughter."

"I don't speak a word of Russian."

"Don't worry," he said, offering to carry my bag. "I'll be right behind you. And I'll stay with you to help translate."

"Thank you," I said and glanced over again, getting a better look this time, as we followed the crowd to the customs area. He was slender and a lot taller than me. His brown hair, even more golden under the airport light, had a few gray strands around his temples. "Has anyone ever told you that you look like Harrison Ford?" I asked, trying not to stare.

"Now and again, but only when I travel."

"Hmm, why's that?"

He shrugged and rubbed his chin. "Maybe it's because I like to walk around with a whip and a fedora like Indiana Jones."

"They're in your suitcase, right?" I teased.

"Yes, and I have several in case I lose one chasing a bad guy."

We inched up and, after going through customs, walked down another long hallway where people stood waiting, some holding signs with names, others leaning forward over the line to get a quicker glimpse of passengers walking by.

Mom! Mom, over here!

My eyes sifted through the room to find Laura. There she was, beautiful as ever, standing near a column off to the left side and waving me over. She wore her hair pulled back in a high ponytail and pink gloss stained her lips, making her fair complexion look even paler and in need of a few extra doses of sunshine.

"You look beautiful. A little thin, though."

"I walk miles a day. And I always take the stairs instead of elevators."

Laura eyed Alexei with a look of intrigue that quickly turned to skepticism, an expression a father would give his teenage daughter's first date. After I introduced them, she spoke to him in Russian and lightened up after they had a quick laugh. He shook our hands and, as he walked off, reminded us to call him before quickening his pace.

"So you're already picking up men, huh?" she teased and winked.

"He was kind of persistent. I wasn't sure if he was just being nice and wanted to show me around."

"Oh, he's interested, for sure. Russian men are pretty persistent. But, we won't hold it against him since he's cute."

We walked through the terminal toward the exit, where several people waited, holding flower bouquets. "Here comes Pavel," Laura said after we walked outside. "His family has been my home away from home. By the way, he speaks about five words of English, so you might have to use some sign language."

We piled into Pavel's dented four-door sedan, and I began taking in the sights. Rows and rows of drab buildings complete with graffiti and black panels flooded my view. They looked cheap and put together quickly, almost like they were made out of cardboard and, with one small blow, would topple over. They slowly disappeared in the distance as similar ones took their place.

"*Krushchovee*," Pavel mumbled before taking a long drag from his cigarette.

"Bless you," I said, trying to make a joke.

Laura rolled her eyes and cracked her window to let the smoke out. "They're called *Khrushchovee*, named after Khrushchev. He wanted to make sure everyone had housing, so he built apartment buildings quick and cheap. He didn't seem to care much about the quality."

"Wow, lots of laundry hanging on those balconies," I said as we passed more buildings.

"Not many people have dryers. We all wear stiff underwear, remember?"

I laughed, recalling the photos Laura sent me. The ones where she laid her clothes all over the room to dry.

"What's going on over there?" I asked and pointed to a line wrapped around a building, a bottleneck I'd never seen before, not even during rush hour on a Manhattan subway platform.

Laura turned to look. "They're waiting to buy bread."

"I didn't realize it was that bad."

"It's the system, and pretty much a horrible way to buy stuff. So get this," she said and turned to me, explaining with her arms flying around like she was directing a plane to the gate. "First you decide what you want from the showcase. Then you stand in line to pay. After that, you go to another line to get the bread with a ticket or receipt. It takes forever."

"You mentioned that in your letter, but I didn't expect it to be so bad." We stopped at the corner in front of the bakery, and I began counting people in line. "I think I've experienced my very first culture shock."

"Don't worry, I'll show you the beautiful parts of St. Pete."

Pavel took a sharp turn, and Laura piled onto me. Before situating ourselves, we had a good laugh like bumper-car drivers who'd knock into each other at an amusement park. We stopped at a light and at the corner, people stood waiting for a bus. In all my years of living in New York, I'd never seen that many people waiting outside for public transportation, even in the worst rainstorm. We passed several buses packed so tight you'd have to be a world's best escape artist to get out.

The city my daughter called magical looked incredibly hopeless and depressing. Would I ever understand the spell she was under? And did it even matter? There was no point in trying to charm me. After all, my trip had nothing to do with magic, unless somehow, my confession mysteriously disappeared and no longer hung over me with the weight of my deceit.

Chapter Seventeen

After driving for twenty minutes, Laura told me we'd reached the center. Another ten and we'd be at the dorm. The crowded sidewalks made it difficult to see the storefronts behind them. We were on the edge of Nevsky Prospect, a long boulevard that took us from one end of the center to the other. At a stop, two husky, gray-haired women stood by the curb sweeping up the city's soot. Kiosks lined the street by a large, yellow building called Gostiny Dvor, which looked like an old palace instead of the largest shopping center in the city.

Even with the brisk temperatures, young women wore mini-skirts and showed off their legs, all of them shapely from either good genes or lots of walking. In a letter, Laura had mentioned the beautiful women and how they and their short skirts caused many fender benders. A pretty girl. A short skirt. And a split second for the driver to look away from the road was all it took. Before seeing St. Petersburg for myself, I expected plump babushkas wearing long wool coats and scarves wrapped around their hair and tied in the front.

We stopped at a red light again with enough time to get a closer look at the crowd. Nobody seemed to smile. Not one soul. But many couples strolled arm in arm. In some ways the culture felt cold, and in others warm and embracing like parts of Central Park.

"Many people call St. Pete the 'Venice of the North' from all the canals and waterways," Laura said as we crossed over a small bridge.

"Seems pretty appropriate, considering how cold it is," I remarked, amazed that it was May but felt like winter.

We turned off Nevsky and onto a side road. Pavel stopped the car in front of an old cream-colored building. He hopped out, took my luggage from the trunk, and gave us a kiss goodbye on both cheeks.

"So, this is it. What do you think?" Laura asked.

The gray concrete crept up the front of the building where the paint stopped in a haphazard way, as if the workers ran out of supplies or decided it was quitting time for good. "It's a pretty street. But needs a facelift," I said and looked across the sidewalk as a man called out. A woman smiled, and he ran to catch up.

"Wait until you see my room. It needs about ten lifts and a tummy tuck."

We walked into the building's lobby, dark and drab, the kind that probably never got good morning light or any light no matter what time of day. Students chatted on a sofa, some read by the window where a speck of light came through, and a few sifted through mail that had piled up on a table in the corner. The attendant at the front desk took my passport, and Laura and I walked down a long hall to the staircase.

"No elevator?" I asked and stopped by the railing.

"Unfortunately, they're fixing it. Actually, this is the first time it's ever been broken."

"They probably knew I was coming," I panted, and as we climbed four flights of stairs, students rushed up, down, and around us.

Along the way, Laura greeted a few of them in Russian while fumbling in a pocket for her key. She unlocked the door and dropped her purse on the table. "Well, here we are. Don't you love the color?"

"Kind of reminds me of the pea soup I had last week."

"Did it also have clumps?" she asked playfully and rubbed her hand along the front wall.

The green paint, dull and dirty from wear, had so many layers. Some had peeled off in a few places, making it easy to tell what color was fashionable from decades—or possibly centuries—ago. Laura's boots, which had a dusting of snow, stood on a mat by the front wall with a pair of sneakers. The hook behind the door held her hat and a light-blue down coat, the ones she wore in a few photos that made her look so Russian. She was embarrassed for breaking down and buying a fur hat but couldn't survive the Russian winter without it. I told her not to feel bad, that it could go to good use when she handed it over to the lady selling wool socks on the street.

Just like the lobby, her room had barely any natural light, and the little that came through reflected on a few apples, a small cassette player, and an electric cooking plate by the window. Books lined up on the floor against the wall and on top of her luggage that acted as a makeshift shelf. On the radiator, socks and underwear laid to dry. I peeked outside to the windows across the way and pedestrians dodging each other along the sidewalk. On the ledge, milk and juice cartons shared space to stay cold in the absence of a mini-fridge.

"Nice, huh?"

I stepped back from the window and let go of the curtain.

"On second thought, don't answer that," Laura said, wiping an apple and handing me one. "Oh, I forgot to tell you. We have to time our showers."

"What do you mean? We'll lose hot water if we shower too long?"

"Not exactly. I only have hot water from five to seven in the evening. Sometimes," she said between bites, "it's from four to six. Or not at all, but let's hope for the best."

"What, the Russian babushkas come and turn it on and off, after they've stood in line for their bread?" I teased but felt bad saying it, for making fun of life that was difficult on so many levels.

But my sympathy didn't last long because, almost right away, I wondered how Laura forgot to tell me about the limited hot water. How precisely she knew the times now, with me here, but how conveniently it slipped her mind before. She said we could use the showers on the first floor where they had hot water all the time, but we'd have to get in line and wait. I decided against it. We probably took too many showers anyways, like her students thought when they asked her that question over and over again.

• • •

Laura filled me in on our plans during my stay, and we decided there was time to meet Alexei for dinner. She arranged our upcoming Moscow trip, and we'd spend a few days sightseeing in St. Petersburg in between. But before all the fun on her end and confession on mine, we'd visit Pavel and his family.

To get there, we took the Metro and switched from one bus to the next. We had to make a run for the first bus, jammed at all corners, with people arguing in the back. Laura raised her eyebrows and smiled. This so-called Venice of the North she'd described earlier hadn't made an appearance. I ached to be back home with hot water, polite people, short lines, and my boring life.

After an hour with three switches and sandwiched body parts, we reached Pavel's apartment. He greeted us at the door with a big smile, showing off his front gold teeth that, if melted down, could feed a filet-mignon dinner to a family of twelve. Pavel's wife Irina was stunning, with long brown hair, black eyes, and wide cheekbones. Her hand, dry and cracked most likely from the harsh winters, reached out for mine during introductions. She waved for me to follow her into the main room.

I'd never been in an apartment this small. Pavel and Irina lived in a room that was half the size of the studio apartment Laura rented after she graduated from college. A hallway held a coat rack, and a tiny kitchen and bathroom took up the rest. Altogether, four people lived in a space about the size of a hotel room.

In the middle of the floor, Pavel stood at the table, counting chairs. Realizing they didn't have enough seats, he grabbed two stools from the kitchen and laid a board over them so they could seat double the amount of guests.

"By the way, I forgot to warn you," Laura leaned in and whispered.

I sat down and eyed bottles of champagne, vodka, and undistinguishable food on the table. "What, they don't have hot water either?"

Laura rolled her eyes. "No, they're going to push the food pretty hard."

"So they're practically all Jewish mothers here," I said.

She grabbed the chair next to me and smiled at Pavel. "They're also big on toasts so keep an eye on your glass unless you want to get wasted."

"Definitely don't need my bed spinning." An oval platter with pink icing caught my eye. "What's that?" I pointed. "Looks good. Some kind of dessert?"

"It's called herring under a fur coat. Has beets, herring, onions, and potatoes. It's covered with mayonnaise and the beets make the mayo turn pink. It's to die for."

"I think I'll pass," I whispered.

"You're no fun."

"Just think, I could be lying on the beach in the Bahamas. Instead I'm wearing winter boots in May, staring at a herring wearing a pink coat. Hey, what do you think the herring looks like naked?"

She grinned and put the napkin on her lap. "You'll only have to suffer another week, but I'll have to hear about it forever."

Pavel, his wife Irina, and their friends joined us at the table, and we began with a toast to friendship. Laura tried to get me to pronounce the Russian word for stuffed cabbage, but after five tries and many laughs around the table, I gave up. Russian was way too hard, and they teased that after a few shots of vodka, I'd be a pro at it.

"Mom, they want to know if you like St. Petersburg?"

"Should I lie and tell them it's simply fascinating?"

Without waiting for me to continue, Laura spoke. I glanced at her and raised my eyebrows. She whispered, "I told them that you love it and want to move here."

I smiled at my hosts and then looked at Laura. "You didn't."

"Just kidding. I told them that so far you like it and the people seem nice."

"That's true," I said and thought how nice a juicy steak would have tasted at that moment.

Two hours later and with bottles of beer and champagne piled up and empty, everyone began singing. With all the excitement, Pavel knocked over his shot glass along with the vodka in it, and they all yelled "*Urrah!*" in unison.

"Do they ever stop drinking?" I asked Laura.

"They practically brush their teeth with the stuff."

"There's no way we're getting home tonight, is there?"

"Are you kidding?" Laura added and picked up her glass. "He's not drunk. It takes a lot more vodka for him to get plowed."

Pavel pushed the chair out and stood up suddenly. He leaned over to grab the bottle of vodka and took off the top to pour.

"More vodka? I understand, yes?" he said with a big smile.

"*Nyet*," Laura said.

"*Nyet*," I copied while putting my hand over the glass.

Pavel shrugged and poured the rest for his friends. Then he wrapped his hands around the bottle, pretending to squeeze it as if he were wringing out a washcloth to get out the last bit of water.

By the end of the evening, Laura was exhausted from all the translating and occasional singing. Pavel drove us back to the dorm and, along the way, I decided I'd tell Laura about Michael when we got back to the room.

I wouldn't wait any longer. I couldn't. It would be the perfect moment. She'd be relaxed and a little tipsy and not quite with it. But by the time I got up my nerve after getting undressed, she was fast asleep on top of the covers with her clothes still on. She used to do that all the time as a teenager. I'd always wake her, make her get undressed and under the covers. But this time, I wrapped her with the extra blanket and, after thoughts of washing my face with cold water, went to bed with my makeup on and my secret still with me.

Chapter Eighteen

The extra glass of champagne the night before gave me a splitting headache. I wanted to stay in bed to ease into the day after succumbing to Pavel's hospitality and heavy hand, but we had plans. As we both lay in bed, me with one eye open, Laura told me we'd be going to the Russian *banya* with one of her students. It's a bathhouse, she said, like a steam room at the gym, but better.

The confession was still front and center, eating away at me. But telling her now or at the *banya* in front of her student wasn't an option. Going to the *banya* was good for your health, she mentioned, a totally different experience than what we had back home. I was up to it, even if it delayed the inevitable.

After breakfast a few doors down on Plekhanova, we headed to the *banya*, one Russian word I could say with ease and repeated in my head on the way there. We entered an off-white, three-story building, walked up to the second floor, and passed an indoor pool on the way to the dressing area, one that shocked me with its openness.

Several young women chatted and walked around naked. They surrounded me with their youth, their beauty, their ease of being uncovered and carefree. With two towels wrapped around me, I followed Laura and Katya into the sauna. We placed our towels on the wooden bench and sat down. Within seconds, sweat dripped down the side of my face and in the middle of my back.

"Not sure how long I can stand this," I puffed.

Laura loosened her towel and leaned her head back. "If it's hard to breathe or your heart beats too fast, go outside." She wiped the sweat away from her brow and swept it up to her hairline. "I stay about ten minutes, take a break, then go in for another five."

Katya left the room and came back a minute later holding tree branches covered with leaves wrapped together with a rope. She handed one to Laura.

"Mom, get up."

"Why?"

"I'll explain," Laura said, pausing for a moment to get a good grasp. She raised the branch and, with a swoosh, hit Katya's stomach. "It's from a birch tree; it's really good for the blood flow."

"I thought that's what jogging's for."

Laura began hitting me with the branch next. "Just give it a shot, no pun intended." She laughed.

"Ouch! That hurts!"

"Oh come on, no it doesn't. Part your legs a little so I can do your thighs."

"Excuse me? Go part the Red Sea instead. Just do my back."

"They say it gets rid of cellulite," Katya mentioned while slathering honey on her face and chest.

"Then I should have started when I was fifteen."

"What do you have to lose?" Laura asked.

"Oh, I don't know. My dignity? And the top three layers of my skin, but who needs that?"

After the birch whipping, I couldn't stand the steam any longer and went to the changing room, showered with lukewarm water, and used the loofah Laura packed.

My daughter was right. I would feel relaxed—afterwards. In the mirror, my cheeks glowed like the time Max and I stayed out in the sun an hour too long during our honeymoon.

"Don't get dressed yet," Laura called out from the shower. "I want you to try the hot and cold pools. You dip your body into one that's really hot then hop into the other that's super cold. It's awesome."

"I think I'll pass," I said and continued to dry off. "I've had enough fun for one day."

Laura pushed aside the shower curtain and grabbed her towel. "Are you sure? How about that birch branch? Do you want to take one home with you?"

"I'm going to use it on you if you keep it up," I quipped, although I really wanted to use it on myself—over my head—to beat out the truth and tell Laura about Michael. *When would I find the right time? Or the courage?* Instead, I chose to joke around, without a care in the world. Truth was, anticipating the fallout had me overwhelmed with anxiety.

• • •

Later that night as we waited for the elevator to meet Alexei in the lobby, I knew it wasn't the right time to tell Laura—yet again. She brought me to Russia to get my mind off my mother's passing, but how would she react when she found out the real reason for the trip? My nerves got the best of me, and hell if they were going to let me spit out the truth. The sightseeing. The strolling on Nevsky. The *banya*. Dinner with Alexei. Staying busy helped me put it off and pretend the real reason wasn't from my procrastination.

Laura pushed the button over and over again, as if it would help the elevator arrive any faster. "Mom, how are you since *Oma*? You holding up okay?"

"I'm doing okay, I guess. I'm glad she didn't suffer," I said, hating the lie, the secret, and the years that flew by.

We got on the elevator, the one that had been broken and fixed earlier in the day. Before we reached the lobby, the elevator jumped and pushed me against the wall. Laura grabbed my arm, reassuring me it jumped sometimes but never got stuck. The elevator moved slowly again and, after the door opened with my fingers crossed behind my back, we walked to the lobby where Alexei stood waiting for us.

Chapter Nineteen

Alexei smiled and right away my face became warm, maybe it even glowed like it had earlier after the sauna. Nothing would happen between the two of us, and I didn't expect it. After all, he'd be in London soon, and I'd be back in DC within a week. But on the way to the restaurant, I was a nervous wreck while trying to convince myself to enjoy the evening and soak in the Russian culture.

We followed the hostess to our table, and Alexei walked ahead to pull our chairs out before we got there. The restaurant reminded me of supper clubs popular in my youth, the ones where you'd lounge, eat dinner, and dance the night away with nobody vying for your spot.

Before sitting down, Alexei spoke Russian by our table and, before long, the waiter brought back a bottle of champagne and a few glasses while another waiter carried over several appetizers. A platter of cheese and cold cuts. Potato salad mixed with peas, carrots, and pickles. Red caviar on top of sliced rustic bread with butter.

Alexei filled my glass with champagne and insisted we try everything he ordered. I agreed in hopes that some of the unusual cuisine would make for great conversation between the three of us. Throughout the evening, young women in short skirts made an appearance, and ladies closer to my age wore colorful pantsuits or black dresses that fell to the knee. A live band played hits one after another, from Whitney Houston to Michael Jackson.

"So, Elsa, what do you think?" Alexei asked as he leaned closer so he wouldn't compete with the loud music and conversations around us.

"About what?"

"St. Petersburg?"

I hesitated and swirled around the last bit of champagne in my glass. "You really want to know?"

"Of course. How do you like our beautiful city?"

"Well..." I hesitated and Laura chimed in.

"She loves it."

"I see." He grinned and topped off my champagne. "You got a little tongue-tied," he teased.

"I didn't want to hurt your feelings."

"You'd never do that," Alexei said, "because St. Pete is the most beautiful city in the world. You'll come to notice, even if it takes a little longer."

The waiter brought more bread and added a new dish, eggplant salad, to the center of our table. I chose a piece of dark bread, broke it in half, and put some butter on top.

"What's the deal with the birch branches in the sauna?" I asked jokingly, not knowing what else to say about Russia. "Isn't it bad enough to sit there and sweat like a pig?"

He smiled. "Ah, *venik*. Laura took you to *banya*."

Venik, I repeated, assuming it meant birch branch until Alexei told me it was Russian for broom. He winked then teased, "We all like a good beating every once in a while."

My face got warm again, and I looked away to hide my blushing. Alexei reached for our champagne glasses and handed me mine. We stared at each other, and I wanted to turn away again. But couldn't. His eyes were on me, looking through me, almost making me forget Laura was still with us. And for a second, I'd forgotten about my troubles, my confession, my years of silent struggle.

"To our meeting," he said as he lifted his glass.

We toasted and drank to the bottom and, when the band started playing one of my favorite songs, I turned around to watch.

"You like reggae music?"

"Who doesn't like Bob Marley?"

"Then let's go dance," he said as he put out his hand and led me to the dance floor.

• • •

We left the restaurant around eleven, and Laura tapped my arm and motioned for me to look up. Interspersed with pink clouds, the horizon glowed with a beautiful blend of peach and purple, making buildings in the distance look airbrushed in soft pastels, a romanticized notion I'd only read about.

I stopped and stared. "Is this White Nights?"

"Almost," she said. "White Nights isn't until June, but it's staying light later and later."

We walked for a few minutes, and after quietly asking me if it was okay to leave, Laura pretended to be tired and spoke firmly in Russian with Alexei as he nodded and looked my way.

"Don't turn into a pumpkin," Laura teased and walked back to the dorm while Alexei and I strolled down Nevsky toward the Hermitage.

Russians walking arm in arm kept pace on the sidewalk. Instead of feeling nervous at night in this foreign city, I felt alive, breathing in the cool air and letting Alexei fold his arm into mine. We reached the Neva River and stopped at the bridge to take in the Hermitage, brushed in a light green and outlined with white like the decorative icing on a wedding cake. The lights from the street on the embankment dashed unevenly across the river and on the buildings alongside it.

"Wow, it's so beautiful," I said and leaned on one of the posts. "I can only take a day or two of museums. But I could stand here forever. In this very spot."

"Ah, see. You've found something. I told you it was beautiful. You know, if you had more time, you could take a trip to Karelia. It's north from here, a short trip by boat, but it is very beautiful. Just quiet, mountainous, green land."

"Maybe next time."

"Oh, so you do like Russia enough to come back?" he asked.

"I don't know. Maybe in a few years to see the places I've missed along the way."

The breeze swept my bangs to the side, and I closed my eyes after leaning on the edge of the bridge. Alexei's hand rubbed against mine, but I didn't move away. I enjoyed the moment, one that I hadn't felt in so long.

After a few minutes, he took off his jacket and placed it on my shoulders. He serenaded me in Russian with a melody that sounded familiar and then hummed the Bob Marley song we'd heard earlier at the restaurant. I smiled and took one last look at the Hermitage before turning to face him.

"We should probably head back," I said with hesitation.

"It's my singing, isn't it?" he teased.

"Are you kidding? You have a great voice."

He winked and fixed his jacket on my shoulders. "You have a great everything."

I closed my eyes and grinned. His boldness amused me and was a warm welcome. "Laura might worry if we don't get back soon," I said without moving, warm against his body as we stood there for a few more minutes.

Alexei let go and held out his hand. We walked back to the dorm, arm in arm, and I felt like a true St. Petersburgian as others passed us by. When we got to the front door, Alexei stopped and took my hand. "Elsa, I really like you."

Embarrassment took over when the words wouldn't come out. Here I was, in my early fifties, acting like it was my first date. Was it because it had been so long without this kind of attention? Or because I'd never been with a man this forward? "I like you, too," I wound up saying, surprised it even squeaked out at all.

"Can we see each other again before you return to Washington?"

Was this Harrison Ford look-alike really asking for a second date?

Was he just curious about American women?

What else could it have been?

"Not sure," I said. "This evening was wonderful, but Laura has an action-packed trip for us."

Alexei stared and moved my bangs to the side. "What about London? Would you visit me there?"

I hesitated for a moment and decided to be honest, at least for once on this trip while neglecting my confession. "That sounds wonderful, and I had such a lovely evening. But it's too complicated."

"I don't see how. If we enjoy each other's company, it won't feel like we're trying. And the flight isn't long," he said.

"I just can't."

Alexei paused and squinted. "Do you have someone waiting for you back home?"

I didn't answer, but my silence gave away the lie I created. He took his jacket from my shoulders and put it back on. "I hope I wasn't too forward."

"No, no. I had such an incredible time," I said while switching my handbag to the other arm, disappointed in myself for lying, for not giving it a chance, even as crazy as it sounded.

He gently kissed the top of my hand. "Thank you for a lovely evening. Perhaps we'll meet again."

"On Nevsky Prospect during White Nights," I said, not because it was believable or that I meant it. But because it was a romantic notion easy to say, one that could distract and amuse me later on when longing for a good memory.

Alexei smiled and held the front door open for me. When I got to the room, Laura jumped up from the chair and begged for all the details. I filled her in, sparing the parts about his request for a second date, and went straight to bed hoping to get a good night's sleep as soon as my head hit the pillow.

But that night, thoughts about Alexei consumed me. How he asked to see me again. How he invited me to London. And how I wanted to spare myself a broken heart, thinking he'd be off to London or Russia or wherever with somebody else when he wasn't with me. Why did I have to travel thousands of miles to meet a guy? Why couldn't I find someone at home and not complicate my life? And why did I have to lie to Alexei? I'd lied enough about Michael. Was I too scared I'd chase him away? Or afraid of the intimacy again after all these years?

Chapter Twenty

The tossing and turning all night left me haggard in the morning, but Laura had everything planned out as usual and that meant sleeping late wasn't an option. We spent the next two days touring the Hermitage, which felt like it could take up five New York City blocks. All the gold-ornamented halls, thrones, and chandeliers made me weak at the knees, but the steep white marble staircase and long hallways had me aching. The Impressionists Laura raved about bored me after a few paintings, so we met up after I joined a group of British tourists and their guide for a good history lesson in the Egyptian room.

After the museum, we strolled up and down Nevsky Prospect and sat at Kazan Cathedral, perfect for a rest and people watching. A few couples embraced and kissed, an old man read a newspaper, and toddlers ran around chasing each other on the grass in front of the fountain. Laura got antsy and talked me into checking out the department store that we passed from the airport.

Inside, Gostiny Dvor looked like a typical store, with electronics in the front, jewelry in the middle, and coats and clothing in the back. As we circled around, we noticed a crowd gathering a few rows deep toward the back of the first floor.

"Wonder what's going on over there?" I asked as we continued to walk toward the crowd.

"Probably a demo of some new electronics. People get all excited to see that stuff."

"But it's mostly women," I noticed. "Maybe they're demonstrating a new microwave?"

We squeezed into the crowd and peeked through. In front stood a beautiful young woman with a blonde bob and fitted red dress with matching lipstick and nail polish. As she spoke, she submerged a tampon into a bowl filled with water.

"What's she saying?"

"She's talking about the tampon."

"I know she's talking about the tampon, silly. What's she saying about it?"

Laura listened closely before translating. "That it's very absorbent. That it can stay in for hours without leaking."

"This place is behind twenty years, at least."

"*Tikha*," the woman in front of us called out with a grimace.

"I think we're in trouble," I whispered. "What did she say?"

"It's obvious, don't you think?" Laura said before translating, "To be quiet."

Laura put her index finger over her lips in a quiet reprimand, and I looked over at some of the women who watched with genuine interest. And at that moment, it made me realize how much we took for granted. Had they never seen a tampon before, something we'd become so accustomed to for decades? How could I have been so insensitive and make fun of their circumstances? "No matter how hard or different this place is, I still love it," Laura said.

I put my arm around her and leaned my head against her shoulder. Laura's passion for other cultures warmed my heart. She was living her dream and sharing her new world with me.

"I'm so glad my tampon days are over," I said as we walked away and to the hat section.

"You sure you're not pregnant?"

"Ha, from what? Watching *Miami Vice* reruns? Nope, no more periods or hot flashes. I am done—and don't miss it a bit."

The Secret We Lost

• • •

Later that evening, we left for Moscow. The train station crawled with travelers dodging each other, and vendors whose old and worn faces abandoned their true age. An attendant asked for our tickets and ID and, after boarding, we found our compartment. It was cozy, with a small table by the window, a pocket door with a lock, and seating that resembled two bunk beds.

Before lifting the seat to place my bag under it, I pulled out a book and crossword puzzle. The long narrow seat would convert to my bed for our overnight travel. As we waited to depart, Russian music blasted over the speakers and people passed through the train with their overnight bags. It gave me time to think, and I decided this was the perfect place to tell Laura about Michael, as soon as the train departed. We'd be alone with no place for us to run or hide.

"Earth to Mom? Hello?"

"What?"

"I called for you like ten times. So, here's the deal," Laura said and put her ID into her pocket. "We've only got two days in Moscow, so we'll just do the touristy stuff. We'll go to Red Square, the Kremlin, maybe the ballet if I can get tickets."

The train finally took off and, soon after, the conductor leaned against our compartment door. He reminded me of Mr. King, my old horrible boss, with his hair, dark and slicked back, and eyes a sliver of brown like a squashed cockroach. Laura passed him the tickets and when he smiled, dull silver caps took the place of his two front teeth. Before leaving, he winked at her several times.

"What's that all about?"

"He asked if I wanted to join him for some champagne later."

"Really? If that happened at home, he'd be fired."

"That's actually the first time a conductor has tried to pick me up. Sometimes I've shared compartments with men who would give me their phone numbers. But, other than that, it has been cool. Hey," Laura jumped up and slipped on her sneakers, "let's go to the club car and get drunk."

"You're joking, right?" I said and followed her after grabbing my purse and closing the pocket door.

We ordered a bottle of champagne and brought it back to our compartment, leaving the drunk men behind and shrouded in their cigarette smoke. I breathed in the smoke on the way out and craved one myself, but being with Laura meant I had to stick to my two-a-day limit. Laura popped the champagne and, after two glasses, I became tipsy and leaned back to close my eyes.

Why was I so afraid to tell her?

I owed it to her.

Maybe she'd have the heart to forgive me, or better yet, not be mad.

I was holding onto that thought and hoping for the best.

The room kept spinning and spinning until the sound of squeaky brakes and morning light awakened me. Nothing, not even the hallway conversations or squealing brakes I'd heard earlier when we boarded, interrupted my sleep.

Laura was curled up with a book open and face down on the side of the bed. She'd never been a morning person and, to this day, preferred to stay in bed as late as possible if she could. I took my crossword puzzle from the table and worked on it until her beautiful face popped up.

"What time is it?" she asked and rubbed her eyes.

"Almost seven. We'll be in Moscow soon, right?"

Laura stretched and let out a hefty moan. "How'd you sleep?"

"Like a log, surprisingly."

"We'll check in and head over to Red Square," she said and fixed her ponytail.

• • •

We got off the train and took a short taxi ride to our hotel. Alexei said Moscow wouldn't be worth the trip. But it seemed less stark and more upscale than St. Petersburg. The vibrant, hustling streets reminded me of New York, with women dressed in their high heels and carrying bags from what I imagined were the finest boutiques.

After settling into our room, we walked to Red Square, where the Kremlin Palace and magnificent St. Basil's Cathedral stood in front of us. We got closer and for the first time it felt like Russia. The Russia I'd always imagined. The one I thought I never wanted to see.

Chapter Twenty-One

Red Square bustled with families, tourists, even brides and grooms posing for pictures. So many people surrounded us, but it didn't feel real. Looking toward the palace's top-floor windows, I wondered who was looking out at us, and if they appreciated Red Square in all its beauty, or if it went unnoticed the way I discounted the grandeur of the museums on the Mall in DC.

I walked for a closer glance at St. Basil's Cathedral and its domes, ones that looked like a kaleidoscope of colorful onions, of multi-colored soft-serve ice cream with gold crosses sprinkled on top. Something so enchanting, so overwhelming that newspapers and magazines couldn't do them justice.

"Pretty amazing, huh?" Laura said.

"Now it really feels like Russia."

"That's because of the media. Think about it," Laura mentioned. "Whenever you see the news about Russia, you see St. Basil or the Kremlin in the background."

"Hmm, never thought about it that way."

"St. Pete is more of a European city than Moscow, and I like it there a lot better. But St. Basil's takes my breath away."

If I hadn't skimmed an article about Red Square before my trip, I would have expected the ground to be covered entirely in red bricks. It turned out that the Russian word for red originally meant beautiful, or at least that's what the English tour guide said behind us in my attempt to listen in. The square was crowded, but everyone moved around easily. Tour guides shared history in various languages, art students sketched on their pads, and more brides and grooms posed for cameras.

"See over there." Laura lifted her chin to point across the way. "That's Lenin's tomb. He's on display for the world."

"Who the heck would want to see that?"

"Just about everyone," Laura said matter-of-factly. "The lines are usually crazy, but it's not too bad today."

"I bet it's fake."

"That's what I thought until I went. Looked like a wax figure. He was embalmed, and supposedly they do something every day to keep it looking that way."

"Ew, makes my skin crawl," I said, imagining waiting in line to see a dead guy, which made standing in a long line for bread seem much more appealing.

"That sounds like a no. What about a tour of St. Basil's?"

We walked even closer to the cathedral when I began to feel that Russian soul Laura talked so often about—but here, in Moscow, not in Laura's St. Petersburg. I wanted to deny it. I wanted the distaste for Russia to remain, at least until the weight of my secret—and its burden and deflection—had been taken from me.

I'd come to Russia for one reason, a lie I couldn't live with any longer. My confession hadn't happened in her dorm room like I'd planned. Or on the train. Or for the past twenty-odd years. It had to happen here, on Red Square, surrounded by hundreds of people and my apprehension.

"Laura, I need to tell you something I've been holding back for years," I blurted.

"What? That I have a twin sister that you gave up for adoption?"

"You have a wild imagination, but can we be serious for a moment?" I said as we stopped just outside the cathedral.

"Can't it wait until we get back to the hotel?"

"If I don't tell you now, I never will."

131

Laura stood there and stared, waiting for me to speak. And that's when I let it all out. How I should have been watching my brother. How my stomach dropped when I walked back to the living room and saw the window open. How his lifeless body on the sidewalk made its way into my memory for good. How it felt when my mother looked up at me from Broadway. And how the relationship with my mother was never the same.

I stood there, trying my best to explain. All those notes and thoughts I had about breaking the news became useless. I didn't introduce it the right way. I just blurted it out. And after that, neither one of us paid attention to the tourists circling around to view the Moscow sights.

"It's horrible," I said, looking down. "I still can't live with myself, but it was an accident."

At first, Laura didn't say a word, trying, I suppose, to let it sink in. *Was she in shock? Was she disgusted by my actions and years of denial? Did she feel sorry for me and our entire family?*

Finally, she spoke. "That's the saddest thing I've ever heard. *Oma* shouldn't have left him with you."

"I believe that too, but I'm wrought with such guilt. It agonizes me." I went to hug her, but she stepped back.

"All this time, all the stories you've told me about her. You made me think there was no reason for your crappy relationship. She was grief-stricken, to say the least."

My heart pounded fast. "What are you saying? That I deserved to be treated like that by my own mother?" I said defensively.

"Her own son died!" she yelled. "What did you expect? And the fact that you never told me?" She turned around and took off, practically pushing people out of her way as I zigzagged between tourists to catch up.

"Laura, calm down. People are staring," I said, out of breath.

"Like I give a damn. Let them stare."

I grabbed her arm, and she stopped. "How do you think I feel? After all these years living with what I did. Michael would have been forty-five. Probably living a beautiful life that I robbed him of."

"Wait a second." She paused, looked up from the ground, and stared at me with her hazel eyes and, for the first time, they had a coldness about them. "*Oma* named her son after her brother Michael?"

I didn't answer.

"Please don't tell me you lied about that, too?" she asked and waited for me to answer before continuing. "So she never had a brother named Michael who died as a teenager?"

I looked down and shook my head.

"How could you do this? Lie to me all this time, making me think she was the bad guy," she cried.

"I never meant to hurt you."

Laura looked straight at me. "Never meant to hurt me? How could you even say something so pathetic?" She paused and turned away. "Well, it doesn't matter anyway."

"What do you mean by that? That you're able to forgive me?" I asked and reached out.

Laura felt my touch and stepped back, putting both hands on the straps of her backpack. "No, I don't mean it that way. It doesn't matter because I'm not coming home. I'm staying in St. Petersburg. Whatever you say, nothing matters."

I couldn't breathe. Like I'd been hit, stomped on, pushed to the ground. I thought she was upset and trying to get back at me.

She turned around and got closer. "I was planning to tell you," she said in a calmer voice. "That's why I wanted you to come here. I didn't want to tell you over the phone."

Suddenly, my face felt warm, and I ripped off my scarf and threw it at her. "You tricked me. You said you wanted to spend time with me and get my mind off Millie."

"True," she said and picked up my scarf. "But I also wanted to tell you in person that I've met someone, and we're in love."

"What? I thought you and Yuri broke up?"

"It's not him. Remember your reaction when I told you about Yuri? It was a little extreme, don't you think? And it made me realize it's not phone conversation."

"It will never last," I spat. "He'll use you for citizenship then dump you after he gets what he wants."

"Sorry, you're wrong once again," she said and shook her head. "That can't happen because he's American. He's working here and will be here for a couple of years. Then, we'll decide what to do. We both love Russia and want to stay."

What the heck was she saying?
In love with an American who also loved Russia?
Had she lost her mind?
Had they lost their minds together?

I'd waited so long to see her and was excited she'd be coming home. I tried everything. I tried telling her that St. Petersburg was dark and depressing. That nobody smiled. That everyone was unfriendly. That the lines were terrible. That the weather was a beast. Nothing worked.

She tried everything, telling me how much she loved Russia. Even its harsh climate, the long lines, the sober faces. She tried to tell me about her boyfriend. How they were inseparable. How he was smart, funny, and treated her well. Nothing worked.

"Mom, don't you think it's better I told you in person rather than on the phone?"

I didn't respond.

"By the way, his name is David, and he's Jewish."

"That's great," I said. "That'll help you a lot, being how much they like Jews around here," I said sarcastically as I walked off.

"What's wrong with you? Why can't you let me live my life and be happy for me?" Laura said as she caught up.

"How'd you expect me to take the news?"

"A hell of a lot better than what you just told me, don't you think? You've lied this entire time, and now you're trying to turn it around and make me feel guilty about staying. You know, you really need to get some help. In a way, you're lucky I'm not coming back," she yelled behind me as I continued to walk off. "With the way you're acting, you obviously don't give a crap about my happiness. And besides, what else have you hidden from me? Is there more to the story about your brother Michael, I mean *Oma's* brother?"

I stopped and turned around. "Don't you ever talk about Michael that way," I yelled. "I loved my brother! He was everything to me."

At that moment, it didn't matter that people stopped to stare. It didn't matter that my entire world had crashed down on me again. The weight of the lie had disappeared, only to be replaced by my daughter's contempt.

"I'm leaving for DC tomorrow. How dare you trick me like this to get me here. And how dare you talk to me that way? I'm your mother, not some piece of dirt on the side of the road."

"Then treat me with respect. I'm almost twenty-six. I'm a grown woman who's going to be happy and not live in the past like you do—when you're not living in denial."

I wanted to slap her, right there on Red Square, right in front of everyone. To make her snap out of it. To make everyone else hit pause on their oh-so-perfect happiness button, to take away their moments of laughter and joyful poses. But all I could do was turn around and make my way back to the hotel, biting my bottom lip hard to hold back the tears along the way. No matter what, no matter how hard, there'd be no tears in front of her.

Laura yelled several times for me to wait up, and I could feel her presence behind me as we stormed back to the hotel. Our sightseeing ended quickly in Moscow. We packed our bags and headed to the terminal to exchange our ticket and hope for an earlier return.

Once on the train, we didn't say one word to each other back to St. Petersburg. All I could think of was getting home to Washington. And if I'd ever see my daughter again.

Chapter Twenty-Two

Before Laura told me her news about staying in Russia, I often reminded her that things seemed magical and exciting because they were new. If she had grown up and lived in Russia, she would have felt differently about it. "Don't take away my great memories," she'd always tell me. I never tried to take anything away but wanted her to realize the opportunities she'd been given.

The great memories she talked about would stay with her, even decades later. But after what happened in Moscow, those memories became littered with lies. And, at least for me, the initial enchantment on Red Square became poisoned with our argument.

Laura and I hardly spoke the next morning when we arrived in St. Petersburg. But later while packing, she tried to talk me into staying. She was still mad—furious, actually, for lying to her—but didn't want me to leave upset. It was too hard for me to stay for the rest of the trip. I couldn't get over her wanting to live in St. Petersburg, of all places. And to stay for love?

She was supposed to go to Russia for the adventure and experience—and a break from a job and life she called mundane, a job and life that I thought she took for granted. Laura was supposed to come back home. She had to come home. That was the plan all along.

Our ride to the airport was long and silent. It reminded me of our trip to the airport when she left home in August. We were quiet and contemplative then, but even with all my worrying, I was impressed with her determination to reapply until she got accepted. And I was at ease about her going, maybe because I knew all along she'd be back a year later.

"Mom, I can't believe you're acting this way. You gotta let go!"

"Don't tell me I haven't let go," I answered while waiting to get in the customs line. "You went off to college and Russia. I let you go and experience life."

"Can you even hear yourself? You said 'I let you experience life,' like you allowed me."

My jacket fell off the top of my luggage, and we both reached down to grab it at the same time. "Laura, it came out the wrong way. I just think it's a mistake."

She rolled her eyes and raised her voice. "You're still trying to treat me like a child."

"It's just that I don't want you to give up your career and independence for a guy." I could feel the tears welling up and that tingle in my nose, fighting them both back by pressing my nail hard against my thumb.

"You're not making any sense. So it would've been okay to stay in Russia without meeting David?"

I didn't answer. People around us started to stare, as if they could feel the tension between us.

"Okay, now you're going to pretend you didn't hear me, or ignore me. Whatever."

Hearing those words hit me in the gut. It was exactly what I'd said to my mother so many times whenever I brought up Michael and wanted to talk about what happened.

"Do what you want," she continued, "but it's not fair the way you're acting."

"You haven't thought this through," I finally said. "It's on a whim. What will you do here? How will you make money?"

"It's like you never give me any credit. I already have two jobs lined up. One's at an American organization as an admin and the other at a hotel. They're both within walking distance from where we'll be living. They'll extend my visa, and David already has his." She smiled. "See, it's all worked out so no need to worry."

"Let me get this straight," I said. "You went to college and got a degree in business to become an administrative assistant?" I thought back to all those years architecture consumed me, and all those times my mother told me going into that field wasn't in the cards. Would Laura be giving up a career for David, one that she chose and went after with nobody telling her to pick something else? "Never mind, it doesn't matter," I continued. "My mother never gave me advice, practically never talked to me. I always thought it was different between us."

Laura held her purse and put her other hand on her hip. "Do you have any idea how controlling you are?" She paused for a moment. Her voice cracked before adding, "You don't really care that I'm happy."

"Of course, I care," I said but couldn't look at her as the words came out.

"This whole situation is crazy. Think about it," she said and folded her arms. "I'm the one who should be pissed. You lied to me all these years about Michael. And you don't want to stay and meet David. Maybe the long flight will give you time to think about it," she added and handed me my jacket. "Bye, Mom."

And just like that, she turned away and left. No hug. No kiss. Nothing. But I couldn't blame her.

Why was I acting like this?
Why couldn't I be happy for my daughter?

∙ ∙ ∙

For the entire flight, I recognized this wasn't normal. A bad relationship with Laura like with my own mother wasn't an option. At least for all those years, Aunt Regina came through and we built a close bond, the kind I wanted with my mother but accepted would never happen.

But so many good things never lasted. My aunt was right that night on her sixty-fifth birthday, even in a joking manner. She did have one foot in the grave. But didn't know it. A few months after her birthday dinner, the one where they teased Max and me to start a family, she was diagnosed with breast cancer. After the bleak prognosis, she said more than once she'd planned to beat it, going to numerous doctors only to hear the same bad news.

She was a fighter, getting up every day to get dressed and put on her makeup. I saw her all the time yet still noticed her dramatic change, which seemed to happen overnight. The hair and weight loss, the dark circles and color drained from her face, the hopeful look in her eyes when she'd say to her doctor, "That's fine, we'll try something else." At the end when she couldn't manage much, I'd come over several times a week to help.

"*Leibshen*, would you put a little makeup on me? I look dreadful."

"No, you don't," I said and reached for some rouge and lipstick.

She held up a mirror, took a look at her reflection, and placed the compact down on the bed. "Don't lie to me, darling. I know the truth when I see it. And it's staring back at me."

"I used to love watching you put on your lipstick, *Tante*."

After applying her makeup, I pulled out a colorful silk scarf from the drawer and wrapped it around her head. Aunt Regina took the two ends and twisted them into one that spilled over her shoulder and onto her collarbone to brighten up her gray cardigan.

"You know, Millie felt horrible about cutting your braid," she said while playing with the corner of the scarf with her thumb and index finger.

I reached for the light-pink polish to paint her cracked nails, the ones that not so long ago looked perfect without hiding behind a coat of lacquer. "How'd you know about that?"

"She told me. Do you know she cried for weeks on end about it?"

"I don't believe it for a minute," I said and shook the polish. "She never apologized."

"Because she was embarrassed."

"Well, don't you think it was drastic, what she did?"

"It was, and I told her. We've known each other for a long time, longer than Gus, who never tries to upset her. I'm her friend and tell it like it is." She paused and extended her hand, allowing me to start on the first coat. "Elsa, you have to understand what she's been through. Having a miscarriage on the ship over and losing Michael just put her in a horrible state. Something clicked, and she has never been the same. Long ago, we lost the Millie we all knew."

"Why didn't she get help?"

"Who in their right mind can help a person who has lost two children? Who, tell me, I want to know."

"Not to take the pain away, but life has to go on," I said and blew on her nails to dry them. "You can't take it out on other people."

"Darling, you are absolutely right. Millie took it out on you. No one remembered the window was open. I didn't. She didn't either," Regina said, lifting her arms slightly to wrap me in them.

"Wait," I exclaimed, "you'll mess up your nails."

"*Liebshen*, it's okay."

We hugged for a long time, reminiscing about her birthday party and how we sang and danced all night to "Georgy Girl."

141

"About Millie, she's a lost soul. Try to be kind to her, even if it's hard. She's still hurting after all these years."

"You find the good in everyone, don't you, *Tante*?"

"I try to put myself in other people's shoes. You never know what it's really like until you try. But enough about that. Let's talk about that husband of yours. That Max, he's a keeper. Does he have a brother for me?"

"I think he's taken, but I'll ask."

"Good. Let me know. But soon, okay?"

"You got it," I told her.

She pulled away and looked at me with her overbearing dark circles, the ones that outstayed their welcome and competed for attention with her red painted lips. "Elsa, I love you so much. You're my favorite niece."

I laughed. "Your favorite. And only."

She tried to laugh back, but I could tell she was hiding her pain by the way she moved her body to find a comfortable spot on the bed.

"Elsa, don't be sad for me. I've had a good life."

"Don't talk that way, *Tante*," I said, attempting to hold back the tears and the tremble in my voice. I tried to be strong, not necessarily for her, but for me, knowing that we'd be losing this beautiful soul too soon.

"I'm not afraid of dying. While I'm still able, I want you to know that, and how much I love you."

"I love you, too."

"I really hope you have a wonderful life. But sweetheart, you need to lighten up a little. Don't take things too close to the heart. Life is so short, have some fun."

I hugged *Tante* and held on tight. She smelled like a mix of mothballs from her sweater and candied apples from the rouge. That was the last time we spoke about my mother. It would be hard to keep her advice about being nice to Millie, but in a way, it was her dying wish. A wish I found hard to keep.

The Secret We Lost

• • •

By the time the plane reached Dulles Airport, my body ached from the long trip. Matt and Greg stood on the side, waiting for me to hurry through the crowd at customs. I'd have to tell them about Laura not coming home. How she chose Russia and a guy over her life in DC. *What will they think about her falling in love with an American guy and staying there?*

"No way," Greg said when he heard the news. "I mean, of all places."

"But she's in love. And happy," Matt added, almost in defense of Laura's decision.

"You're always so damn romantic." Greg paused and touched my elbow. "So she's not coming back, at all?"

I shrugged. "Who knows. I have a letter in my bag for you guys."

"Can't wait to read it, but first, how'd you like Russia?"

"Red Square was gorgeous, but the rest? How could anyone fall in love with that country?" I said as we continued down the hallway. "Nobody smiles, the lines are long, and they're behind twenty years. And the food? It's like one smoked fish after another."

"Sounds like you loved it and want to go back next week."

"Oh yeah, sure, let's book the ticket while we're here," I teased and remembered Alexei. "I did meet an interesting guy on the plane. He took me out for dinner."

"Oohh," they said in unison.

"Don't get your hopes up. He lives in London."

Greg put his arm around me. "You'll have to tell us more. Don't forget, we lead pretty boring lives, so we're living vicariously through you."

"Ha! My life is about as exciting as waiting in line at the post office."

• • •

When I got home, I tossed my coat on the bench and checked the messages left on my machine, hoping Laura had changed her mind about staying. But no such luck. Susan had called to check on me and the hospital needed more insurance information for my mother. I eyed my suitcase in the foyer and, instead of unpacking right away, threw myself on the bed and stared at the television for hours. Watching Indiana Jones again made me think of Alexei and took my mind off the emptiness, even for a brief moment.

I missed the comforts of my apartment while away—my bed, the hot water, the food. But not the silence. Funny how I wanted it for so long, but now the privacy and feeling of having my own space didn't feel right. I was no longer caring for my mother. And Laura was thousands of miles away. The space was all mine, with the silence so deafening. It wasn't supposed to be quite like this.

People always said things can change, and ultimately our own choices created our destiny. In my case, it was the lack of good choices—and the loss of loved ones—that changed mine. First, Michael then Max then *Tante* then my father and, in between it all, the loss of my mother on an emotional level. Was I falling into a depression or was it the sadness from a lifetime of grieving on the inside?

Laura was right, yet again. I needed to live my life, not the life of Elsa the caretaker, or Elsa the widow, or Elsa the mom. Just Elsa. But where would I start? How would I begin living my life?

Chapter Twenty-Three

I'd been back for several weeks when Laura started leaving messages on my answering machine. She often called while I was at work or out shopping. The crazy time difference made it impossible to connect, or at least it gave me a good excuse for not talking. I wanted to call her back. I even picked up the phone and dialed but never went through with it. What would we say to each other? Why couldn't she understand why I never told her the truth? Was I a bad mother or a bad person for not telling her? For granting my mother's wish to never speak of it? The phone stayed untouched and a week later, I got my answer.

July 12, 1994

Mom,

I'm hoping this letter reaches you; I sent it with a friend visiting her family in Delaware. I tried calling a couple of times and left the number where you could reach me. Thankfully, we have a phone in our apartment! Why haven't you returned my calls? Why do I feel like I'm chasing after you in vain and feeling guilty? I've done nothing wrong.

This is, or rather should be, a very happy time for me. I'm with someone who's wonderful. I'm having great life experiences; I'm learning Russian and absorbing the culture. In case you're wondering, I'm doing really well. Except for the fact that you're mad and won't talk. Why are you treating me like I've committed some heinous crime?

You're acting like you'll never see me again. I told you that I'll probably be here no more than two or three years, and that I'll visit long before then. Right now I'm concerned. To be honest, if you're going to be this way and not supportive, what would be the purpose of ever visiting you? To see you frown? To be told of my so-called mistakes? To not hear you accept David?

I know that it may take time for you to come to terms with my decision, but you didn't even call me back. What if it were an emergency, and I really needed to talk to you? If you don't put this behind you, it will hurt our relationship in the long run. It was so hard for me to understand why you lied to me about Michael for my entire life.

Think about it—for twenty-six years, you made up some lame excuse about Michael being Oma's brother. Really? But, I'm grown up enough to accept that you were hurting so much from the pain and guilt, and Oma not wanting to talk about it made it worse. I can only imagine what you, Oma, and Opa went through. How hard it must be for you, still. But just because you're hurting doesn't mean the whole world has to stop for you. It's normal for kids to move on in life and have adventures. That's what I've done. I'm living my life. And so should you.

Please think about what I've said. When you feel like talking, you know my number.

Love,
Laura

I crumbled the letter and threw it at the wastebasket. It hit the side and fell on the floor. *The ball was in my court, for a change. I had control of it and our relationship*, I thought and reached over to pick up the letter and put it on the nightstand.

I was always the one who looked like the bad guy. First, with my mother; now Laura. My head began to throb. I went to the cabinet in my mother's old bathroom and took out the extra-strength aspirin. Sleeping pills sat next to them, an entire bottle's worth from when my mother had trouble falling asleep. She swore them off, never wanting any help, always claiming chamomile tea did the trick, not some pill a young doctor had prescribed. I took the bottle from the shelf and dumped some pills on the counter.

I counted them out. And I eyed them for way too long.

What am I doing?

My life is no worse than anyone else's.

My life is good.

It always has been.

I cried out and flushed the pills and the rest from the bottle down the toilet, and ran for the phone.

"It's Elsa. Can you come over?"

Chapter Twenty-Four

I confessed everything to Susan in the middle of the night. All about Michael. The relationship with my mother. The lies thrown at Laura. My trip to Russia and what happened there. Everything. She sat and listened without a word until I stopped and looked up at her.

Susan grabbed a tissue, dotted her eyes, and insisted a strong cup of coffee would do the trick. We went into the kitchen, and she fumbled in the cabinet to find the filters for the machine. While we waited for the coffee to brew, she sat next to me and took my hand.

"Elsa, I'm so sorry. I wish you'd told me sooner so we could have talked about it. Maybe it would have helped?"

"I couldn't figure out how to get it out. I couldn't even tell my own daughter, can you believe that?"

"Stop beating yourself up. Don't you think you've done enough of that already?"

It felt so good, a relief really, to tell someone who wasn't affected by my secret. Someone who wouldn't be hurt by my lies. Someone who wouldn't judge me.

Susan got up and filled two mugs. She brought one over to me and leaned against the counter. "Have you thought about talking to someone? It could help."

I was already talking to somebody, at that moment. But it wasn't what Susan meant. And now, was it too late?

It had crossed my mind a few times, but I'd put it off for so many years after Michael's death. I don't know why I was so against it. Maybe because it wasn't the "in thing" to do for my generation. Often, it was frowned upon and thought of as unnecessary.

Talking to someone could help, to help me realize changes needed to be made, not just about opening up, but letting go. We sat together until dawn and when both of our yawns became the topic of conversation, Susan handed me her therapist's card, gave me a long hug, and went on her way, begging me to give it a try.

After she left, I fell asleep on the sofa and woke up to the sound of a vacuum outside my apartment door. The television also hummed in the background and before reaching for the remote, I picked up a pad and pen from the coffee table and began doodling. I stopped for a moment and looked down at the sofa where the therapist's card had fallen between the pillows. *Would I be willing to talk to someone? Really talk to someone and spill my guts? And would I be ready to make a change?*

Part of making a change was coming to terms with what I'd done and reaching out to the person I loved the most. To the person willing to forgive me. I shaded the last box on my doodle, ripped off a piece of paper, and wrote my heart out.

July 30, 1994

Dear Laura,

Thanks for your letter. I actually wasn't avoiding your calls. Believe it or not, I was out every time and came back to your messages. I'm writing instead because I needed time—and the courage—to think this through. In a way, writing is a cop-out because it's easier than actually saying the words. The big news is that I reached out to my friend Susan. She recommended that I start seeing someone who will help walk me through all my issues and take me out of this fog. I was always embarrassed to ask for help. I know the ordeal with Michael is at the crux of it. No matter how painful, I need to figure out how to live with it.

Dr. Livingston specializes in grief counseling, and that feels right for me. Tomorrow, I'm going to make an appointment. Susan has been seeing him for a while now. She said part of his theory is to talk about it, but then you need to let go of things you can't control, especially things in the past.

It's also embarrassing that, as a mother, I have to tell you all this. The last thing I've ever wanted was to argue and for me to become a burden. You're wrong—I want you to be happy. I was just shocked when you told me your decision to stay. I know you'll do great things, and your happiness is so important to me. Anyways, I'll be in touch and let you know how things are going.

Love,
Mom

• • •

Two weeks later, I started working on myself with the help of Dr. Livingston and, after a few visits, began calling him Jay. We met once a week for an hour. The experience was different than expected; I always thought therapists asked, "How do you feel about how you feel?" Instead, Jay taught me the steps of the grieving process. Although he didn't think there should be a time limit, he believed it wasn't healthy to continuously mourn. The more we met, the more we discovered my sadness wasn't that simple, not just from the death of Michael and Max. I was grieving the lost relationship with my mother. I was grieving the relationship that stopped short with Raymond. I was grieving for my father and Aunt Regina, the two who showed me the most love.

During one of my sessions, I blurted out something so vile—that deep down, I sometimes wished my father and aunt had outlived my mother. Being truthful, I discovered, turned out to be the best medicine.

"I hated my mother for how she treated me," I told Jay one day, no longer willing to beat around the bush or avoid the truth.

"But you still took her in when she needed you."

"Oh, that's different." I waved in the air, brushing away the notion. "It was obligatory," I responded.

"Even so, you still did it. Not that many kids take their parents in these days. It shows me that you didn't really hate her. You were still probably trying to get her approval or at least some type of relationship to form."

"Oh no. I was horrible because she was horrible to me for so long. My daughter hit it on the head when she told me she understands why my mother treated me that way."

He looked away and made a note on his pad. "Why would she say that?"

"Well, I did hide it from her. I just told her recently about what happened to Michael."

"That must have been hard," Jay said, putting down his pad and leaning forward in the chair. "How'd she take it?"

"Not very well, but luckily, she can't hold a grudge as long as me."

Jay got up when his assistant knocked on the door, apologizing for the interruption. I glanced over at the shelf behind his desk lined with books, knick-knacks, and a framed sign with the word *Breathe* centered on a light-blue background. *Breathe.* It seemed like such easy advice to give coming from an inanimate object.

"Look, you had no control over how your mother treated you after the accident," he said, and I tried to hold onto every word. "That's one thing I want you to remember. Often we have no control over the way people act toward us—or even how they perceive us. Don't be hard on yourself for not telling your daughter or for what happened. You didn't know the window was open. Honestly, your mother should have reminded you."

I reached for a tissue when Jay passed me the box. "So many children watch their siblings and nothing happens."

"It's a horrible tragedy. You know, one way to stop worrying is to imagine the absolute worst thing that could happen and when you realize that, you'll worry less. In your case, the worst thing actually happened. You lost your only sibling in an accident. Your life has never been the same and you never had a chance to resolve it with your mother."

Jay got up and walked over to his cabinet. He pulled out a new box of tissues and placed it on the table. I looked away because I couldn't stand looking at him while crying. He was my therapist and had probably seen a thousand people cry, but it still embarrassed me. It made me feel out of control.

"Elsa, I need to be honest with you. There's no mending the relationship you had with your mother. I wish I could have helped you with that sooner, but we'll never resolve that in our sessions. What we need to do is decide how you'll come to terms with it. Lying about your brother or making excuses about the way your mother treated you has to stop. And denial never works. You need to say, 'Hey, I did the best that Elsa could do, and that's that.'"

"Easy for you to say."

"Okay," he whispered, with an air of disagreement. "Let's discuss some ways for you to come to terms with it. I believe when we do, you'll feel this heavy load lifted off."

I left his office that day thinking about his every word, and to get over the tragedy, I'd need to stop feeling guilty over the accident and the way my mother and other people in my life made me feel. Jay never mentioned it, because we always talked, but writing helped. Instead of keeping a journal, though, I wrote letters.

For six months and while working with Jay, I wrote several to Laura, faxed to her every other Monday as we'd done before. We were still working through our issues—actually my issues, making an honest effort to let her live her life and better my own in the process. Then, at the end of those six months, I wrote another letter.

January 15, 1995

Dear Raymond,

Hope you're well and your grandkids are growing like weeds. I'm fine and have been making changes in my life. I know you've never really believed in counseling, but I've begun to see a shrink, as we've always called it. He has been a huge help in dealing with my issues. One of those issues has been you, believe it or not.

When we met in 1971, I fell in love with…your office! I walked through the door and knew right away I wanted that job. Then I met you and fell in love with your great personality, charm, and sense of humor. Even before we became involved, I liked you as a person and boss. I'm so glad that I have all these great memories. It came at the most perfect time, the time I needed help getting over the loss of Max.

Even though you told me that you'd never leave your wife, I was hoping you'd change your mind. I can't say I was happy with your decision, and I never truly accepted it by proof that I held onto our relationship all those years. I'm grateful that you have been part of my life.

With the help of my shrink, I'm starting to move on. I've been opening up and have allowed myself to put you in a different category. Sorry about the lack of a better word choice! You're now in my "past relationships" category, and now I can move on to find new ones. I can't believe it has taken me this long. Part of the reason, I think, is that I put other people first. I put Laura first all those years. Then, I took my mother in. Now, my mother has passed. Laura is living her life. And now I need to live mine. I'm sure you're happy for me.

Elsa

I addressed the envelope and read the letter again. But, looking for a stamp gave me second thoughts. Why send the letter when it made me feel better just to write it? *Remember, Elsa, you need to put yourself first. It shouldn't matter how Raymond feels. Besides, he already knew all this. I was the one who needed convincing.* Instead of sending the letter, I folded the stationery and placed it in my nightstand with the ones from Laura.

Chapter Twenty-Five

The letter stayed in my drawer and every once in a while, when I pulled it out, it helped me with positive thinking, something Jay asked me to focus on. It helped me get through the cold winter, the part of the year that crept through my bones. I pushed myself out of bed, even on the coldest day, and ventured out on the weekends rather than reaching for the remote and clicking through the channels like before.

I'd bundle up and go out, trying not to compare my Wisconsin Avenue strolls to the Madison Avenue of my youth with Max or Raymond. I was trying to live in the present.

During one of my walks, I ran into Susan on the way to my corner coffee shop. We caught up and realized how much had changed since the time she came over late that one night. I'd taken her advice and started getting help. And she'd taken mine, overcoming her fears of meeting someone new who could take her husband's place.

As we chatted, a guy who looked familiar came up from the Metro's escalator. As he got closer, it dawned on me. It was Sydney, someone I'd been out with for dinner who never called me back after our first date. He didn't notice me at first, but once Susan called out his name, he froze, not knowing what to do, whether to stop in his tracks or continue toward us.

"Is that the new guy?" I asked in a playful way, pretending not to know him.

She blushed and fidgeted with her scarf. "Yep. Let me introduce you."

He walked up, and we shook hands. Before he could utter a word, I said, "So nice to meet you. Susan was just telling me all about you."

"I sure was. Elsa, why don't you join us for a movie?"

"Wish I could, but I have a gazillion things to do today," I fibbed.

We said our good-byes, and they walked arm in arm down Wisconsin Avenue. Susan turned around to wave, and I gave her a thumbs-up. That moment, for me, was a true test on my road to finding peace. Six months earlier, I would have found a hundred reasons to bad-mouth Sydney, to find fault within myself for him not returning my calls. Instead, I was happy for Susan, for both of them.

It made me realize I needed to put even more energy into my personal life. In my professional one, with the exception of my horrible boss before Raymond, I didn't take anything personally and had a thick skin. Everything rolled off my back. If I had that attitude with my personal life, things could improve. I still needed to work through many issues but decided everyday stuff wouldn't get to me anymore, like blaming my middle-aged body for my lack of dating. Or getting my feelings hurt when people were rude to me on the Metro. Staying positive was helping me get my life back. So was talking with Jay.

Proud of my progress, I told him during our next session. He mentioned for all these months, we focused on how to get over the grief, how to be more positive, and move on. But he noticed I never talked about good moments in my life other than the time seeing Sydney and Susan happy together. It was time, Jay said, for me to open up.

"You want me to talk about good times? That's so unlike me."

"Now wait a second. You were making such good progress."

I laughed while fidgeting with the zipper on my jacket. "I'm just kidding. See? I can make fun of myself now. Isn't that progress?"

He smiled and waited for me to continue, not letting me off the hook so easily.

"Where do I begin?" I said, looking up at the ceiling and out the window for some ideas to hit me over the head. "There are so many I'm sure, but I don't know…"

"Why don't you lie down and close your eyes. It will take you there," Jay said.

"You're joking, right? That sounds like such psychobabble to me."

"Never mind. Stand up. Stand on your head. Whatever works."

It didn't matter where or how I stood. What mattered was the person I remembered and spoke about. My father's name was Gustav, but everyone called him Gus. Except for me. I called him *Vati*. We took those Sunday trips to Marty's once a month. Of course we loved our sweets and wouldn't pass them up, but spending time with my father was the best part of my life growing up.

From what *Vati* told me, we started taking those trips when I turned three. It began on my birthday. We turned them into our little monthly getaway, with me circling every first Sunday on my calendar and wishing it would hurry up, wishing we could go every Sunday, but *Vati* told me he had to keep his girlish figure. At the time, I had no idea what he meant, but it made me laugh anyway.

He always knew what to say. And he always took time to say it, to sit with me on my bed and talk. After Michael died, he sat with me numerous times, telling me it wasn't my fault. When my mother cut my braid, he told me he liked it, saying, "It's the new look; all the fashionable women have short cuts." As much as I remembered good times with my father, every moment was tainted by living with my mother. Until I moved out and got married.

Instead of Marty's on Sundays, we started meeting at Fort Tryon Park close to my parents' apartment to play chess every other weekend. All of his friends would huddle around while smoking their pipes to see who would win. It was hard to beat *Vati*, but I did a couple of times. And when it happened, I'd prance around and do my victory dance, and his friends would laugh along. When we had Laura, his life changed. He couldn't have loved anyone more and beamed every time she called him *Opa* in her squeaky little voice. He wanted to start the Marty's tradition with her, but by that time, it was hard for him to make the trip. He had bad arthritis and asthma that took a toll on him. The *Vati* I once knew began to age very quickly. So instead of Marty's, I'd pick up the sweets on the way to the park, where we'd enjoy them.

We'd meet *Vati* every other Sunday and chat with him while eating our donuts. Laura had good taste and always went for the chocolate covered ones. *Vati* devoured the others with strawberry jelly inside and powdered sugar on top.

On those Sundays and when Laura got older, she'd grab the chess pieces and run around while I chased her to get them back. My father would laugh his head off watching me try to catch her. He'd egg her on by calling out "I'm going to get you," which made her only run faster.

Jay said I was only allowed to remember the good times, so I won't mention the last time I saw my father, when I was chasing Laura, when my father told his friends he felt dizzy and had pain in his arm, when his friends asked me to keep Laura distracted. I'll only tell you that Laura saved me that day. Because the last memory I had of Vati was his roaring laugh.

When I told Jay that first story, it helped me open up. Many stories poured out about my father after that. Trips to the Bronx Zoo. Holidays at Brighton Beach. And singing tunes on the bus to Marty's.

"You really miss your father."

"We always miss the ones we love."

"Interesting," Jay said, tapping the pen on his notepad. "You said that you love him, not loved him, as in past tense, like he's still around."

"I wish he were."

"Sounds like you had a great relationship. Why haven't you mentioned him before?"

"I don't know. It's bittersweet to remember. Or, maybe I'm a glutton for punishment," I answered.

"What do you mean?" he asked.

I shrugged. "Maybe I don't think I can have good times again," I said and tried to brush it off with my assumptions.

"Of course, you can," Jay insisted. "Remembering is healthy, and it's great you're talking about your childhood. But what about when you were older?"

I didn't want to talk about Raymond. There were plenty of good times, but the embarrassment of dating a married man overwhelmed me, a relationship I held on to for all those years, wishing for more as the typical and pathetic "other" woman. So instead of Raymond, I dug deeper.

Chapter Twenty-Six

At first, I didn't want to think or talk about Max. There wasn't one bad moment with him. It just seemed too painful to remember the good times. And there were so many. Living in denial never worked, Jay taught me again and again. So, I rediscovered Max, the love of my life, in my therapist's office.

Growing up, Max and I lived a few blocks away from each other. But we didn't meet until many years later. He lived in a modest apartment as the youngest of three. His father owned a deli and his mother worked as a seamstress on the side. They went to a different synagogue so we didn't know them, but one Saturday night, the Jewish Community Center hosted a social for teenagers. My parents were very religious and didn't let me go out often, but they wanted me to find a husband and knew it wouldn't happen if they kept an eye on me at home. Besides, I wasn't interested in any of the men the *yentas* threw my way at our synagogue.

I almost didn't go to the social that evening. After all, at nineteen, I was almost over the hill by then. My friend Anna dragged me along, almost begged me, because she didn't want to go alone. Max was there and kept eyeing me from across the room. Finally, he got up the courage and asked me to dance, and that Max could move. "Let's Twist Again" was all the rage. Everyone hit the floor, screaming and singing along. You should have seen Max go. I thought I'd break a hip when we twisted so fast. But he held onto my hand and never let go.

After that first dance, he was ready for more. And, of course, with my luck, "Jailhouse Rock" came on next.

"Come on, Elsa," he said. "We've just started!"

"I can't. I'm dying."

"What? I can't hear you," he pretended as he grabbed my hand and pulled me farther out on the floor.

After that night, I went along with Anna each month in hopes Max would be there. He showed up every time. Whenever I saw him, my stomach dropped, my heart pounded. Once we spotted each other, we'd smile and head straight to the dance floor and stay there all night.

A few months later, he asked me out on our first date. With my father's permission, we went to the nearby diner for dessert. We discovered we had a lot in common. For starters, we loved root beer floats. But not the usual kind with vanilla ice cream. We loved ours with chocolate ice cream and extra whipped cream. "Leave off the cherry," we both said in unison, which made us laugh with amusement.

While dating, we didn't get to spend a lot of time together because of our studies. I was going to secretarial school, and he was becoming an electrician. On one hand, I secretly hoped he'd go to college and have a more professional-type job. But when Max finished trade school, he began working as an apprentice electrician. Three years later, he got his license and started making a decent living.

I was dying to get out of the house and out from under my cold-hearted mother but wasn't dying to get married. I loved Max and wanted to spend every moment with him, but I felt so young, and the thought of settling down, even with Max, made me apprehensive. Then, on New Year's Eve, Max and *Vati* whispered to each other in the corner of our living room and, before long, Max got down on one knee and asked for my hand. My father and Aunt Regina clapped and hollered for joy.

We got married the next year at my parents' synagogue and took a short trip to Niagara Falls for our honeymoon. But the biggest, most spectacular surprise came just a month later for my twenty-fourth birthday.

After dinner, Max hailed a cab, and as we got into the back, he handed a note to the driver. Then he made me close my eyes.

"Come on, Max. This isn't fair. You know I get motion sickness," I yelled playfully and tried to peek through with one eye before he caught me.

"You do not! Remember *Maid of the Mist*? You asked to go back twice."

"Just tell me where we're going. You know I hate surprises."

"Don't worry. You'll love this one," he said and took my hand.

"You're lucky I don't give you a knuckle sandwich," I joked.

We rode for what seemed like forever and, when the taxi came to a stop, Max told me to keep my eyes closed until he gave me a cue. He took my hand, helped me out of the cab, and stood me in position.

"Okay. Now you can open your eyes."

As with any New York street, people passed by in a hurry on their way to who-knows-where, with horns blasting and cabbies yelling at other drivers to get out of the way. But it didn't take long to notice we were in the theatre district standing in front of St. James's. I looked up at the sign that read *Hello Dolly*.

"Sweetheart, the one and only Carol Channing, for your birthday." He turned me back around, and we kissed for a long time without a care in the world until someone whistled and Max broke away and laughed.

• • •

The two of us had such a great life, going out dancing, and seeing movies often. But we also loved staying home, sitting next to each other on the sofa and watching TV. *Perry Mason* was our favorite until *I Dream of Jeannie* came along. He had a secret crush on Barbara Eden and wouldn't miss an episode. Every time we watched it, Max would say, "I dream of a little Kartchner." His wish came true, and on January 10, 1968, Laura arrived.

People always said it's not the quantity but the quality time you spend with someone. When it came to Max, it was both. Max could have worked overtime to make more money, but he always wanted to spend more time with us. He was home every night for dinner, and we spent every weekend together.

Even though we had a toddler at the time, we didn't want to give up our love for bike riding, so Max attached a basket that fit on the front of his. At first, I was a nervous wreck putting her in it, but after watching them and seeing Laura laugh, it made me so happy. I could still picture it—with me on my own bike following them. We'd often stop at the park and have picnics, and the two of them would run around as I watched and giggled my head off. Our weekend bike riding had always been one of my happiest moments.

Jay said I'm only allowed to remember the good times, so I won't mention the last time I saw Max, when he was on the floor playing with Laura, when he looked at the clock and rushed out the door realizing he was late for an appointment, when that unforgettable knock on my door by police moments later terrified me. I'll only tell you that Laura saved me that day. Because the last memory I had of Max was him playfully pulling on Laura's stubby toes while reciting This Little Piggy.

"So there you have it. Are those the stories you wanted to hear?" I asked Jay.

"Those were really great. How did it feel talking about them?"

My eyes grew heavy and my nose tingled again, the way it always had before the tears flowed. I reached for the box in front of me, pulling it closer to take a tissue. "Mixed feelings," I said. "Really happy recalling them, especially that first dance with Max. But I also felt sad."

"Why?"

"Because I won't have moments like that ever again. Like there's not a care in the world."

"By telling yourself you won't ever be that happy again, you won't be," Jay said. "The mind plays games with us, you know. We give out positive or negative energy. I think, whether we've lost someone or not, we all get to that age in our lives when we remember the good ole days, when we were young and carefree, going out with our family and friends, and having a good time."

Jay got up from his chair and walked over to the window. He peeked outside then pulled on the cord to lift the blinds. The sun came through the office, and its light scattered onto the coffee table in front of me. Dust flew around in the air and settled on the spot where the tissue box once sat.

"Max may have been the love of your life, but it doesn't preclude you from being happy again. It's okay to feel sadness when you remember him. But, hearing you share those stories, I can tell you're a passionate person. You have to find that again. That joy for life."

Jay paused, expecting me to agree or at least have some response.

I looked out the window and watched people at the crosswalk, hoping something would come to me, something that would help me find that joy.

"Elsa, I know it's not easy. But now that you've rediscovered those happy times, you need to rediscover Elsa."

"You're right. I really have been trying to stay more positive, so that's a start."

Jay snapped his fingers and pointed at me. "Yes, that's a great start. Now take that positive energy and do something with it. Make a list of your hobbies. And before you know it, you'll be living your life again and finding joy in it."

It felt more like a necessary pep talk instead of a therapy session and, as I left Jay's office that day, it was the first time I agreed with everything he said. It was time to find myself again, find my hobbies, discover what made me happy. I'd known this for a long time, but always figured a way to talk myself out of it. As the Red Line approached, I made a list in my head and blocked out the lousy excuses.

Chapter Twenty-Seven

I got home and wrote everything down. Reading. Doing crossword puzzles. Eating. Well, Eating shouldn't have been on the list. Maybe Eating Out would be better. Or Eating Out and Dancing, like the supper clubs of my youth. It reminded me of Max and, more recently, of Alexei and our night together. I often thought about Alexei since the trip, and that night was just about perfect, how we stood on the embankment by the Hermitage and looked at the airbrushed sky.

Every once in a while I considered calling him but never got up the courage. Nothing would come of it, so why try? And why contemplate my life while trying? His business card sat nearby in my nightstand, and I looked at the front enough to remember it had two numbers on it, one for London and another for St. Petersburg.

I decided to play a game of fate. I'd call London and if he answered, I wouldn't chicken out and hang up. My heart raced while the drawn-out beeps played out, like the ones I'd heard when calling Laura in Russia several times before. By the third beep, he answered.

"Hi, it's Elsa," I could hardly get out and, for a split second, considered hanging up after hearing his voice.

"Elsa, hello! What a nice surprise."

"I've been meaning to call," I lied. "Just been busy."

"How's Laura? I'm sure you're glad she's home."

"Actually, she's still in Russia," I said, playing with the phone cord. "She decided to stay longer."

"Ah ha! She got the St. Petersburgian bug," he said, almost boastfully, while I deliberately left out the details of our horrible fight.

During our talk, we laughed a lot and got to know each other a little better. Speaking over the phone took some of the edge off, allowing me to be myself and not get nervous in front of him. Alexei mentioned he'd been spending most of his time in London and only traveled back to Russia once. He asked about my boyfriend back home, and at first I'd forgotten about the white lie that night in St. Petersburg, the one to spare myself a broken heart. It seemed so easy to make up stories, one after another. After all, I'd done it my entire life.

"I have some news also," Alexei said after hearing my relationship, the make-believe one, had fizzled out.

The TV caught my attention in the background, and I reached for the remote to turn down the volume. "Oh really? I hope it's good!"

"I'm coming to Washington in March for a conference. Maybe you'd like to play tour guide?"

I giggled nervously and reached for his business card, flipping it back and forth when he told me the news about his trip. We joked some more, reminisced about our night together and, right before hanging up, we decided to call each other every other Sunday at eleven in the morning, my time, until March when we'd see each other.

I looked forward to those Sundays, and it became a nice routine where I'd walk to my neighborhood café for coffee and a bagel and be back before eleven for our call. We continued our Sunday chats every other week, and I hadn't laughed that hard since my days with Max.

But I was realistic. Nothing would come of it, so I stayed on the positive track Jay suggested and rediscovered my hobbies. I joined a book club. Took belly dancing classes, figuring that would be easy since my hips and belly were made for it. Met friends for coffee where they chatted about their kids and their husbands' annoying habits. And even let Donna and the girls at the office talk me into a last-minute Happy Hour—in the middle of the week on a Wednesday.

Donna suggested the Mayflower for our gathering, a place with a cozy lounge and the best Bloody Marys in DC. The girls had to finish up a few things at work and asked me to go down and grab a table since Wednesday nights always got busy.

I left the office, grabbed the Red Line, and walked a couple of blocks to the hotel. Before heading to the bar, I made a quick stop in the ladies' room for a touch-up that my hair and makeup needed after a long day.

The hostess chose a table large enough for the four of us, and the waitress came by to take my order, a Bloody Mary, one with a kick and celery stick perfect for stirring. She returned with my drink and placed it down with a napkin and a small envelope with my name on it.

"What's this?" I asked.

She shrugged and turned around to attend to her next customer. My eyes followed her to the table where she made small talk with a few out-of-towners. Maybe it was a note from the girls saying that they were running late. *But why wouldn't they just call my cell?*

I flipped the envelope over and ripped it open. The note was written on Mayflower stationery and underneath the letterhead, there was one sentence that read:

Do you have a whip and fedora I could borrow?

My heart raced. I'd only heard these words one other time, in Russia while standing in the customs line with Alexei. I looked around, but didn't see anyone familiar. I stood up and peeked around to the far right corner of the bar, where Alexei sat. When he saw me, he lifted his drink as a cheers, stood up, and walked my way.

"You about gave me a heart attack," I said and kissed him back on both cheeks.

"I'm glad you didn't, since I failed medical school."

"How'd you arrange this? I didn't expect you for a couple of days."

We sat back down, and while sipping on his Scotch, he shared the details. How he wanted to come early to surprise me. How he called the office and spoke to Donna who arranged the whole thing. And how he couldn't wait to see me.

"So what made you come to DC for a conference? Don't they have them in London?"

"Not like this. I'm dying to see the new products they have coming out."

"Like what?"

"The newest in robotics and surveillance devices."

"Sounds sexy."

"Not nearly as sexy as you," he said and pulled his chair closer to mine.

I laughed and reached for my drink, hoping the Bloody Mary would calm my nerves.

"What's so funny?"

"You're very forward. I'm not used to it."

He stirred his drink, reminding me of the first time we met on the plane. "You're the one who mentioned the word sexy. I was talking about my conference."

"You have a point."

We stared at each other for a few seconds until I looked away first.

"So what really happened with the boyfriend?" he asked.

Instead of making up an excuse, I shrugged and kept the lying at bay, using silence again as a way to let him make his own assumptions.

"Well, whatever happened, it's his loss," he said as he clanked my glass with his. "Drink up."

"What's the rush?"

"No rush." He leaned in and whispered, "You're so beautiful."

My pulse quickened. I could hardly concentrate as we talked about the books and movies we loved. He teased me about my romance novels, and I teased him back about the far-fetched spy thrillers he devoured. Turned out we had the same taste in movies, old classics, so I invited him over to watch one. Alexei paid the waitress, and we held hands as we walked through the lobby and onto Connecticut Avenue to grab a cab back to my place.

Chapter Twenty-Eight

As we rode up in the elevator, I could hardly talk, anxious as heck, slipping over my words, anticipating what would happen next. Here I was, a grown woman—fifty-something if we're counting—still tipsy from my Bloody Mary, nervously awaiting my first kiss. We walked down the long hall, and Alexei laughed after I tried shoving my key into an apartment on the fifth floor instead of my own on the ninth. He took the keys and twirled them between his fingers, and we headed back down the hall to wait for the next elevator going up.

When we reached my apartment, I gave Alexei a quick tour then excused myself while he admired the view. I closed the door behind me and sat on the bed to get my bearings. It was just Alexei and me, the two of us, and nobody else. Not my daughter. Or my mother. The last time I brought a man home, and it was just for coffee and dessert, my busybody mother acted like a chaperone at a preteens' sleep-away camp.

At that time, I'd hesitated inviting anyone back to my place, but loved my apartment, loved the view, and thought, what the heck, why not invite my date Sydney over for coffee and dessert. It was the same Sydney who came up that day on the Metro, the one who'd started dating Susan, the one who never called me back, and it always made me wonder if my mother had anything to do with it. That night, as soon as we walked in, my mother immediately came out when she heard a man's voice. After introducing herself, she stood by her bedroom as Sydney hung up his coat. Her shadow fell across the floor, her hand gripping the doorknob as she eavesdropped on our conversation.

While I fixed the coffee, Sydney sat in the living room, already under interrogation as if he were picking up his date for the high school prom.

"What is your name again?" my mother asked.

"Sydney," he answered politely.

"What do you do?"

"I'm in the Marines."

"Ah, the Marines, wonderful." She paused then continued, "You like my daughter, yes?"

"Mother." I darted out from the kitchen and sat down next to him. "It's almost ten. Shouldn't you be in bed?"

"Sheldon, let me tell you something," my mother continued, ignoring me.

"Mother, it's Sydney."

She paused and touched her forehead. "That's what I said. Sydney. My father was in the German Army. Let me go look for pictures. I know there is one with him in his uniform."

"Mother, the physical therapist is coming in the morning. Let's show Sydney the pictures another time?"

She walked back to her room and stopped at the front door. Before turning the corner, she waved good-night.

I was about to get up from the sofa to get the coffee and dessert when Sydney took my hand. "Wait a minute," he said and pulled me close.

Sydney leaned in and was about to kiss me when my mother called out. I ignored her, but she called again a minute later.

"Maybe you should check on her?"

I agreed and walked down the hall to her room.

"Is everything okay out there?" she asked. "It was so quiet."

"Mother, thank you for being the nightly guard, but everything is just fine. Don't worry so much."

She asked me to find a missing pair of slippers, which turned up under her bed, and to make sure the blinds were closed all the way. I said good-night and walked out, where Sydney stood in the foyer, putting on his jacket.

"I should get going," he said.

"But you just got here."

"I didn't realize it was so late. I've got an early start in the morning."

After saying good-night, I shut the door and pulled the chain across. My mother's bedroom door stood ajar and a dull light from the television shined through and across the hallway floor, with its sliver of light—and life—suffocating me.

"Please go to bed." I sighed, realizing that I'd never be able to invite a man to my apartment with her around.

Now, with my mother no longer with me, I could look back and make light of it, even laugh a little, and finally let go of the life that used to define me.

"Elsa, is everything okay?" Alexei called from the hallway, snapping me out of my previous thoughts and attempts at intimacy.

"Yes, just a minute," I sang and dashed to the bathroom to wash up, brush my teeth, tweeze the few unwanted hairs, and shave my bikini line with a razor that had collected dust on its handle.

I looked frantically through my dresser for the best bra-and-panty set, plunging my hands deep into the drawer, making a mess of it all. I'd planned to go to Victoria's Secret before Alexei arrived, but his surprise visit got in the way, in a pleasant way. At the bottom of the drawer, a black silky bra surfaced but its panties were missing in action. I dumped my mismatched underwear collection on the bed and rummaged through it to find something close, settling on the black bra and dark-blue panties. With luck, the lights would be dim enough, so Alexei wouldn't notice.

I changed and sat down on the bed to feel my legs, making sure the razor had done its job in my frantic attempt to enjoy this moment and what was about to happen. *What did someone so handsome—and a few years younger—see in me?* I never believed it when, ten years before, women told me to enjoy my thirties and forties because when you hit fifty, something happened. You started feeling your age and looking it as well. The weight stayed on. The crows' feet found their permanent place. The age spots from the sun looked more like dirt stains than cute freckles. I shook my head, told myself to snap out of it, and went out to join Alexei.

"I thought I lost you in there," he teased. "The movie's ready, just waiting on you."

We started watching and through the first half of Hitchcock's *Rear Window*, I felt Alexei's eyes on me many times—as his leg brushed against mine, as he put his hand on my thigh, as he pushed my hair back behind my ear.

I finally turned to him, and he leaned in for a kiss. It reminded me of the first time Raymond and I kissed on the sofa in his office. But this was so much better. This was in my own apartment, not hidden away in some married man's place. We lost ourselves in the moment before Alexei picked me up and carried me out of the living room.

"No, turn left then another right," I said, trying to direct him.

"Oh, you mean my other left," he teased and lowered me on the bed. As he kissed my neck, I started giggling.

"You and your giggles. What's so funny this time?"

"I'm ticklish."

"Oh, it's too soft. You like it rough, yes?" he asked and nibbled my ear.

"No, it's perfect, but let's dim the lights a little," I said and reached for the lamp on my nightstand.

He took my hand. "Wait, I want to see you. You're so beautiful."

I lifted my arms so he could take off my blouse and for a moment I felt so self-conscious, wishing I'd had an extra drink to help me unwind, wishing he'd let me turn down the light.

"How do I get this off? Is there a special combination?" he teased while trying to unfasten my bra.

"I forgot it. Too many numbers."

"Don't worry. I have teeth like wolf." He growled, turned me over, and kissed my back, making his way to my bra. He pretended to gnaw at the hook. "I might need my glasses for this one."

"Let me help," I offered.

"No, don't move an inch." He tried again and, without success, ripped the hook and threw my bra across the room.

"I'll buy you another one like that. And three more that fasten in the front."

The moment overwhelmed me, and I let myself go, remembering the last time I felt this happy. It was first with Max and then Raymond—both so long ago. And now it was Alexei, with only a thick, Russian accent giving his good looks competition.

• • •

The sun poured through the side curtain and near the bathroom where Alexei gathered his clothing, trying not to wake me.

I stretched my arms over my head and watched him get dressed. "Where are you going?"

He came over and kissed me before leaning over to put on his socks. "*Meelaya*, I'll see you later. I'm headed to the conference."

"Can I make you some breakfast?"

"No thanks. I'll get something along the way."

He leaned in for one more kiss, a longer one this time, winked, and left. I pulled the covers over my eyes and did a wiggle. Then, realizing it was Thursday and not Saturday, I jumped out of bed and into the shower, singing along the way.

At the office, the girls jumped from their cubicles and ignored the phones that rang off the hook when they saw me. "How was it?" Donna asked. "He sounded so sexy on the phone."

"How could you keep it a secret?" I asked, realizing after it came out that I'd kept a dark secret for so long. But this was different. The secret Donna kept, of Alexei's visit, was the good kind, the kind that made lying more than okay.

"Oh, that was easy," she said. "I just imagined what it would be like to have that kind of surprise."

I started from the beginning and gave them all the juicy details, from the first moment at the Mayflower, to the last when he came back to my apartment.

It was hard to get any work done at the office. I kept daydreaming and reliving every moment. Getting the note at the bar. Looking over and seeing Alexei sitting there. Riding in the elevator together. The way he carried me to the bedroom. The way he undressed me. Our first morning kiss. The wink before he left.

After work, I made a quick stop home to change before meeting Alexei for dinner. The mailman passed me with his empty bins and a big hello. He'd been our mailman forever, and we often chatted. We always greeted each other by first name, and he knew all about Laura's departure and the letters I longed to receive.

"There's a little surprise in your mailbox," he said as he made his way to the front door.

"Oh goodie, I think I already know what it is," I teased and thanked him before making a quick stop to find Laura's letter leaning against a few bills. She usually faxed them, but whenever she could, she'd find someone coming to the States to mail the letters from here. I opened it on the way up in the elevator but with no time to read, I stuffed it into my purse for later and got ready to meet Alexei.

Chapter Twenty-Nine

The few days with Alexei flew by. Most evenings, we stayed at the Mayflower. He had to return to London on Monday, so over the weekend, we visited the Mall, taking pictures in front of the Washington Monument and stopping for ice cream. We acted like tourists, but we did it while holding hands and stopping along the way to kiss. It was nice, for a change, not to have a care in the world.

Before leaving, Alexei asked if he could come visit me again the following month. He was asking my permission, instead of telling me where and when we'd meet like Raymond had done all those years with his weekly notes. I said it would be perfect and, as we waited for the cab to make its way up my long circular driveway, he kissed my ear and lingered there. The driver popped the trunk, and after Alexei put his luggage in, walked toward me for one last kiss.

"Bye, *meelaya*."

"What's *meelaya*?"

"It's like sweetheart. But sweeter."

I waved good-bye and walked to the Metro. While searching for the pass, I discovered Laura's letter in my purse, the one I'd put there a few days earlier. It was the first time, in all the time she'd been gone, that I'd forgotten about it instead of holding onto every word and reading them more than once.

March 12, 1995

Momitchka!

Happy International Women's Day! Remember we celebrate that on March 8. I love this holiday. All the women walk around with flowers and for one day out of the year, you actually see women smiling on the streets.

How's the weather in DC these days? Here, it's still snow and ice. As much as I love this city, I get tired of all the cold weather. But when May comes along and the snow's gone, I really miss it. It's like my first kiss at the roller skating rink: really sloppy and messy but when it's over and I think about it again, I miss having that "first."

Everything is great. I'm staying busy with my jobs, and David likes his. Even after these months of working at the hotel, the guards at the front door still stop me and ask where I'm going. Seems like they have a different guard every time. Supposedly, they have a problem with prostitutes entering the hotel to get it on with the international businessmen, so whenever they see women walking alone into the hotel, they stop them. Every time I tell them that I work there. Not "work" there, but really work there—at the front desk.

But seriously, I enjoy the job because I can get good use of English and Russian. I'm glad I decided to stay this extra time because one year would not have been enough to learn the language. Finally, I'm able to converse well and I can read the newspaper!

On another note, David has been approached by a few American companies to work in Moscow. I'm thrilled for him, but he's not sure if he wants to move. Supposedly, the companies consider it a hardship assignment, which means they'd pay him extra for it and provide an apartment. I think he should do it because it will look good having international experience. It's an exciting time, and

I'm really enjoying it and the people I've met. But it feels like forever since I've seen you. Please write back and fill me in on what's going on, and how you're doing since Oma died. Are your sessions helping to deal with stuff? Did Alexei come for the conference?

Love,
Laura

I folded the letter and put it back in my purse. They always made me laugh. But this one concerned me. She talked a lot about David and his job and his opportunities. Was she going to stay just for him? Was she forgetting about herself and her opportunities?

Not another thought.

She was more than old enough to live her life and make decisions. *Besides, negative thinking wasn't part of my new path, my new plan*, I thought, and got off the Metro and walked two blocks to Jay's office.

• • •

"So, how's everything going?" Jay asked as I took off my coat and sat on the sofa.

"Couldn't be better."

"You look happy. What's been going on lately?"

"I took your advice although, to be honest, I wasn't really expecting advice from a therapist."

"Ouch, that hurt," he said while laughing hard, and it made me laugh back and notice his good sense of humor because he could take a joke about himself. "So what advice was that?"

"I started a bunch of new things. Joined a book club, oh and belly dancing."

"Sounds fun. What else?"

"I told you I have a new boyfriend, right?"

Jay sat up. "No, I'm pretty sure you left that part out."

"Let me take that back. He's not really a boyfriend. I met him on my way to visit Laura." I paused, collecting my thoughts, wondering what would happen between Alexei and me. "I don't know, not sure it's going to work out since he lives in London."

Jay told me it was okay to be realistic but reminded me to believe in people again. Living in this positive manner challenged me, but staying on course was my only choice. I still pictured my first visit with Jay, more than six months earlier, and how hard it was to find something good to talk about, about my brother, and the relationship with my mother. And now, I'd mostly come to terms with most of that baggage, trying hard not to live in the past.

"So, Elsa."

"Yes," I said with hesitation.

Jay continued, "I'm really proud of you. You've made so much progress that—"

"Are you breaking up with me?" I teased.

He smiled and closed his leather-bound notebook. "No, I'm not breaking up with you. It's just that you've come a long way since opening up. That's all you really needed."

"So you don't think I need to come back?"

"Honestly, I don't." Jay put his pen and pad down on the table. "It's always good to have someone to talk to. So if you're not ready, maybe we could cut back to once a month."

"I don't know what to say. I've become used to our visits."

"I know. Sometimes it's hard. That's why it's so good to have friends in your life, people you can talk to." We stood up, and he walked me to the door. "Listen, it's just food for thought. You don't have to decide now."

And with that, I took a long look at the framed sign with the word *Breathe* and left his office. Jay was right. I'd made progress, thanks to him. But if I stopped seeing him, I'd miss our meetings. It was as if I'd gained another friend, even though, in a funny way, I was paying for it. But I didn't have to decide at that moment. I had time and more interesting things to wonder about. My book club. My belly dancing class. My next visit with Alexei.

Chapter Thirty

*L*olita was next for our book club and though it was just a coincidence, Alexei loved Nabokov and had mentioned it more than once. I'd never read any of the Russian authors, the ones Laura loved and devoured, the ones Alexei read besides his spy thrillers. I planned to pay attention to this one, not skim through or skip pages like the times our teachers assigned the classics in high school. I couldn't wait to surprise him, show it off on my coffee table during his next visit, maybe even impress him with a few quotes.

The book club, my job, and the belly dancing: they all kept me busy. But Alexei was always first on my mind. I'd be in dance class and while the instructor said "move your hips this way instead of that way," I imagined rolling around under the covers with him. When it was my turn to read from *Lolita* for the book club, they asked me three times to begin. My mind was elsewhere. And it wasn't such a bad place to be. I liked the new Elsa. I'd like to think the new me started to arrive before Alexei showed up, but he was a big part. I felt like a hypocrite with Laura, the time we argued when I told her not to live for some guy. And here I was, counting the days before Alexei's April visit, like the countdown before a long-awaited spring vacation.

I'd already been to the grocery store to get his favorites, coffee, and oatmeal with fresh fruit for our morning breakfast. He used to be a meat and potatoes kind of guy, but cut back when he put on ten unwanted pounds when he turned forty.

Now, he watched his weight and what he ate. But he never hounded me about mine and poked fun at my chocolate obsession when he found several bars stashed in my nightstand during his last visit.

After cleaning up the apartment, I washed the sheets, freshened up, and waited for his seven o'clock arrival. When it became 7:30, I started to worry. Not the type of worry that made me think something bad had happened. It was my negative thoughts rearing an ugly head.

In a matter of minutes, I convinced myself that he didn't want to see me again. That he thought I was too old. Not smart enough. Not educated enough. Not cultured enough. Too American. Too old-fashioned. Too set in my ways. Too far away. And then the phone rang. It was Alexei apologizing, telling me he'd just landed and would be at my place within the hour. *I'm such an idiot*, I said out loud and poured myself a glass of wine, gulping it down in two takes.

When Alexei arrived, he wouldn't let go. "*Zaika*, I missed you so much."

"I missed you, too," I said, neglecting to tell him about my worrisome fit. I wanted him to believe in the confident, independent Elsa he met in Russia. And I wanted to believe in me, too.

"So what should we do?" I asked.

He raised and lowered his brows.

"That's all you can think of?"

"With you, yes." He walked over to his suitcase and took out a package. "I told you I'd buy you new lingerie with friendlier hooks. Wait, there's one more thing," he added and handed me a box out of his pocket. Inside, a necklace with an oval-shaped ruby sparkled between pastel pink tissue paper.

"You're spoiling me."

"Here, let me help," he said and took the necklace from the box. "I chose ruby because it symbolizes passion and good health." Alexei fastened the clasp and kissed the back of my neck.

"You shouldn't have," I said and walked over to the mirror to take a closer look.

"It's beautiful, like you." He came up behind me, wrapping his arms around my waist. "Let's leave the rest for later. I'd love to take a walk. My arse is numb from sitting so long."

"Your arse?"

"Okay, my ass, as you Americans say. Better?" he said as he grabbed mine. "*Pashlee.*"

"What's that?"

"It means, let's go."

"Okay then, let's go," I said, choosing a sweater as we headed out the door for an evening walk.

• • •

"*Zaika*, let it ring," Alexei said the next morning as he kissed my chest, making his way down to my stomach.

"What if it's important," I replied while staying warm under his touch.

"That's what the answering machine is for. It's an amazing invention, don't you think?" he teased.

The phone rang a few more times then stopped. A minute later, it rang again. David, Laura's boyfriend, began leaving a message, and I jumped up and over Alexei to pick up the receiver.

"Hi, David. Is everything okay?"

"Everything's okay, but Laura doesn't know I'm calling."

"Calling about what?" I said, trying to stay calm.

"I've been trying to tell her she needs to take a break, maybe visit you or some friends, but she won't listen."

"What happened? Did she lose her job?"

"I really hate telling you this over the phone."

"Damn it, David. Stop beating around the bush already and tell me what's going on!"

"She was attacked."

"What?" This time I screamed. "What happened?"

Alexei jumped up, threw on his pants and asked me in the background what was going on. I had to put my hand up a few times for him to be quiet so I could hear David's explanation. Supposedly, she was at a party in the dorm where she used to live. When she got ready to leave, some guy started flirting with her.

"He was really drunk. She told him to stop bothering her, but he didn't get the message. He was peeved that she wasn't interested so he roughed her up a bit. Luckily—"

"What do you mean 'roughed her up'?" I asked and fumbled through my nightstand for a pack of cigarettes. "Where the hell were you?"

"At home. She went with friends, but she was ready to leave, and they wanted to stay."

"Great friends. What did he do to my little girl?"

David sighed and continued. "He put a cigarette out on her cheek."

"What? Let me speak to her!" I demanded while Alexei paced.

"She's at work. I can't convince her to take a break."

"Well, I'm dragging her home by her hair if I have to. Whether she likes it or not."

"Elsa," David said in a much calmer voice than mine. "I don't think that's a good idea."

"Ask me if I care." I hung up the phone, threw on my pajama pants, and turned to Alexei. "I have to go back to that godforsaken place again."

Chapter Thirty-One

A week later, I had my visa, expedited and expensive, and could hardly eat or sleep once on the plane. Alexei tried to comfort me but nothing helped. I hadn't seen Laura's face yet, trying to prepare myself for the worst, all while wanting to kill the guy. Alexei insisted on going with me and skipped some business meetings he'd arranged back in London. I needed a shoulder to cry on but held it together and didn't break down in front of him—my anger taking over the sadness. My jaw, clenched so tightly, had me searching my purse for extra-strength anything.

We got a room at the Nevsky Palace Hotel on the main prospect and, based on the price alone, it could have been a ten-star hotel. But Alexei insisted we weren't going to stay in the dorm where I stayed with Laura last year, with its sporadic hot water and unreliable elevator. The hotel's location was perfect, just two blocks from where Laura worked and a ten-minute walk the other way to their apartment.

David didn't want me to come and didn't have a chance to tell me during our heated talk if he'd planned to tell Laura about my arrival. But it didn't matter. I was ready to storm down to the hotel where she worked and make my case. Alexei stayed behind, on my request, so I could convince her on my own to come home. He didn't want me going alone, but it was a straight shot up Nevsky, a street I'd walked once before.

Into the hotel I went, past the front doorman Laura said stopped hookers. Past the valet. Past the beautiful women carrying Chanel bags. And past the businessmen and tourists until I saw my beautiful daughter standing behind the check-in desk. She still wore her hair the same way, up high in a ponytail, and when she turned around, the end of her ponytail flipped and landed on her shoulder.

"Mom?" she yelled, almost puzzled, as if she were seeing double. "What the heck are you doing here?"

"Surprise, surprise," I said nervously, almost smirking, but not at her: at myself for believing I'd storm right in and drag her away, save the day for my only daughter, the one I still wanted to protect and treat like a child. I paused, not knowing what to say next. Laura always pulled away whenever the lecturing began. I got cold feet at the last minute and decided not to tell her the real reason for the visit. So I lied. Again.

"Alexei had some business, so he talked me into coming. It was very last minute."

"Obviously. I never thought you'd set foot in this place again."

"That makes two of us."

"Why didn't you tell me you were coming?" She turned to grab a document from the printer, revealing the mark on her cheek that she unsuccessfully covered with makeup. She also looked pale, with purple circles sunken under her eyes.

"Sweetie, you look tired. What happened to your face?" I asked, changing the subject about my surprise visit.

"It's nothing. I'll tell you later."

Maybe she didn't want to relive it. Maybe her employer didn't know. My beautiful daughter had been hurt, and I wanted to wish away that awful scar and her memory of it.

"I'm not off for few hours, but we can get together later," she said and handed a coworker some documents from the printer. "Are you sure they haven't cloned you? I'm still shocked you're here."

"Well, people can change, right?"

"I hope so," Laura said before we made plans to meet later at her apartment.

• • •

It was the end of April and still chilly in St. Petersburg. The snow and ice had started to melt, and the locals had exchanged their heavy coats for sweaters and lighter jackets. While dodging slush to make my way back to the hotel, I walked down Nevsky Prospect where several vendors, in their entrepreneurial spirit, sold framed paintings, jewelry, and nested dolls.

When I got to the room, Alexei was in the shower, and it gave me time to unpack the rest of my belongings. Before pulling out my clothes, I went to the dresser to figure out which drawers he'd taken, and something came over me. At first, I wanted to blame it on the jet lag or my anger about what happened to Laura, but it was my irrational lack of trust that made me start snooping through Alexei's drawers, paying careful attention to the way he arranged them.

Alexei sang his favorite Russian folk songs but would be drying off any minute, so my snooping had to happen fast. What was I looking for?

Evidence of another woman?

A clue of infidelity?

Like a phone number or a business card, proving he was with another woman when he wasn't with me?

As I carefully lifted the shirts not to make a mess, a metallic glint caught my eye. Alexei had put a handgun between his two sweaters. I wanted to pick it up, to feel it in my hands, but I'd never held a gun and was afraid it might be loaded. My heart raced when the shower turned off.

"Alexei, I'm back," I said and evened out the sweater to cover the gun, closed the drawer, and began folding my pants. Alexei came out naked, drying his hair with a towel. He threw his towel and picked me up and onto the bed.

"Hey, I was unpacking," I said as he got on top.

"I'll unpack you instead."

"Not sure what that means."

"Well, you know, English is my second language. Maybe I should teach you some Russian."

"Oh yeah? What would you teach me?"

"Hmm, let's see. I need some inspiration first."

He kissed my neck and shoulders and began unfastening the buttons on my shirt. But I could only think about the gun.

Where did he get it so fast?

Why was he hiding it?

What would he need it for?

"Shit," I said out loud, forgetting the moment.

"*Meelaya*, is that your attempt at dirty talk?"

I moaned and sighed and wished I'd never come back to this horrible city.

Chapter Thirty-Two

On our way to Laura and David's apartment, we took our time, past an antiques store, shoe boutique, and a bakery that reminded me of Marty's from my childhood. As a woman left the shop, the door stayed open for a moment and a trail of vanilla and toasted almonds tumbled out with her.

We crossed over the Bank Bridge that sat above Griboedov Canal and Alexei insisted on some photos, making me pose with the golden-winged lions perched on the edge of the bridge. As I looked back toward the bridge and the small boats that lined the canal, I finally understood why they called it the Venice of the North.

Laura's cozy flat, as Alexei called it, was on the ground floor with boots and umbrellas lined up by their front door. We took our shoes off before entering and, with Alexei's help, David moved a table by the wall to the center of the living room. They opened it up and moved dishes, shot glasses, and vodka from the cabinet. The smell of chicken soup came through from the kitchen, and the whistle from a teapot drowned out the loud chatter outside in the hallway.

"Why'd you have to call her?" Laura asked David after he fessed up.

"I was trying to protect you," he said.

"That's funny," I interrupted. "If you wanted to protect her, you would've gone to the party." I reached for my wine glass. "How could you let her go alone in a foreign country?"

David was about to answer, but Laura jumped in.

"Mom, this is my home now. My country, not a foreign one. I don't need protecting."

"You're actually defending this place and what happened to you?" I snapped back.

Laura rolled her eyes and rested her head in her hands. Alexei sat quietly. And anytime he tried to say something, one of us would interrupt and take over the conversation. So instead, he watched us like a tennis match in overtime.

Laura got up and walked to the window. She pulled the curtain back and peeked out. Her scar showed even more now that her makeup had started to fade.

"Mom, really, I'm okay."

"No, you're not. You're not thinking straight. You were attacked, and you're acting like nothing happened."

She let go of the drapes and turned around. "Yes! I was attacked," she yelled and made me jump. "There, are you happy now? But I'm not like you where I dwell on things for forty years! Well, actually, pretend they never happened, which is worse."

I looked over at Alexei, hoping he wouldn't ask me what Laura meant by her comment. Alexei still knew nothing about what happened to Michael, and I had no idea how long it would take for me to open up.

"Laura, calm down," David said.

"I'm not gonna calm down. She wants to come and save the day all of a sudden."

My defensiveness got the best of me. I was aching for her to understand and to forgive me for the second time. "I did what any mom would want to do," I wound up saying.

"No, you're trying to control my life again. Look, I put myself in a bad position. I shouldn't have walked in the hallway that late. But I'd done it so many times before. It didn't seem like a big deal."

"Laura," Alexei said calmly. "Can you tell me what happened?"

Laura didn't answer. In a calm voice, Alexei spoke to her in Russian. She looked down and played with her fork. A moment later, she opened up.

She only knew his first name. Sergei. A guy in his early twenties. She'd seen him a couple of times before and was pretty sure he had a room a few doors down from where she lived on the third floor. He looked pretty typical Russian, whatever that meant. About her height, maybe a couple of inches taller, good-looking, slender, dirty-blonde hair, deep-set blue eyes. Alexei continued, asking if he had any particular marks or tattoos, which we all thought was the oddest question.

When Sergei first arrived, he seemed kind of quiet, but as he got drunk, he got louder and tried to pick up several women at the party. He kept eyeing Laura but wasn't causing any trouble until she got up to leave and walked to the door. He came up to her, reeking like alcohol and a dirty ashtray.

"What did he say?" Alexei asked as he stayed calm. It seemed to have a positive effect on Laura.

"I don't remember. It was something like: 'Where are you going? You just got here; it's too early to go.' Something like that. He stood in front of the door with his arm up, preventing me from leaving."

Laura came back to the table and sat down. David put his hand on her arm and started rubbing it. "I asked Sergei to move. He opened the door, and when I left, he came out with me and continued with his bullshit. For a split second, I thought about going back to the room, but it didn't cross my mind that he'd do anything. Then, before I knew it, he held me against the wall, and leaned in to kiss me. That's when I started going off on him. I couldn't believe anyone from inside couldn't hear, but the music was pretty loud. He was really drunk; I was surprised he could still stand, let alone hold me like that. That's when I kicked him in the balls and ran."

"That's my girl. What happened next?" Alexei said.

"He caught up to me, called me *suka,* and put his cigarette out on my face. Finally somebody heard when I screamed bloody murder."

"You have to go to the police," I interrupted.

"You're kidding, right? First of all, they'll say it's my fault. Then, he'll find out I snitched, and I'll look a hell of a lot worse than I do now."

"Laura is right," Alexei agreed. "She can't go to the police."

"What's wrong with you two? He can't get away with this."

"Elsa," Alexei said and came to sit next to me. "Going to the police will not help."

"Okay. Then, pack your bags. You're coming home with me."

Laura got up and started pacing while biting the skin around her nail. "See, I knew it. David, seriously, why'd you have to call her? I'm not going to the police or home. I'm not going anywhere!" she screamed and walked off. "When are you gonna let me live my life? It's enough already!"

She stomped down the hall to the other room and, when she slammed the door, we all jumped. Alexei tried to comfort me by rubbing my shoulders while the three of us sat in silence. I couldn't make Laura come home with me. Obviously, it was the last thing she wanted.

Funny, though, to think that while on the plane, I had it all arranged in my head. I'd waltz into this strange city, march into her apartment, pack her things up, and whisk her away. Just like that. Just as if she were five years old again. As if she had no life of her own. What was I thinking? Could I have really dragged her home by her hair? Why did I even come here to try to convince her? I sighed and got up to look around their apartment.

They had a beautiful flat in the center of town, just a ten-minute walk from the Metro station, although you could walk practically everywhere and wouldn't need a car or public transportation. From what David told me, their apartment was large by Russian standards. They had a long hallway that led to two rooms. From the entrance, an alcove to the left led to a living room and to the right, was an office. Down a hall and around the corner was one bedroom and a bathroom separated into two rooms, one for the toilet and one for the sink, bath, and washing machine.

The long hallway reminded me of my childhood apartment, the one where I grew up in New York. Any time someone rang the bell, my mother would walk from the kitchen or living room to the front door. No matter what, she'd always know which way to turn the seven locks, as if she'd memorized the combination to a bank vault.

Her steps were etched in my memory. It always took twenty-two of them for my mother to reach the front from the kitchen. After I got married and left the house, Max and I could tell what room she was in by the amount of time it took her to greet us whenever we came for a visit.

• • •

By the time Laura came out of her bedroom, we were in the kitchen drinking tea while David told us more about his job. She'd been crying. I couldn't stand looking at her this way. Did she feel like we were ganging up on her? Rather, that I was ganging up on her? She didn't want to relive it, and now hearing about it and seeing her like this, I wanted to drop the whole ordeal. I couldn't take her away from a place she called her home. I couldn't drag her down to the police station to make a statement, even with my best intentions.

"Mom, you have to promise you won't do anything. You just need to go home and leave it alone."

"But what if he does this to someone else?"

"What if I told you that you'll make it worse for me if you do something? Seriously, you have to promise."

"Okay, okay. I promise."

"Promise what?"

"That I won't do or say anything."

"And you'll keep your word?" Laura asked.

"Yes, I promise. Are you happy now?"

"Want some tea?" David asked and grabbed a mug from the counter.

Laura nodded and cut a huge slice of chocolate cake. She cut some more pieces and passed them around the table.

"Chocolate is the best medicine," I said.

"Wait a second," Alexei chimed in. "I thought it was laughter."

"Whoever said that never tried brownies," Laura joked.

Hearing Laura laugh made me feel better, knowing my old daughter had found her way back. That made me happy but only for the moment. I was still mad as hell and determined to confront Sergei, no matter what Laura said.

Chapter Thirty-Three

Alexei followed me down Nevsky Prospect, past our hotel, and toward the dorm. The late evening brought colder temperatures and sent chills down my body. The vendors began packing up their belongings, and the light from the street lamps left a warm yet fragmented glow to the city's bleakness.

"Elsa, please," he said. We stopped, and he took my hands. "You're cold. Come on, let's go back to the hotel. Or, to a café to get some *chai*."

My fight wasn't with Alexei. I adored him, but he wouldn't convince me to change my mind. Whether he liked it or not, Sergei was about to have an unexpected visit from an angry mom.

"Don't do this. You promised Laura, remember?" Alexei reminded me.

"Why is everyone making such a big deal? He's an ass and shouldn't get away with it."

"Right, but what will you accomplish by confronting him? Have you thought about it? You don't even know which room or what he looks like."

"I have a good enough idea by the way you interrogated Laura," I said, letting go of his hand to continue my walk down Nevsky.

"Don't make this your battle," Alexei snapped. "Laura's a big girl. Can't you respect that?"

I stopped to face him. "What if that happened to someone you loved more than anything? Wouldn't you want to do something?"

"Sometimes we can make things worse by getting involved."

"You make a good point," I said.

He smiled, almost out of relief. "So you'll come back to the hotel?"

"No."

I passed Kazan Cathedral, with its large, semi-circular shape and columns that stood triumphantly. It reminded me of my previous trip the year before. The city was warmer then and the prelude to White Nights kept the sky the color of lightly roasted marshmallows sprinkled with pink. Now, it was dark, bleak, and gloomy as hell. My hatred for this city, and what it recently stood for, clouded my thoughts.

I walked down Plekhanova Street and entered the dorm, where an attendant greeted me with a grunt and, in return, I fed her a lie about visiting a friend. Lying in this country, or at least to people other than my daughter, seemed so easy.

When a few students passed speaking English, I asked if they knew a guy named Sergei who lived on the third floor. They walked with us down the hall and pointed to the room. As I lifted my hand to knock, the door opened and a young man fitting Laura's description stood in the doorway, looking surprised. He closed the door quickly, turned his back to me, and locked up.

"Sergei?" I asked.

"*Da. Kto hochet znat?*"

I knew almost no Russian but knew that *da* meant yes and by Laura's description that it had to be him. He stood there and, while waiting for me to finish yelling at him, cocked his head back to look me over. A second later, he put the key in his pocket and walked off.

"Hey, wait a minute," I screamed. "Where the heck are you going?"

Alexei stepped in and spoke to him in Russian. Sergei stopped, turned around, and came closer. They began a heated discussion, and Sergei got into Alexei's face, spitting words and clenching his fist.

As Sergei walked off, he turned around and smiled, said a few words, and left. One of the words, *suka*, jumped out at me. Laura used it when she described what happened in the hall that night.

"See, I told you nothing good would come out of this," Alexei said as we both watched Sergei stride down the hall and disappear.

"What does *suka* mean?" I asked as some students poked their heads out from a few rooms.

"It's not important."

"Just tell me."

Alexei leaned against the wall and fixed the collar of his coat. He translated, hesitantly, saying that Sergei called Laura a bitch and that she came onto him at the party before changing her mind. "Elsa, it's obvious he's bullshitting. Just be happy nothing worse happened."

"Oh, so putting a cigarette out on her cheek is okay?"

"That will heal, and she'll have her beautiful face back."

"I can't believe everyone is so nonchalant about this, even Laura."

"That's not true. But this isn't the way. Remember, I grew up here and know what it's like." He pulled me close and wrapped his scarf around my coat. "Let's go have some champagne and chocolate in bed, okay?"

"I'm not in the mood."

"I can persuade you," he said and smelled the back of my wrist.

"Are you always this romantic after a confrontation?"

"That was nothing," he said, and I believed it, especially after discovering his gun.

Chapter Thirty-Four

The next morning when we got up and out of bed, Alexei pulled the drapes back to let the sun in, and we watched people come and go. You could tell the tourists from the locals. The tourists always held onto their bags with extra caution and wore smiles instead of desperation. Life seemed bleak and the weather even more depressing. I was crazy to come here and more than ready to leave. Laura made her point loud and clear: Russia had become more than an adventure. It had become her home, part of her soul, her spirit.

We ate breakfast at the same bakery we passed the day before, with its showcases overflowing with cakes and pastries that reminded me of Marty's, even more so on the inside. I chose chocolate cake, a little decadent for the morning, and Alexei helped with every other bite.

On our last day, Alexei wanted to show me Peterhof Palace and its spectacular cascading fountains. Or the town of Pushkin with its gold-ornamented palace once used as the home of the Tsars. Instead, he took me to the Russian Museum for a tour of paintings by Rupin and a stroll to the Church of the Savior. It was a copycat of St. Basil's on Red Square, with its vibrant domes and golden crosses, a bitter reminder of my confession in Moscow.

Had I really made that much progress like Jay mentioned? Was I really able to let go and let Laura live her life? I thought I'd made strides but this trip proved otherwise. Convincing myself to let go seemed so easy that day in Jay's office and on his comfortable sofa.

In the evening, Alexei surprised me with tickets to the ballet, and after the performance, cars lined up like taxis as people poured out of the Mariinsky Theatre. Alexei approached a sedan and opened the back passenger door for me. In one of Laura's letters, she mentioned how people made extra money by giving rides. A person would flag down a car and they'd negotiate a price to a destination, something that hadn't caught on back home yet. Even though hitchhiking used to be popular, to me, it seemed odd to get into somebody's car you didn't know.

"*Zaika*, did you like the ballet?"

"It was wonderful. I love how you surprised me," I said and remembered the time Max took me to see *Hello Dolly*, making me hide my eyes in the cab along the way to St. James's Theatre so long ago.

"We're not done yet. Hope you're up to having a light dinner."

Alexei leaned forward and spoke Russian to the driver. At the light, he turned and as we drove by Laura's old dorm, anger settled in. Sergei was getting away with the attack, and he clearly had no remorse. Laura and Alexei didn't want me going to the police and said it would make matters worse. True, I knew nothing about the way things worked in Russia and how people ticked. *What goes around comes around*, I hoped and held on to the idea for dear life.

"I'm taking you to Literaturnoye Café. They have the best *blini*, especially when you combine it with caviar and champagne."

"What's *blini*?"

"You don't know? It's what the French call crêpes. But we make them better," he said when the driver came to a stop. Alexei got out of the car and put his hand out to take mine.

As we passed several tables on the way to ours, couples enjoyed their *blinis* with sour cream and black caviar. Some chose tea and others had shots of vodka. In the corner, musicians played the piano and a violin. Burgundy drenched the walls and green velvet lampshades dampened the light, making the room cozy and elegant. By the window, a mannequin with wavy hair sat contemplating his thoughts while writing a letter. His dark curls and long sideburns reminded me of Max.

"Who's the guy?" I asked.

"That's Alexander Pushkin, the most incredible poet who has ever lived."

The hostess brought us to the back corner and placed the menus down on a table set for five.

"Are we expecting someone?" I asked.

"It's a surprise."

"You know I hate surprises. Well, except when it comes to the ballet."

"Let me tell you more about Pushkin."

"I love how you changed the subject," I said.

He smiled and placed the napkin on his lap. "You worry too much. It's a good surprise."

After we ordered some tea, Alexei told me about Pushkin, how he published his first poem when he was just fifteen, and how the entire Western world had him to thank for his lyrical works.

"When did he live?" I asked while eyeing the front door.

"In the early 1800s. He died during a duel over a woman."

"How romantic."

"Not exactly. Pushkin thought his wife was having an affair. He challenged the guy to a duel, but didn't make it, wound up dying a couple of days later." Alexei paused and looked toward the front of the restaurant. "I'm not sure what happened to his wife. His house is a museum now, not far from here. Ah, here they are," he said as his words trailed off.

Alexei smiled and got up from the table to approach a young man and woman who looked in their late twenties with a child about four years old. They hugged and greeted each other before walking back to our table.

"Elsa, I'd like you to meet my son Dima, his wife Natasha. And this is my wonderful grandson Misha." Alexei picked Misha up to give him another hug.

"Wow! What a beautiful family." I was shocked. I knew his family lived in St. Petersburg but didn't expect to be meeting them and wondered why he hadn't told me.

Before long, I found out that Dima was a twenty-six-year-old engineer and his wife Natasha, an elementary school teacher. Little Misha was five years old with gorgeous red hair he inherited from Alexei's ex-wife.

When I asked more about her, Alexei changed the subject. But it didn't stop me. And when I pushed a little, he opened up, saying nothing out of the ordinary happened. "We just grew apart," he added. "In Russia, it's very difficult to find an apartment, so you live with your parents until you get married. That's why many people get married so young, so they can get out of the house. And why so many end in divorce."

Misha got up from the table and walked over to sit on Alexei's lap. Misha had Alexei, *deydooshka* as he called him, wrapped around his finger. Alexei bounced Misha on his knee and pulled on his ears while making funny noises.

"You spoil him, like all good grandparents," I said.

"Of course, I spoil him," he said in a cute voice. "He loves the video tapes I bring back from London, don't you, Mishka? *Da?*"

Misha nodded.

"Wow, he understood."

"Not really. I said *da,* so he nodded."

I couldn't stop staring at Misha and his floppy cinnamon hair and connect-the-dot freckles. He had two teeth missing in the front, and whenever he smiled the gap showed, making me smile back. It was hard to communicate with his family, but as we sipped on our tea and ate *blinis*, Alexei shared stories about Dima as a kid.

At the end of the dinner, I could tell Alexei didn't want them to leave. Saying good-bye was hard, especially when it came to Misha. Alexei bent down and whispered something to him while we put on our coats. Misha tried to close his own, fumbling with the buttons but not giving up.

"Good-bye, Mrs. Kachna," Misha said.

"Kart-ch-ner," Alexei repeated.

"Kartchner."

"*Moladets!*" they all said, and Alexei bent down to give him a high five.

We said our final good-byes in front of the café and strolled down Nevsky arm in arm.

"They're such a nice family," I said while looking down to step over some slush.

"They are, but I was such an idiot when Dima first married her. Such an idiot that we didn't see each other for two years," he confessed as we crossed the street on our way back to the hotel.

Loud laughter from a young couple distracted Alexei from his story, and we waited for them to pass us before he continued, telling me how he didn't want Dima to make the same mistake by getting married too young. Alexei learned quickly how he had to stop being so controlling and let Dima live his life. It reminded me of my relationship with Laura and made me wonder if Alexei was sending me a subtle message.

"Put it this way, I acted like a fool," he said.

"I'm sure you weren't that bad."

Alexei was more than a fool, he told me. And Dima wouldn't put up with it. They kept their distance and before

203

long, Alexei realized he had to change his ways if he wanted a relationship with them, especially with Misha. He finally accepted Natasha and now everything was forgiven.

"It must be hard, not living close by. Why'd you decide to move in the first place?"

"When the Soviet Union collapsed, I was working in the London Embassy. They didn't need me there anymore. After I lost the job, I didn't know what to do. But I knew I didn't want to go back."

As we walked, continuing our way to the hotel, he opened up more. "Life here is very hard. Especially now with the horrible inflation. So through my connections, I established a security business with offices in London and St. Petersburg. I have a better quality of life, and I'm able to help my family much more. I miss them, but it's only three hours away."

"Tell me more about your business."

"We protect people and places."

"Anybody famous?" I asked.

He brushed my hair to the side, ignoring my question at first.

"You're not going to tell me, are you?"

"It depends. What will you give me?" he teased.

"You're adorable, but not as much as little Misha. Could he be any cuter? And, I love the name."

"It's short for Mikhail. That was my father's name."

"Oh, like Mikhail Gorbachev."

"Yes, like good ole Gorby."

We walked in silence, enjoying each other's company. A block down, the hotel's façade glowed from the light escaping the guest rooms, like a back-lit bar that comes to life once dusk settles in and customers arrive for a cocktail. Alexei reached for our room key and, as we approached, I thought of the wonderful time with his family and little Misha.

Even though Misha looked nothing like my brother, the evening made me think about Michael again, how cute he was with his dark-blonde curls and brown eyes. He never made it past four, and the memory of his short life would remain. He was four years old forever and to everyone—to all who loved him and to those who never had a chance to meet him.

"I had a little Misha in my life once," I blurted out, the first and only time I'd mentioned it to Alexei.

"Really? Was he your first love?" he teased and put his arm around me as we entered the hotel lobby.

"He was my brother."

"Where is he now?"

As we rode the elevator to the eleventh floor, I told Alexei about Michael and how he died that September day. He pulled me close and held onto me, allowing me to let go of my childhood memories that had unwillingly become a part of me. The elevator stopped on our floor, and we hadn't noticed until a moment later when, after the bell rang, the door closed on us. Alexei reached over and pushed the button again and during these few minutes, he continued to hold me. He didn't ask for more details. He didn't say a word. And he never let go.

Chapter Thirty-Five

We sat on the edge of the bed with the TV on in the background, with its quiet hum getting our attention. Alexei rubbed my shoulder with one hand and checked his watch with the other. Being late was one of his pet peeves, and he avoided it whenever possible.

"Are you sure you don't want me to stay?" Alexei asked after turning off the television. He hesitated and, especially now that he knew about Michael, wanted to hold me in his arms and make everything better.

I didn't want him standing up his friend. "Don't be silly. You won't have another chance to see him."

"I feel bad leaving you."

"And I'll feel bad if you don't go. I'm fine, really."

He kissed me good-bye and threw on his camel-colored wool coat and plaid scarf. After he left, I jumped up to check if the gun was still there. The shirts sat neatly folded and flat with nothing underneath them. Either he moved the gun or had it on him. I searched the room, from one drawer to the next, under the mattress and in his suitcase, and came up empty.

Instead of getting undressed and in the shower as planned, I grabbed my coat, hat, and scarf and headed for the elevator, not sure what had come over me. Alexei seemed to adore me, but I still had my doubts from all those years being second fiddle to a married man. Was Alexei meeting an old lover rather than an old friend? But why would he take the gun? He mentioned that it was dangerous walking alone at night. Maybe he brought it for protection.

I took the elevator to the third floor and stairs the rest of the way before exiting. The temperature had dropped below freezing, and I pulled my hat down below my ears and rubbed my hands together to warm them up. A man wearing a trench coat and fedora bumped into me, continuing on his way without an apology. The native New Yorker in me took over, patting down my coat pockets to make sure nothing had gone missing.

I was about to turn around and head back to the room for my shower but spotted Alexei halfway down the block. I continued along Nevsky, following him like a crazy lady who took everything for granted or, even worse, a lost soul who had everything to lose. He stayed on the main prospect, and walked past the Metro stop, small shops, and Dom Knigi bookstore he mentioned earlier when we visited Kazan Cathedral. Once he got to the corner, he turned left onto Plekhanova toward the dorm.

Shit.

Was he planning to go to the dorm? To confront Sergei? Or maybe he was telling the truth. Maybe his friend, the one he'd plan to visit, lived on Plekhanova or another side street.

Alexei stopped by the edge of the dorm and looked around. I had to think fast. I stopped and slowly moved left to wait near Kazan Cathedral. He stood by the side of the building for a few minutes before a man joined him. They walked toward the back and continued to talk. It was hard to see, so I tiptoed to the left side of the cathedral and stood by the passageway next to the canal. As I stepped over paper, debris, broken glass, and God only knew what else, I covered my nose with my scarf, almost gagging from the smell of urine.

While chatting, Alexei handed his friend something. They talked for a few minutes, had a few laughs, and kissed both cheeks. Alexei started back down the passageway toward Nevsky Prospect, and I tucked myself behind a column until he walked by. *How would I get back to the hotel before him without knowing any shortcuts? How would I pretend I'd been sitting in my room, all cozy after my shower, waiting for his return?*

I kept my distance and pulled down my hat. Alexei walked slowly, stopping suddenly when he saw Dom Knigi on the other side of Nevsky. I panicked and stood still, pretending to fix my scarf. He waited for the light to turn, crossed the street, and entered the bookstore. Earlier he'd mentioned Dom Knigi and its great collection, and it gave me time to calm down and make my way back to the hotel.

I rushed to the room, threw my clothes off, and jumped into the shower. A short time later, the door opened, the shower curtain moved to the side, and my Russian stood naked in front of me.

"Let me help you," he said as he washed my hair and pushed away the lather from my forehead.

"How's your friend doing?" I asked.

"Doing well. He couldn't stay long, so I stopped at Dom Knigi on the way back and bought some Pushkin for you."

Alexei wasn't lying, really. He had met a friend or an acquaintance—even if it was on a dark side street instead of a bustling café.

He rubbed my shoulders and started speaking Russian in between kisses. "*Daragaya*, I will recite the most beautiful poetry until you fall asleep."

• • •

I quickly realized from my short visit to Russia that my daughter wouldn't be coming home. Even after the attack, after a cigarette burn that marked her beautiful complexion, she continued to call St. Petersburg home. She was happy here.

With David. With her jobs and friends. Even with Russian winters, which had come to make her happy and, when the last bits of snow and ice disappeared, she missed them and longed for their return.

As we sat at the airport awaiting our flights, Alexei asked me about his next trip to DC. I already missed Laura and would miss Alexei even more but had a hard time figuring out last night. What was he keeping from me? What if he passed the gun to the person he met? And how much should it matter? Should I dwell on it or just enjoy my life and pretend I didn't see anything? Living in the present was one thing, denial another. But can't denial be a good thing? To act like it never happened? I wondered what Jay, my therapist, would have said to that one, knowing how denial was the crux of my mother's despair.

"Elsa? I called your name three times, even said George Clooney was sitting next to you," Alexei teased.

"Sorry. Deep thoughts."

"Are you still worried about Laura?"

"Actually, Sergei."

He ran his hand through his hair then rubbed the side of my arm. "You don't need to worry."

"What if she bumps into him again at the dorm?"

"That won't happen."

"Of course, it could. She goes there all the time. I'm such an idiot. What was I thinking going over—"

"Elsa," he interrupted. "Sergei was arrested this morning. I don't know the whole story, but police found a gun and drugs in his room."

I paused for a few seconds. "Really?" Almost doubtfully, I added, "How do you know?"

"I have my sources."

"What does that mean?"

"Okay, I confess. While you were having lunch with Laura today, I went to the dorm to talk to him, and they told me at the front desk."

"I thought you said we should stay out of it?"

"I had second thoughts."

"I'm not going to hold my breath," I said. "He'll come up with some story and be out in a day or two."

"Not here. They're very strict about drugs. Plus the gun. Here, you're guilty until proven innocent." Alexei pulled his newspaper and reading glasses from his bag. "Don't worry. I've seen guys get locked up for two years just for a bar fight."

At that point, I wanted to confess about following him. I wanted to ask if he gave the gun to that guy on the street. If Alexei planned it, he took a huge risk to make sure Sergei paid for what he did. But was it fair punishment? Could I keep my silence and forget about it? It seemed so much easier to deny these thoughts. To push them way back, keep my mouth shut, and convince myself that he wasn't involved. It was easier and made sense. Besides, it was time to enjoy my life, not complicate it.

Chapter Thirty-Six

The receptionist took my coat and led me back to the office. The leather sofa had been replaced with a more comfortable plush version in a greenish-gray that matched the walls so perfectly, as if a swatch was brought to the counter at Sherwin-Williams.

It had been a week since I'd been back from Russia and two months since my last session. Jay always told me to call whenever I needed to talk. And after what happened in Russia this second time around, it was the right decision to have another visit.

I explained how Laura wouldn't come home after her attack, how I flew there more or less by the seat of my pants, trying to control everything, including my daughter. It didn't take long for me to get to the point with Jay. What took longer was realizing that just because I thought Russia was a horrible place didn't mean Laura couldn't love it.

"I suppose if I were attacked in DC, I wouldn't leave either," I finally got out.

"Exactly. Because in life, you can't run from things. If you can't get over them emotionally, they will follow you no matter where you live."

Jay was right. But I kept double-guessing my actions. Treating Laura like a child and wanting her close by to protect kept gnawing at me.

"We all second-guess ourselves, especially as parents," Jay added. "We always wonder, 'Am I doing the right thing?,' 'Did

I say the right thing?,' 'Am I teaching them the right things?' Even when they're grown up and out of the house."

The light flashed on Jay's phone, and we both looked over. Its orange glow distracted us for a moment and from our conversation about Laura. It wasn't a bad thing, and it made me realize how much time we spent talking about her, as if she were still the center of my existence.

"So, what else is new? Are you still seeing Alexei?"

"So far so good." My smile disappeared. "Just don't know if I can trust him a hundred percent."

"Did he give you a reason not to?"

"Not really. When we're together, he gives me so much attention. He's so romantic."

"Then what's the problem?" Jay asked.

I'd been honest with Jay all these months, so what was the point in changing that now? Come to think of it, he'd been the only person I'd been completely honest with this entire time. "I don't know," I wondered. "What if he's with someone else when he's not with me?"

"Elsa, based on your previous relationship, I can see how you'd feel that way. But it's not a healthy way to start one. You had an affair with Raymond but lived in the same town with him and his wife. You don't have to be a thousand miles away to have an affair."

"I like him so much, you know? I'm afraid something will go wrong," I admitted.

"You know who are some of the happiest people in life? The ones who don't worry or sweat the small stuff."

"Yep," I said and stretched my arms up and back before putting them on my lap. "And I'm forgetting how much progress I've made. I'm not gonna screw it up."

Jay nodded and gave me a thumbs-up. He waited for me to continue, knowing there was something else on my mind or the need for reassurance on my own.

"I'm going to enjoy what I've got, no matter how long I've got it," I said, reaffirming my decision not to tell Jay about the gun, how I followed Alexei that night, or the likely setup of Sergei. And I'd never mention it to Alexei either or ask how he spent his time in London without me. Many things had complicated my life before that were out of my control. I wasn't about to risk complicating my own life—on my own.

When we finished our session, Jay opened the door and his assistant waved as she took a call. To me, my relationship with Jay had become second nature, so easy to have him there at a moment's notice to lean and count on. What a bittersweet moment, the way I walked out of Jay's office for the last time, up the hall, and down L Street to catch the Metro.

Chapter Thirty-Seven

The summer months flew by. My job kept me busy booking travel for conferences, while Alexei's visits and Laura's letters kept me company in between. We took turns corresponding, and Laura wrote hers every other week on Tuesdays. To follow tradition or just out of habit, she still took advantage of the fax machine at work to send me hers. I never underestimated, for all those years, the sheer joy of looking forward to something as priceless as a letter from a loved one.

August 27, 1996

Mamachka!

I love calling you mamachka, it sounds so cute!! I can't believe I've been here for three years! It's amazing how time flies. I'm sorry I can't be there with you during the Jewish holidays. David and I will be going to a small service at someone's apartment. Believe it or not, some people are still scared to show their Judaism in this country.

So...the news of the week is a certain someone, who shall remain nameless, is still in jail. I was pretty shocked about the whole thing, but to be honest, it's a relief. And, that's all I'll say about that subject, because we don't know who's reading our faxes—or my thoughts! The summer here was fantastic. For a couple of years, they've been repairing the fountains at Peterhof, but finally, they're working and I was able to see them in all their glory! I'll have to take you there (if you ever decide to come back—ha!). I also spent time in part of the country I'd never been to. I went with one of my coworkers her hometown, a place called Vyborg, which is in Russia right across from the Gulf of Finland. It gets so cold in the winter that you can walk on the gulf and drive a car on it. Um, no thanks! I think I'll stick to the sidewalks. I've become so used to the temperature here that when it's just forty degrees, I go out with just a sweater. In the summer, when it's seventy, I'm hot as hell! What will I do whenever I return home and it's ninety in the summer?

Speaking of coming back, I'm so excited that you'll help me plan the wedding. I'd really like to have it in the spring, maybe in March? I know that only gives us about six months, but maybe since we're having it on a Sunday, we'll be able to get a place. How about I let you pick the location? I'll give you a list of the people we'd like to invite, which is only about forty or fifty, which includes David's family and friends. He has a small family, which let's be honest, keeps the cost down.

Anyways, I need to run to work. Not really run, I'll walk fast. This week, I'll sit down with David and we'll put our list together for the invites. I'll fax it to you next time.

Lots of love!
Laura

The last time we spoke on the phone before getting her latest letter, Laura broke the news, the good news that David had proposed. It was time. She was twenty-eight, the perfect age to get married. I'd dreamed of this moment, helping her plan a wedding—but together. She'd given me so much authority to choose everything, and it made me nervous. Being in Russia, she didn't have time to fly home and plan it all, so she sent me a picture of a dress she liked along with her measurements and asked me to pick something out.

The following weekend, I looked up bridal stores in the local phone book, and chose one in Chevy Chase, a couple of miles from my apartment, on a side street filled with boutiques. The shop's window sparkled with crystals, sequins and lace, full skirts and slim bodices, all beautiful collections but nothing close to Laura's choice. She wanted something fitted, simple, and elegant with a short train. The door rang out when it opened and two ladies looked up over their bifocals to greet me.

"Is this the first time you've ordered a dress without the bride around? It makes me a bit nervous," I admitted.

"You should see the requests we receive. Besides, we've been here in this very spot practically since lace was invented," the shop owner said and asked me to follow her to the back of the showroom. "We've even chosen gowns over the phone, sight unseen until the brides come for their fitting a week before the wedding."

"Really? I can't imagine," I said and followed the trail of dresses, vails, purses, and pumps along the way.

"This is the one," she said, pushing aside gowns and pulling a sample from the row. "It's perfect and not too expensive."

The light-pink price tag flipped around when she brought the dress over to a separate rack. Five hundred and ten dollars. I'd heard some gowns ran thousands, enough for a serious down payment on a car, so the price helped settle my nerves. But would Laura like it? I compared the dress to the one in the picture.

"Don't worry, it comes in bright white. It's a little hard to tell, but this one's eggshell."

"What do you call this, the way it goes out?" I asked and felt the silky fabric.

"Mermaid, but some say trumpet. I just love the scooped neckline and subtle beading at the top; it's exquisite."

"You have a great eye," I said.

"It's your daughter with the good taste."

We laughed and walked back to the counter, where she wrote down Laura's measurements. She recommended ordering the dress a size up, in case we had to do some last-minute adjustments.

Laura wanted every detail to be simple but elegant so, with the owner's help, we picked out a veil and full-length satin gloves, and ordered white roses for Laura and the bridal party through her florist-friend connection. We said our good-byes after both ladies wished me well and told me to call on them with any questions or advice for the upcoming celebration.

For the next month, I stayed busy planning the rest of the ceremony, faxing the details to Laura and making sure she approved. We booked a small reception hall in Silver Spring, ordered elegant invitations with a black border that looked Art Deco, and chose the menu. Then I sat down to make my part of the guest list.

Creating the list seemed easy at first. My boss, friends, and a few relatives. To keep it small and the expenses down, I came up with a system, using my address book and with each name, marked how long we'd known each other and how long it had been since we'd spoken. If it was more than a year or if we spoke once in a blue moon, they'd end up in the "maybe" category with a final decision at the end.

And then there was Raymond. We'd known each other for decades, and he'd known Laura for most of her life. He was my boss then we were lovers. We were lovers then friends. The closeness between us remained and oh-so familiar, like the only two people in a room who understood an inside joke.

As the years went by, we only spoke twice a year on our birthdays. But we were still in each other's lives to a certain extent. Would he be comfortable around Alexei and should it even matter? Raymond was one of the few still alive I'd known the longest, the one who helped me when times got tough. Inviting him felt right. I finished my list, with Raymond added to the end, combined it with Laura's, and counted seventy-two people.

It would still be a couple of months until the invitations had to be addressed and sent out. The list sat in the top drawer of my nightstand next to Laura's letters. Every once in a while, I'd take a few out to read. This time, I pulled out the whole pile and read through them one by one. They made me laugh, get teary-eyed, and miss her even more.

When I got to the bottom, it wasn't one of Laura's. It was the letter I wrote to Raymond but never sent. It had been a long time since I'd looked at it. What was I thinking? Writing about how I always wanted to be with him and wished he'd left his wife?

For all those years, denial took over. Waiting and hoping Raymond would get a divorce, even when he was always honest with me that he never would. But I held on for hope, for a change of heart, for a love that could be strong enough to replace the family he'd built. After finishing the letter, instead of folding and putting it back in the pile, I tore it up and threw it away.

No more dwelling on the lost chances or proving how far I'd come. But there was one thing I still hadn't taken care of, something that couldn't be avoided any longer that had nothing to do with Raymond. It had been more than two years since my mother died, and I hadn't been back to the cemetery. The first year passed, like that, without an unveiling of her tombstone, a solemn ceremony that should have been done at the anniversary of her death.

It had been hard, and I avoided it at all costs. Why put myself through it and the extra anguish? But my parents deserved the respect. And so did Michael. I checked the calendar and noted the upcoming Jewish holidays. It was customary to visit the gravesite during the week between Rosh Hashanah and Yom Kippur, and it was time. I made a note to take a Sunday trip to New York at the end of September.

Chapter Thirty-Eight

Susan parked her car near the cemetery's office, and we hiked up the driveway that curved around the building. Along the way, a man holding a prayer book reached into his pocket for a yarmulke, and two women stopped at a stand to choose stones that could be left at the grave. Most memorials stood large and upright with Stars of David and Hebrew etched into them. I tried to decipher the words but many years had passed since I'd read Hebrew or even prayed.

We reached the family memorial—with Michael's as the first one in the row. It left a rising soberness after we read the dates on his tombstone, subtracting the four short years between death and birth and the years so wistfully taken from him.

"Thanks for coming with me," I told Susan as we stood in front of the gravesite.

"It meant a lot that you asked. What got me through losing my husband were friends. And talking about it."

Being at the cemetery reminded me of the one time my mother and I had visited *Vati* and *Tante*, except she never wanted to talk. My mother only made one remark, to say how visiting paid respect to the dead. I always thought it was for the family to feel better, to have a place to remember our loved ones and feel comforted at the same time, not for those buried there.

Over the years and while Laura was in school, I used to visit the cemetery without my mother knowing. Without her, I spoke to my dearly departed, wishing they could hear me. Sometimes I'd ask my father, as if he were standing there, why he had to leave so soon. I'd ask him why he couldn't be around as long as my mother, feeling guilty for even thinking it, let alone saying the words out loud. I'd also ask him why he was able to forgive me for what happened, but my mother never could.

Then I'd talk to Michael. I'd ask him to forgive me and tell him all about my life. How I met Max and left our parents' apartment as soon as I could. How we had our beautiful Laura. And how Max was taken from us as payback for not watching Michael that day. I would say the same things over and over at each visit. The only difference was the stories got longer with details about that particular year, whether it was Laura going off to college or the type of music or food popular at the time. I knew he couldn't hear me. But it was the only way to apologize and have any relationship with my brother. Most people would bring prayers and stones to the graves. I brought words and asked for forgiveness.

But this time I wasn't alone. And when I spoke, it was with Susan. She made me remember. And made me laugh and cry at the same time.

"Why do you think we bring stones instead of flowers?" she asked.

"No idea. Probably a way of remembering? Because they'll be around a lot longer."

Susan opened her purse and pulled out a small gray stone with metallic flecks and placed it on the top of my mother's memorial. "I brought a special one from Germany. We moved a lot when Peter was in the military, and we spent a lot of time in Berlin. The kids loved it, and our littlest one was so into rocks and digging. He had quite the collection, and whenever we moved, we'd put them in little bags labeled with the location. I'm all sentimental, so I kept the box and have rocks from Japan, Italy, all over the place. I thought I'd bring one from Germany since your family was from there."

I hugged her and looked down at my mother's grave and then at Michael's, thinking about the fall and the horrified expression on my mother's face when she looked up at me. For so long to get myself to sleep, I'd have to block it from my mind and think of good thoughts, like going with *Vati* to Marty's or dancing the twist with Max. With Jay's help, I'd come to terms about the terrible accident. But it was still painful to see those four short years etched in stone, as part of our tragic family history.

When we returned to DC, I wanted to call Jay but didn't want to feel needy. I'd made progress and no longer had to search for distractions or have the TV on to keep my mind from going to that dark day. But I thought about the fall again and my mother looking up at me from the sidewalk. Had the cemetery visit set me back? Or was it normal to feel this way after the trip?

I wound up leaving a message and Jay called me back first thing Monday morning. He asked more about my trip after listening to my detailed message.

"It was hard because my whole family is there—well, except Laura. I'm an orphan now." I paused, not sure how much to share before deciding to continue. "I'd made such progress with our sessions, but I thought about it again after going to visit."

"Thought about what?"

I lit my morning cigarette and took a drag. "The drapes moving, and the moment I realized the window was open in our living room." I blew the smoke out and could feel the tingle in my nose again, the one that came as a warning sign to keep my emotions in check.

"Elsa, do you want to come in today?"

"No, I'm fine," I said. "It made me realize that ever since seeing you, I haven't had all those thoughts at home. I miss Michael but think of the fun times we had together. I'm able to sleep better now."

Jay repeated what he'd mentioned so many times during our sessions, that all I needed was to talk to someone. "Your mother conditioned you to keep quiet, but it wasn't fair to you. If you had opened up much earlier," Jay added, "you wouldn't have suffered all these years."

"Well, you really helped me. And I'm just calling to say thank-you."

"You can call anytime, and hey, I won't charge you."

I laughed and doodled on my pad. "That's mighty kind of you."

"Take care of yourself, Elsa. You deserve to be happy."

Jay was right. I should have opened up a long time ago. I should have told Susan and Laura. Even Raymond. They could have helped me get through it. They could have reminded me that it could have happened to anyone.

Jay was right about something else. I deserved to be happy.

Chapter Thirty-Nine

Alexei sat next to me, reading the *Washington Post*. He put the newspaper down and folded it neatly before setting it on the coffee table. On the other side, his black leather jacket and green cashmere scarf sat draped on the back of the sofa.

It was New Year's Eve, and he'd already shared stories about the crazy celebrations in Russia, all the drinking, dancing, singing, and staying up all night until dawn. We had plans to meet Susan and Sydney in a few hours but had started celebrating at home with caviar and champagne.

"*Daragaya*, your yawn is contagious," Alexei said while covering his mouth to hold back his own. "Are you sure you want to go out? We could celebrate right here."

It was tempting to stay home and cuddle in front of the TV, but we'd already promised to join Susan, and we weren't about to break those plans at the last minute. I reached for Laura's latest letter and handed it to Alexei.

"Are you sure it's not girl talk?" He snickered while putting his glasses back on to read the letter.

December 27, 1996

Dear Mom and Alexei:

Happy Hanukkah, Merry Christmas, and Happy New Year's! Did I forget anything? Oh yeah, the next one, Valentine's Day or also known as the holiday I have always despised. I mean, really, why do they have it? To make women who don't have a boyfriend or husband feel like crap? That's why I love International Women's Day. No matter if you're married, have a boyfriend (or girlfriend) or are a mom, you can celebrate.

All is well here in St. Pete. I'm freezing my butt off, as usual, but I've become more used to it, especially when I think of the first winter I spent here. I remember that week in January where it was about ten below zero. It was something I'd never experienced before. Getting ready to go out would take about thirty minutes just to get dressed: tights, regular socks, wool socks, leggings, jeans, bra, tank top, T-shirt, turtleneck, wool sweater, scarf, coat, hat, gloves, boots. Did I forget anything? By the time I was ready, I looked like an inflatable balloon at the Macy's Thanksgiving Day Parade. But that's when I bought all my great jewelry on the street at the kiosks. Virtually no one was out shopping, so I got some awesome deals!

We're planning a New Year's party at our place this time. It will be a lot of work, but fun. I plan on taking a really long nap, so I can stay up. Last year, we were out until four and I was so pooped I slept the entire day. We're having about ten people, a couple of Americans but mostly our Russian friends. I mean, no one knows how to party for New Year's like Russians!

I love the dress you picked out for me for the wedding! It's beautiful and almost exactly like the one from the photo. And everything else you mentioned in your letter about the flowers and table arrangements is perfect. I'm also glad we're able to keep the guest list small; that way, it won't be crazy expensive. But let me know if I can pitch in for anything, or if you need help from David's parents.

Can you ask the bridal shop how far in advance they can make alterations before the wedding? I need to know so I can make my travel plans.

I can't wait to see you! I miss you so much! Alexei, thanks for keeping my mom out of trouble. You know, she's wild and crazy, if you haven't noticed. (Just kidding!)

Love,
Laura

After he finished the letter, Alexei handed it back to me. "I'm trying to imagine Laura like an inflatable balloon. Might not be her best look."

"Of course, she's exaggerating like always. I'll try to find a picture to show you next time," I said and remembered the Macy's parade, the one so dear to my heart that I watched while growing up. My father always had it raring to go, and we both settled in front of the TV to watch the balloons go by, the singers and dancers perform, and Santa Claus make his appearance at the end.

"Speaking of next time, when are you going to visit me in London?"

Alexei's question caught me off guard. It had been a few months since the last time he asked, maybe because I always shrugged it off or he wanted a change of pace from visiting me. I reached for my champagne and took a sip. "Oh, I don't know. Not sure if I can handle all that rain. Doesn't it rain all the time?"

"Sure. But it wouldn't matter if I'm with you."

"Aww, that's sweet."

Alexei took my champagne glass and put it on the table as I was about to get up. He pulled me close to him. "Where do you think you're going?"

"To get more appetizers."

"My appetizer is right here," he teased. His sexy Russian accent made him sound adorable no matter what, no matter if it sounded borderline cheesy.

"We'll be tired when we get back," he said and ran his finger along the back of my arm. "So let's have dessert now."

"You can be so, I don't know…" I paused, trying to find the right word.

"Irresistible?"

"I was thinking more like goofy."

"Goofy? Me, goofy?" He leaned over and began tickling.

"No, no. Not goofy! I didn't mean it. Stop or I'll pee in my pants." I wriggled and tried to escape.

"Really? That's sexy."

"You're crazy," I said.

"Grab the glasses, and I'll show you just how crazy."

I picked up our flutes and, as he carried me to the bedroom, we left a trail of champagne and a thousand giggles along the way.

• • •

The following morning and after a late night out with Susan, we slept in. After all, it was New Year's Day, and we earned the right to be lazy. I woke up to Alexei kissing my neck. He raised his eyebrows a few times before reaching under the covers when I asked what he wanted to do on his last day.

"You have a one-track mind," I said.

"That's not true. I think about champagne, too."

"And that adorable little Misha, right?"

"He's something else, isn't he?" Alexei turned on his back and reached below his head to raise the pillow. "Elsa, there's something I've been wanting to ask you."

"Uh oh."

"No, it's nothing to worry about."

He played with the edge of the pillowcase and looked up at the ceiling. "Remember when we were in Russia and you told me about your brother?"

I nodded, but he didn't notice. He stared up, deep in thought, trying to decide whether he should continue. "Were you upset that I didn't ask you more about him?"

"Not at all. Actually, I enjoyed just being held. My mother never wanted to talk about it, but it was because she blamed me. She didn't want to relive it."

"It must have taken a lot of courage to tell me."

It was true. It had taken courage. And it was interesting that Alexei used that word because no one had ever said that to me—that it took courage to talk about it.

"I kind of understand what you've been through—to a point," Alexei continued.

I sat up. "Your brother also passed away?"

"No, but when I was about the same age, something horrible happened. Something I couldn't talk about for the longest time."

I sat up higher. "What happened?"

Alexei sighed and opened up to me.

Chapter Forty

Alexei was eleven at the time. He and his best friend Sasha would spend hours together where they lived in a suburb twenty minutes outside of St. Petersburg. They'd get home from school, quickly do their homework and, after a snack, their grandmothers would send them out of the house to get some fresh air.

They spent hours together riding their bikes, throwing rocks in creeks, and running away from bullies. Every day on their adventures, they had to cross railroad tracks to get to their favorite playground in another neighborhood. Sasha was always more daring than Alexei, and he would come up with games along the way. One day, Sasha decided they should play dodge with the train before crossing the tracks.

Alexei didn't want to do it. He was scared, thought Sasha was crazy. But Alexei was the follower. And he basically listened to everything his friend said. They waited and waited. Alexei tried to talk Sasha out of it, but when Sasha teased Alexei by calling him a little girl, he had to go through with it. They waited for what seemed like hours and finally a train approached.

"Get your lazy butt on the track," Sasha said.

"I'm not doing it."

"Come on, it'll be fun and you can tell everyone at school."

"If I make it back."

"Of course you will! We'll jump off in plenty of time. Come on," Sasha said as he got on the track. Alexei followed, and they both waited. As the train approached and the conductor blew the horn, Sasha danced around while Alexei stood nervously.

"Sasha, come on, let's go," Alexei said and stepped off the track.

"Ha ha! I won, I won!" Sasha said.

"Get off the track now!" Alexei screamed.

"Okay, okay, I'm coming." Sasha started to panic when he tried to move. "My lace is stuck. I can't get it out!"

He bent down and wiggled his ankle, but his shoe still wouldn't come off. He tried again, but the lace was so tight, it wouldn't budge. The train kept blasting its horn, and while Alexei stood on the side deciding what to do, he looked around for someone, anyone, or anything to help. Too scared to go on the tracks, Alexei kept screaming for Sasha to take off his shoe. The last thing he remembered was Sasha crying for help. Alexei turned away right before the train hit, leaving his bike and running all the way home, too shocked to cry, too scared to scream out for help.

• • •

We sat in bed, in silence, when Alexei finished his story. The heat turned on and off with a click, and in between, we could hear the running water from my neighbor's apartment. All those months and years of having the TV on for companionship hid these sounds. And now the silence from the shock and sadness made me notice its annoyance.

"Oh my gosh," I finally said, feeling so stupid for not simply saying *I'm sorry.*

Alexei sighed. "I've relived that moment so many times in my head. I should have tried to help him."

"Come on, what could you have done?"

He shrugged. "I should have done something."

Alexei tried to make sense of it, but what could he have done? Get on the tracks with an oncoming train? He was young and scared. What a horrible memory—to see his best friend die right in front of him. "It's tragic, but it's not your fault," I said and kissed his shoulder. "Please don't blame yourself," I added, realizing how much I needed someone to say those words to me when I was ten.

"The worst part," he added, "was that Sasha's parents blamed me. Hearing your story made me think about it again. No one can really relate unless they've been through it. I just wanted to find the right time."

"Definitely not something you talk about at parties."

We both giggled, mostly out of nervousness, and then giggled again thinking about the absurdness of actually mentioning it at a party.

"I can still picture Sasha's mother and how her face was all swollen and red from crying," Alexei said and turned around to wrap his arm around me.

I wanted to tell him how, for so many years while trying to fall asleep, I could see my mother's face when she looked up at me from the street. And how I couldn't, for all that time, understand and accept the pain my mother went through. Was it because she never forgave me? And so she chose to forget because it was too painful to forgive?

"Let's make a deal," Alexei said.

"What's that?"

"We won't live in the past, but if we ever want to talk about it, we shouldn't feel ashamed."

"Deal," I said and added, "Honestly, I only want to remember the good times with Michael now, not the actual accident."

"Why don't you share them with me?"

We held each other, and I poured my heart out. When Alexei's Misha was trying to say my name at the Russian café, it reminded me so much of my brother. Michael was only three but had a good vocabulary. He understood German and spoke it with my parents, but we always used English together. Our parents always got irritated and asked me to switch to German, but it would only last a few sentences. Michael, since he loved me so much, wanted to speak whatever his big sister spoke. But he couldn't pronounce all the words. He went through these stages where he said them differently or mixed up the letters.

He'd say *yewow* instead of yellow.

And *wove you* instead of *love you*.

And *mazagine* instead of *magazine*.

It was the cutest thing.

"Misha did the same with magazine," Alexei said. "In Russian, *magazine* means store. He always flipped the z and the g. Pretty neat that they both did that with the same word."

"Now tell me about Sasha."

He was a hooligan, Alexei told me, a class clown, and even though the schools were strict and most of the time kids behaved, Sasha would do something every month that would get him sent to the office. Once he brought a frog into the classroom and let it loose. The girls went crazy, and the boys laughed hysterically. But he wouldn't confess to it. So the teacher said that if someone didn't speak up right away, the whole class would get detention and notes sent home to their parents. After that, Sasha caved; the poor kid got in so much trouble at home. Alexei stopped and smiled while remembering how the girls ran around the classroom hopping on chairs and desks to get out of the frog's way.

After sharing some more stories about Michael and Sasha, we fell asleep and woke up just in time for Alexei to pack and have a late lunch before leaving for the airport. As we waited outside for his taxi to arrive, he smiled and touched my cheek. "You're so beautiful. Your eyes are like the sun's reflection on Lake Baikal."

"Now you're making me blush. Pushkin might have some competition after all."

"It's true. Not the Pushkin part, the beautiful eyes part," he said and hesitated a second before continuing, "Elsa, I don't want you to visit me in London."

His comment took me by surprise. "Oh, okay, I thought—"

"Let me finish," he whispered. "It came out wrong. You've forgotten that English is my second language." He started counting with his fingers. "Actually, it's my fifth, and now I'm getting distracted." He paused and looked away for a moment when the taxi pulled up. "What I meant was that I don't want you to just visit. I want you to move there permanently, with me."

It had been almost a year and a half since we began seeing each other, and I never expected this. We loved each other's company, but every once in a while, I still had those thoughts, those terrifying thoughts that he wouldn't want anything more and was perfectly fine with a long-distance relationship. I even wondered how long it would last before he'd want to find someone new. But that day, while waiting with him at my circular driveway, the same place he left every time, I found out how much more he really wanted.

"I'll think about it," I said.

He kissed me good-bye. "*Daragaya*, do more than think about it."

One of my neighbors walked up the sidewalk as Alexei got into the taxi.

"You guys make a cute couple," she said and smiled.

I smiled back and thought about moving to London. Alexei's invitation caught me off guard, so much so that I hadn't noticed the UPS guy and his boxes trying to make their way around me.

Chapter Forty-One

Before Alexei rode off, he put his head out the window and asked me to really think about London, saying that he wasn't joking or in a tough moment after sharing his story about Sasha. I told him he was crazy. He agreed, only adding that he was crazy about me.

I'd never been asked to move anywhere for anyone. I was set in my ways and living alone, for the first time in many years. I loved living in Washington but sometimes dreamed about living with Alexei or at least in the same city.

But London wasn't on my list of places to live. Not sure why. Maybe it was the climate or being outside of the country, or it was the driving. I wouldn't learn in a million years how to drive on the other side. And after what happened to Max, what if I forgot to look the other way while crossing the street? Anxiety, nervousness, fear—all hiding behind each other—became one excuse after another.

But different could be good; different could be positive. Something new and exciting instead of something tried-and-true, like before. But how could I give up my life in DC and move to another country at fifty-four? I couldn't do it.

One visit from Alexei led to another and, before we knew it, Laura flew home. It was the beginning of March, and she came back a week before the wedding to spend time together and tie up loose ends for the ceremony.

Laura appeared from around the corner, rolling her suitcase behind her. She looked the same, pale and thin as usual with her hair high in a ponytail that swung from side to side. We hugged until she broke loose and gasped. After seeing Matt and Greg walk up, she ran and gave them a big hug.

"I can feel your ribs," Matt said as he held on to her.

"You're just jealous from all the stairs I have to climb." She let go and added, "But don't worry, I'll gain it all back—and then some—after a few days."

"You definitely lost a few pounds," Greg said. "I think it's from all that sex."

"If you're talking sex, you should ask my mom."

"Laura!"

"Oh yeah," Matt said. "The Russian from London with love."

"I knew that joke was coming sooner or later."

"I can't believe you've lived in Russia for almost four years. Are you crazy or what?" Greg said and reached for Laura's bag, throwing the strap over his shoulder. "So when do we get to meet David?"

"The day before the wedding. He went to Chicago first to visit family."

Matt smiled and elbowed Greg. "Oh good, then we have time to throw you a bachelorette party!"

"Without strippers," Laura demanded.

"Come on, you're taking the fun out of it. For me," Matt said.

• • •

Greg gave us a ride to my apartment and when we reached the circular driveway, it made me think of the ride back from the airport when Laura left. Honestly, back then, I thought she'd be calling, pleading, begging to come home after hearing too many stories about the bleakness and difficulty of life. Instead, she took advantage of everything the country offered and now called it home with no immediate plans to return to DC. Even after the wedding, they wouldn't be staying long, with a quick stop in Aruba for their honeymoon, and back to Russia.

Laura put her luggage in the extra bedroom that used to be my mother's and came into the living room. "I love this view," she said and walked over to the window.

"It's the best part, isn't it?"

"So, tell me more about you and Alexei. He's visiting you a lot."

"I'm crazy about him. He's quite the romantic. But he's also fun and makes me laugh."

"Maybe you should ask him how he feels?"

I paused as a smile came across my face. "Don't have to. He asked me to move to London…it literally just happened."

"Oh my God, seriously?" she said and jumped in place. "Mom, that's wonderful."

"But my life is here."

"Remember what you told me? That I could come back anytime? Same goes for you."

I stood up and joined her at the window. "I don't know. Not sure if I can give this up."

"Give what up? Your apartment?"

"My independence."

"What's so great about independence? Having someone to share your life with is so much better. Independence is what people say when they're too scared to get close to someone."

Laura had a way, with her unusual look on life, to enlighten me. We both stared out the window and onto Wisconsin Avenue. The street bustled, not quite like New York, but it lived and breathed. It created memories, for all those who looked out their windows, like us, and those who walked up and down Wisconsin Avenue many times, like me.

"You could keep your apartment for a few months, just to make sure you made the right choice."

"Ah, choices. You never know when you're making the right ones."

"I totally agree," Laura said and leaned in for a long hug.

What about your choices, I thought, but didn't dare ask. The last thing I wanted was for us to get into it, especially right before the wedding. Laura let go and walked over to the other side of the room where her plant still flourished, the one she left with me.

"I know you're worried I'll be moving around with David and giving up my own stuff," she said, practically reading my mind. "But I'm thinking about my opportunities, too. And I love Russia. I get homesick when I'm away."

"I'm glad David is moving up in his career and will be able to provide," I said, thinking about my lost chances to become an architect and wanting to make sure Laura didn't miss out on her dreams. "Remember, I'm a mom. I'm going to worry a little."

"A little?" she teased.

• • •

After we had lunch and Laura freshened up, we headed over to Kate's Bridal for the fitting. I almost didn't want to see her in the dress that day; it seemed better to take in all her beauty at the wedding, the glow from her happiness that always outlined her smile.

Over the past few months whenever there was a show about weddings, I'd stop and watch. It was always the same scene, where a mom waited for her daughter to appear in the dress during the fitting. I'm not sure why I traded in *Seinfeld* for those shows. It would have been much better to have a few good laughs instead of a half-empty box of tissues by my side. But somehow I convinced myself it would prepare me for seeing her in the dress and, when the time came, those tissues would be history. Kaput. But I was wrong.

"I'm glad you ordered a size up," Laura said as she opened the curtain and walked out to the sitting area. "Mom, are you okay?"

I could hardly get the words out. "You look so beautiful."

She faced the mirror, turning several times to catch her reflection at different angles. My daughter, all grown up and living so far away, stood in front of me after being gone for so many years—three and a half, to be exact.

A small part of me wished she was still a teenager. To ask for my advice and then dismiss it. To negotiate a late curfew while raiding the fridge. To borrow a few bucks for a movie, promising and failing to bring back the change. I wanted to freeze that time, just for a moment, as she stood in front of me, all twenty-eight years of her, looking stunning in her sleeveless satin wedding dress that brushed the floor when she turned.

Laura placed one hand on her stomach and twisted her hair up with the other to see how she'd look with a bun. "I love it," she said and, while turning around again to look in the mirror at different angles, added, "Mom, you did good—the dress, all the planning, everything is perfect."

She stepped down from the platform and came closer. "I wish Dad could have been here to see me get married."

"I wish the whole family was here. And Michael," I said so freely, without a crackle in my voice, not realizing how less painful it was to say his name out loud since opening up. My mother was no longer around to be hurt by the words or memories.

"I know," Laura said and walked over to hug me. "I'm sorry I got so upset when you told me about it. I just couldn't believe you lied. I didn't understand at the time how painful it was."

"Well, I acted like an ass, too."

"Let's forget that it even happened."

"Don't think we should," I said. "I need a reminder not to keep secrets. It hurts everyone around me. And I can't torture myself and think people can't help me."

As we walked out of the store, I stopped and turned to Laura, telling her that she needed to learn from my mistakes. I didn't believe in people. Or trust them. I didn't think anyone cared enough. My mother didn't want to talk about it, but I could have still opened up. I would have been a much healthier person. "Sweetie, make sure you let people in, even if it's just a shoulder to cry on. They'll help you get through things in life. Trust me, I know."

"That's great advice," she said, and we walked down the side street. "Hey, I wanted to ask you something," she continued. "Why don't you ever talk about Dad anymore?"

"That came out of nowhere."

"Now that I'm getting married, I'm thinking more about him. And I don't really know much."

"Sweetie, what would you like to know? We met when I was nineteen, and he died when you were only two."

"I miss not having a dad," she said. Her voice trembled, like mine that day on Red Square when I told her Michael was everything to me.

"I know. I miss him, too. He was the best husband and father anyone could ask for."

"Was he anything like me?"

I smiled and found myself holding back tears, sharing the similarities. She was so much like her father. Laura had his eyes. And his independence and adventurous side. Max was protective but would have thought going to Russia was a great life experience. Not like me, who, at the time, thought the idea was crazy.

"Maybe we could put some pictures of him on a table at the wedding."

"What a wonderful way to honor him," I said, knowing that as time went by I thought less about Max. Somehow life took over. Then Raymond kept my attention. The passage of time made me forget some of the memories, at least the bad stuff. Then it dawned on me that I could easily block out Max's accident but couldn't do it with Michael's. I kept holding onto the tragedy, partially from self-pity, partially because every time I saw my mother, I thought of him.

As we leaned against the Metro's escalator, people rushed around us to get to their train. Laura held a light-pink shopping bag with white tissue poking out above her white pumps.

"So, you and David are moving back to DC after the wedding, right?" I teased as we moved closer to the edge to let people pass.

"Good try, Mom."

"There's an apartment available a few doors down on my floor."

She nudged me with her elbow and grinned. "Yours might be available, too, if you move to London."

"Listen, don't say anything to Alexei about it, okay? I don't want him pressuring me."

"Not a peep, I promise. But maybe I should keep my wedding dress for you."

I laughed, imagining the effort it would take trying to get into Laura's dress, which was at least two sizes too small. "Please. Even if I could get it over my hips, I'd bust the seams within five minutes."

"Yeah, with those boobs."

"No, my ass. Or, as they say in London, my *arse*."

Chapter Forty-Two

I checked Laura's makeup twice and reapplied her lipstick with a soft pink that matched the stain on her cheeks. Her faced glowed, like the times she'd run around the park or skip next to me on a cold day when she was younger.

She slipped on her satin gloves and pulled them up to her elbows before leaning on the table where she sat with David and the rabbi who recited a blessing. As the groom and rabbi left the holding room to meet up with David's uncle, the two of us stood up. Her look of content, of complete happiness overwhelmed me. *How did I raise such a beautiful, level-headed woman?* One who, in many ways, showed more maturity beyond her years and beyond mine.

We were interrupted by a quick knock before Matt entered the holding room. Laura chose Matt to walk her down the aisle. With no father or siblings, she felt closest to him, and I would be on her other arm, as it was a Jewish tradition to have both parents walk the bride down the aisle.

Matt closed the door behind him. "Okay, ladies. The guests are seated. It's time to get hitched."

After she pulled down her veil, Laura grabbed the chair and pretended she couldn't see. "Help. Somebody turned off the lights."

"Was she this much of a goofball as a kid?" Matt asked as he grabbed her arm and they walked toward the door.

"Only when she had too much sugar," I smiled and remembered fondly.

"Don't make me laugh. One false move, and I'll have a slit up to my eyebrows."

"Oh good," Matt said and rubbed his hands together. "I'd better get my camera ready for the funniest wedding video."

As we left the room and walked down the hall for the ceremony, a familiar voice called out my name from behind. It was Raymond, dressed in a gray suit with a light-blue tie. He had exchanged his round tortoise-shelled glasses for blue rectangular ones.

"I'm so glad you could make it." I walked over and hugged him. "But you're not supposed to see the bride yet."

"What bride? I didn't see one. Is there a wedding here today?" He leaned closer and whispered, "I'm more excited to see you."

I stepped back. "How's your lovely wife?"

He paused for a moment. "I've been banished. We're no longer together."

"Mom, sorry to interrupt. Do you want to meet us by the door?"

"No, I'm coming." I turned back to Raymond. "I'm really sorry to hear that. We'll catch up in a bit?"

The three of us continued down the hall and, a few moments later, we entered the room to walk down the aisle, with Laura in between Matt and me. To each side, a river of faces smiled and women dotted their eyes with tissues. Alexei winked as we passed and took our places under the chuppah. I hardly remembered the vows, or the rabbi's words of wisdom. Only the cantor seemed to break through to me with the same spell he cast weeks earlier while singing "Sunrise, Sunset" that brought me to tears.

Moments later, David stomped on the glass and everyone yelled *mazel tov*, and that's all it took to put everything into perspective. My little Laura, who was all grown up and a Kartchner at heart, had become Laura Klein on a Sunday afternoon in March.

We made our way to the reception and while they served lunch, I visited every table to thank our guests for coming, saving Raymond's table for last. I was tempted to call him when visiting the cemetery back in the fall but changed my mind. We still had our couple of calls a year to wish each other a happy birthday. Finally, that was enough for me, for my life, enough to recall some of the memories that were lost with time.

It had been many years since we'd been involved. But as with any relationship, I'd never forget the first time, the time in his office when he lowered me on the couch and threw his toupee in the plant. It made me giggle, remembering the sweat dripping from his brow and onto his glasses that day when he showed me how to use chopsticks.

"What's so funny?" Raymond stood up and asked as I approached his table.

"Oh, nothing. Just a happy day, that's all."

"Can you believe your little girl just got married?"

"It's unbelievable how time flies." I paused before continuing. "I'm so sorry about you and your wife. Why didn't you call?"

"You were planning the wedding, and I didn't want to bring up bad news."

"You should've called. How are your kids?"

He got up from his chair and put the napkin on it. "They're all great. Sammy's still single. He's always traveling the world, dating a different girl every week, so it seems."

"Let him have some fun."

"But he's thirty-five, and my only boy. I want grandkids to keep the name going."

"You men. Always thinking about yourselves," I teased.

"So, when are you coming to the city again?" he asked flirtatiously.

I held back my irritation. He never asked me to visit like that when his wife was around. But I didn't want to leave a scar on this beautiful day, to poison it with bad thoughts, to get irritated by his untimely and unwanted forwardness.

"Sorry, Raymond. Now's not a good time; it's crazy at work." The waiter buzzed by us and filled up water glasses. I moved out of the way and scanned the room, watching people enjoy their lunches. "I should be getting back."

We hugged a little longer than usual, and I walked to my table, smiling at guests along the way. All this time, all these years, Raymond only thought about himself. I was too much in love with him before to notice. Alexei kissed me and caressed my back when I sat down.

"Who's that devilishly handsome man?" he whispered.

"An old friend. By the way, we don't say devilishly handsome anymore. It's kind of old-fashioned."

"Well, you said it was an old friend, right? Maybe it fits him."

• • •

"Get me down from here!" I screamed as Alexei, Matt, and Greg lifted me up high. Laura, who sat in another chair, held onto a linen napkin while I grabbed the other end. Every few seconds, the guys would prop the chairs higher and straighten them, so we wouldn't fall off.

"I'm dying! Let me down!" Laura said as the Klezmer band played.

Finally they lowered the chair, and I playfully slapped Alexei with the napkin. "I almost lost my lunch up there."

"Jewish weddings are the best," Alexei said.

"You're next," I teased but before we could get him situated, Laura grabbed my arm and led me to a circle in the middle of the floor. It was time to dance the *hora* and my childhood friend Fiona was a sight to be reckoned with. She earned the nickname "Foxtrot Fiona" growing up, and it looked like she was still holding on to the title. She hopped in place, moved her legs to the front and back and, in between, ran up to the center with the energy of an eight-year-old boy.

"Look at Fiona go," Laura mentioned.

"Isn't it great? She's been like that since we met when we were thirteen." I stopped in my tracks and guests fell into me. "I should hook her up with Raymond. They'd have a blast."

Laura pulled me aside. "Mom, seriously? Can you focus on your own life now? Let Fiona find her own happiness. She's probably not even looking," Laura said and took me by the arm. "Come on, let's get back in there."

As we spun around, Alexei watched from the sidelines, laughing and clapping along. I went around the circle again and looked for him but he had disappeared. He wasn't near our table either, or by the bar or the band. Finally, I spotted him. He was on the other side of the floor, dancing the *hora* with just the men, their arms intertwined, their laughter contagious. Every once in a while, we caught each other's eye, and he winked and smiled each time. And it was there, at that moment at Laura's wedding, that I realized I'd fallen in love with him.

Chapter Forty-Three

The following evening, we all sat at the airport and awaited two flights: Alexei on his way to London, and Laura and David headed to Aruba for their honeymoon. At Dulles Airport, yet again. It seemed like my second home these past few years, saying good-bye to loved ones as they went on their way and on with their lives. Sure, I was part of their lives, but in a way that left too much space in between and a yearning to be closer. I fumbled in my purse to find a mint and tried to convince the kids to stay longer.

"Maybe you can come for a visit in the summer? We can take you to see the fountains at Peterhof," David said.

"I don't know. I'd love to lie on the beach, somewhere warm with my toes in the sand. That's always been my plan."

"Can I come?" Alexei asked while putting his arm around me.

"Of course, *daragaya*," I said.

"Ah, your first Russian word. Wonderful! But it would be *daragoy* for me. Don't worry, I'll teach you."

"Just what we need, a fifty-four-year-old speaking Russian with a New York accent."

"I'm sure you'll sound as cute as you look," Alexei said.

"Geez, you guys. It's like puppy love," David teased.

"Puppy love? What's that?" Alexei asked.

"When you fall in love when you're young."

He smiled. "Well, I do feel like a teenager again. Your mother makes me feel young."

"That's because you are," I said.

"What do you mean? I'm fifty-one."

"And almost four years younger than me."

"But you look better," he added and softly brushed my bangs away from my eyes.

"You guys need to get a room already," Laura joked.

Alexei smiled and looked at his watch before gathering his belongings. He said good-bye to Laura and David and asked me to walk with him for a moment. We went toward his gate, and he dropped his bag to the floor to wrap his arms around my waist.

"How will I last the month without seeing your beautiful face?"

"You'll be fine," I said. "Just stay busy, like I do."

"You always give good advice."

"Too bad I waited so long to take any."

Alexei let go, but I could still feel the warmth of his touch. He put on his jacket and picked up his bag. "*Maya lybeemaya*, I'll see you soon."

"My love, right?"

He smiled and winked before giving me a thumbs-up for getting the translation right. It had been close to two years since dating, and my heart still felt heavy, in a good way, whenever he was near. Before he left, I told him I'd think about London and make my decision soon. He turned around and waved before disappearing at the gate. I'd been saying a lot of good-byes over the years and still wasn't used to them. I walked back to join the kids, with just a few minutes to spare before they also had to leave.

"Okay, Mr. and Mrs. Klein. Get the heck out of here before I start crying."

Laura hugged me and whispered, "Take a chance on London. What's there to lose?"

"It rains all the time," I reasoned.

"What's the weather have to do with it?" she said before David picked up their bags, and they walked to the boarding area.

My daughter was all grown up, married, and starting the next chapter of her life. And finally, I was more than okay with it. After watching them walk into the passageway, I turned to look out the window. Drizzle fell, doing its best to remove dirt from the plane's wings.

Seeing Laura leave reminded me of the time my father watched me get on the bus with Max after we got married. *Vati's* bloodshot eyes, and his red nose from holding back the tears, were etched forever as a bittersweet memory. Was *Vati* sad to see me go? Or was he trying hard to accept that he'd been replaced? God, how I missed all the men who were no longer with me.

Chapter Forty-Four

For a few weeks in March, I took extra walks in my neighborhood. Even though my Tenleytown surroundings didn't have the same pulse as New York, it had grown on me. I spent many years in DC, met new neighbors, and saw shops and restaurants come and go. I walked a thousand times up Wisconsin Avenue and back down again and again.

And during those years, I was tempted many times by the chicken with snow peas at the Chinese restaurant and spent week after week at my favorite coffee shop reading the *Washington Post*, chatting with the baristas and tourists. Sometimes those chats turned into debates about politics or the humid Washington summers, but we always connected.

It never failed that I ended up with a great window seat and, when not chatting or reading, would watch people walk up from the Metro. You could tell which ones were the tourists. They would emerge from the escalator, look around, check their maps, and come into the coffee shop for directions. The baristas were great at getting the tourists straight and often times would send them back on the Metro for getting off at the wrong stop.

On March 28 and right before Alexei's next visit, I lit a memorial candle for my Aunt Regina as I'd done every year since her death. She was a fighter to the end, even when she lay in the hospital hooked up to all kinds of machines. I couldn't bear the thought of seeing her like that. Our talks comforted me, and I'd never forget some of her last words, something she always said: *That Max, he's a keeper.* The day she died, I'd gone to the hospital to visit her. But my mother and father were already there with the rabbi saying a prayer by her bedside. The sheet was pulled up, covering *Tante's* face. I ran out of the room and threw myself onto a chair.

"Sweetheart, I'm so sorry," my father said as he sat down beside me.

"I just saw her two days ago. We were having a little laugh about Max," I cried.

"Elsa, she was ready to go. She was in a lot of pain."

"I'm going to miss her so much. Why did this have to happen?"

"I know," he mumbled. "We're all going to miss her."

Vati followed me back into the room after the hospital staff removed *Tante's* body. My mother started gathering her belongings. She handed me a picture of Aunt Regina and me at Coney Island. Before taking it, I grabbed a tissue from a box on the windowsill.

"We had a blast that day. She was trying to ride a bike but couldn't figure it out, so they gave her one of those huge tricycles. She got a lot of attention on that big thing."

My mother didn't answer. She kept tidying the room.

"Do you remember that?" I grabbed another tissue to blow my nose. "We were going to get Michael a tricycle once, remember?"

She still wouldn't answer. The weight of the burden, the guilt, the sorrow from losing *Tante* made it difficult to breathe.

"You're never going to forgive me, are you?"

"Forgive you for what?" she finally responded.

"You know exactly what I mean. Forgive me for what happened to Michael."

She still wouldn't answer. At that point, my father, who had been leaning by the door, approached me.

"Elsa, please, not now," he said in a soft voice.

"*Vati*, you're always worried about her feelings. What about mine? I've lived through this, too!"

"We know." My father came closer and whispered, "Now's not the time."

"*Genug*," she uttered.

"Fine, Mother. Don't talk about it. But don't ever say I didn't try. Just remember I loved Michael more than anything. Why did you have to leave him with me?"

She continued to get my aunt's things together, folding her sweaters and tucking them and a pair of slippers in a small suitcase.

"You know, I'm glad I had *Tante*. She was more of a mother to me."

"Elsa, please," my father demanded. The bags under his eyes held so much burden.

I stood there and waited for my mother to talk to me, but she wouldn't say a word. She continued to pack in silence. I tried to remember what Aunt Regina said. *Be kind to your mother. Put yourself in her shoes.*

That day, the day she died, I tried hard to listen to those words, to put myself in my mother's shoes but kept thinking, *How could she detest her own daughter so much?* At the time, only anger and guilt overwhelmed me. And at the time, I couldn't see my mother's sadness, the kind Aunt Regina talked so often about, the kind Aunt Regina hoped I'd understand one day.

Chapter Forty-Five

My two suitcases stood by the front door, like the time Laura stacked hers. Four years ago when she left, everything seemed large and overdone. The chocolate croissants. The tampons stuffed into the boots. The Cup-a-Soups lining the luggage wall. The distaste for my mother. The lies and deceit. All of it was overdone—except for the indifference. The indifference never became part of me. It would have been so much easier not to care or not have a care in the world. But indifference wasn't a part of my world.

I walked over to the windows, the ones that overlooked Wisconsin Avenue. I loved my view and my corner apartment on the ninth floor, with wall-to-wall windows that took up two full walls shaped liked an inverted L.

A lot happened in this space and in DC. I continued my life as a single mother. I took my mother in then had her taken away. I discovered therapy could help, when open to it. I even tried to discover love, but it discovered me first. In the end, though, it was only a space, an apartment. And nothing in it defined me.

Alexei was on his way for a visit, and this time I wouldn't wave good-bye and watch him ride off in a taxi from my circular driveway. I'd go with him to the airport. And not just to the airport, but to London. And not just to visit, but to live there.

I would have never thought in a million years I'd want to live in London. I loved the United States. I loved DC and already missed my coworkers. I even missed my walks on New York's Madison Avenue. But that was long ago. It was a different time now. It was my time, my new adventure, with my belongings packed, and my heart open to the idea.

In a few hours, Alexei would be landing, so I stopped by my corner café for the last time to enjoy my favorite coffee and a croissant. This time, I wouldn't need to eat two of them to help me face the emptiness from Laura's departure. I sat at my usual spot, watched people come and go, smiled at familiar faces, and said my final good-byes to the regulars and baristas.

While finishing up my last-minute packing back home, I put my makeup, a change of clothing, and a few magazines in my carry-on bag. They sat on top of Laura's letters and some family photos in case something happened to my checked luggage or the rest coming later.

My boxes stood, all lined up and in order, ready for their next destination. I sat on one of them and realized that just within the last year or so, I'd been able to overcome the fear of living my life, finally putting myself first and enjoying where life had taken me.

I pulled out my address book and thumbed through it. When reaching the *Rs*, I contemplated whether to call Raymond. *Would he be happy for me? Or would he put me in a sad mood before leaving? But how could I move without telling him?*

As I dialed his number, Susan knocked on the door. She'd volunteered to coordinate with the movers and had come over to pick up a spare key. While waiting for Raymond, I motioned for her to sit down.

"Hello, stranger," I said when he answered.

"Did you survive the wedding?"

"It was wonderful. Hope you had a good time."

"Indeed I did. So, who was the handsome man sitting next to you?" he said, cutting to the chase.

"Oh, that's Alexei."

Susan grinned and raised her eyebrows a few times when she heard Alexei's name. Then she mouthed, "Is that Raymond?" I nodded and continued to listen.

"Alexei," Raymond repeated. "Sounds Russian. How do you know him?" He continued before letting me respond. "Let me guess. He's a spy and you uncovered his covert operations."

I laughed and brought Susan a can of soda from the kitchen.

"I bet he put a chip in your arm so he knows where you are at all times."

"Good one. We met on a plane, and we've been seeing each other for almost two years now."

"You and a Russkie. I'm happy for you."

"Are you really?"

"Why wouldn't I be?" he asked, his voice rising in pitch.

"Because you kept trying to get me to come up to visit you."

"Just wishful thinking on my part. But really, I couldn't be happier for you."

"Thanks." I paused, eyeing the boxes and luggage by the front hall. "He asked me to move to London. I'm leaving today."

"Wow, Elsa! I have to hand it to you. You've become quite adventurous. Are you sure you don't want to come to New York for one last visit?" he teased.

"I'll have to pass, but I'll miss you."

"Me and my toupees."

"You said it, not me," I teased back as a final nod to the time we had together, a great relationship with complications. But candor was never an issue, at least from him. He was always honest about his intentions from the beginning.

After we hung up, Susan opened her bag and pulled out a bottle of champagne. We toasted to our friendship and to my new adventure. She promised to visit me in London, and I couldn't wait to show her around after getting settled.

253

Before long, we finished off the bottle and started laughing about the time I saved her goldfish Spitzy, the one she named after Mark Spitz. Her building wouldn't allow pets, but Susan was determined to have something she could take care of after her husband died, so she got Spitzy. One day, she called me, all frantic, saying Spitzy had jumped out of his bowl and onto the carpet. I ran across the street to her apartment and saved the day and poor little Spitzy, who wound up dying a week later.

"I wonder if Spitzy died from all that stress," Susan said while cracking up and downing her champagne.

"Spitzy stressed? What about me, trying to grab his flapping body to fling back into the bowl?" I said, standing on my tiptoes, holding my thumb and index finger together, leaning over a make-believe fish tank.

"Spitzy was dear to my heart. And all the Spitzies I bought after him."

It was silent for a second then we started laughing. And we couldn't stop, both of us rolling over on our sides, sitting on the boxes, holding our stomachs it hurt so badly. I looked back over and Susan was crying.

"It's okay." I got up to hug her. "Do you miss Spitzy? You can get another. Or five."

She laughed and, after wiping tears that ran down the side of her nose, she grabbed a tissue from her purse. "I just realized something," she added. "Have you noticed you've been the one saying good-bye all these years? Now you're the one leaving. I'm gonna miss you."

"Gonna miss you too," I whispered, thinking about her remark and holding back the tears. I had been the one saying good-bye all these years. To everyone I loved. And for way too long.

• • •

Alexei came up from behind. He put his arms around me like the time we stopped on the embankment overlooking the Neva River by the Hermitage. He asked me if I wanted more time before we left my apartment. I didn't need any. I was ready to go.

Alexei moved the few boxes against the wall and took one last look out my window. He walked closer and, when something caught his eye, leaned down to pick it up. "I might need this soon, the way I'm aging," he joked and handed me what turned out to be my mother's hearing aid.

It was the one we paid a pretty penny for, the one she was too vain to wear. Who knew how it got all the way in the corner of the living room? I thought of the many times my mother couldn't hear because she'd forgotten, or rather refused, to wear it. At the time, I rolled my eyes. Now it was a bittersweet memory.

"*Daragaya*, you're leaving all sorts of treasures," Alexei said when he bent down to pick something else up. "I think this would match my outfit perfectly," he teased, walking toward me holding up an earring.

My pearl earring. The one I'd lost so many years ago. I tried in vain to find it, looking in every nook and cranny, putting signs up in the lobby, even asking at the office. It seemed gone forever. But I refused to get rid of the other one, which stayed securely in my jewelry box along with a few others missing their pairs. *Tante* had given me the pearls for my sixteenth birthday, and I'd never throw out something from such a beautiful soul. Who knew? Maybe it would show up one day. Maybe in the back of a drawer or at the bottom of my purse. But on my living room floor? It turned out to be my lucky day.

"Babe, you have no idea what this means." After pulling my jewelry case out of the luggage, I found the other earring and put both on.

255

"Pretty sure I do," he said and double-checked the posts, making sure the earrings were secure. "*Lubeemaya*, are you ready?"

I thought I was. Or at least that's what I told Alexei. Leaving everything behind—it seemed so easy, so practical to get on the plane and say good-bye to it all. The past. The lies. The broken hearts. The guilt. I'd already worked through it with Jay, but there was something about moving out of the country that marked a permanent departure to these bitter thoughts.

There was one memory I'd always dismissed, that of my mother's sorrow. Seeing her swollen face and bloodshot eyes wasn't enough for me. Hearing the deafening silence whenever I mentioned Michael's name in front of her wasn't enough either. For all those years, why couldn't I accept her anguish? Not just from losing Michael, but from having her miscarriage on the ship over from Germany?

When it came to my brother, I wanted my mother, just once, to say it was an accident. That it wasn't my fault. That it was her fault. Or that it was our fault, together. To really move on and away, I had to let go of these memories and accept my mother for the way life turned out for her—as a grief-stricken woman, as one of the lost souls of her generation.

"Please don't be mad," I said to Alexei and pulled away from his embrace.

"Are you having second thoughts?"

"No, never. I can't wait to start our new life together. It's just that I need to take care of something before we leave."

"Okay," he said with some hesitation. "What is it?"

I sighed and took his hands into mine. "How hard would it be to rearrange our flight?"

Chapter Forty-Six

Alexei and I made two stops, the first one to Max's grave, where I placed a few stones and caught my first love up on his daughter's recent adventures. Talking out loud to my dearly departed always consoled me, always helped me make sense of the senseless and sudden passing when he was around Laura's age now. Not once did Alexei make me feel uncomfortable talking out loud. We were a pair, like Max and me when we were young, like the earrings from *Tante*.

After visiting Max, we made our final stop to my parents' gravesite. The stones that Susan left on our last visit remained untouched and provided a foundation to the ones we'd put beside them. In the past whenever we visited, I always looked from left to right, the way the tombstones were situated by my family's departure. This time, I started from the right side and stopped in front of my mother's to read the inscription.

Beloved wife, friend, and mother.

I had to do it. I had to put those words on her stone. She was a companion to my father, a friend to my Aunt Regina, and beloved mother to Michael—and to me before the accident. My mother, so hurt from the miscarriage and the loss of her son, was a lost soul, just like *Tante* had described and begged for me to understand.

She never forgave me for what happened, even if she never said it outright or used those words. All those years ago, *Tante* told me to try to understand what my mother had been through—how sadness, not anger, had taken the life out of her.

Like the last breath a person takes underwater, my mother had no strength left. Sadness had swallowed her up, and I couldn't accept it until four decades later.

Alexei bent down and cleaned the area in front of my mother's grave, pulling grass that had grown around the edges too close for the mower to reach. Then he did the same for the other three graves and wiped the dirt that had accumulated on top.

"I wonder how your friend Sasha's mother is doing."

"I don't know if she's even alive. What made you think of her?"

I shrugged and started weeping.

"Come here," Alexei said and pulled me close. "It's okay to forget."

"I know." My voice cracked as I continued. "The hardest part is forgiving."

My purse fell off my shoulder and onto the grass. Alexei slid it out of the way with his foot. "There's no right or wrong, only what's right for you. You don't have to forgive her."

"But that's why I wanted to come here. I want to forgive her and tell her I finally know why she treated me the way she did. It gives me closure."

I picked up my bag and pulled out an old picture, the last one with all of us. Aunt Regina must have taken the photo because she was the only one missing. In the black-and-white picture, my mother and father sat on each side with me in the middle and Michael on my lap. Michael had the biggest smile, showing a small gap in the bottom where he'd already lost one of his baby teeth. Aunt Regina probably did a little dance or jiggle to get him to smile, so he could get back to playing. He could never sit still, and how I wished I'd remembered that so long ago on that tragic day.

I walked the few steps to my mother's grave and put my hand on top. It was warm to the touch, and as the sun beat down I decided which stones would be best used as a paperweight. The photo would eventually be washed or carried away, but for the time being—and for however long it remained there—it would keep the memory of us alive, even to strangers who passed by on their way to visit their loved ones.

I picked out the stones and placed the photo underneath them. "I miss you all so much."

I continued in a whisper. "Mother, I'm sorry for what happened to Michael. And I'm sorry for what happened to us. I wish you could have found peace."

After a few minutes, Alexei came over and rubbed my back. He held my bag in one arm and wrapped his other around me as we walked to the car and headed to the airport.

London, my new home, our new home, was waiting for us.

Chapter Forty-Seven

The Arrival
London: 1997

It didn't take me long to feel at home. Little by little, Alexei showed me his Maida Vale neighborhood. He showed me the shortcut to the Underground. The bus stop where I could get pretty much anywhere in the city within a half hour. The corner market and coffee shop. The synagogue just fifteen minutes away. And it was there in London that we decided, instead of going to the synagogue on the anniversary of my family's deaths to honor them, we'd go on their birthdays—to celebrate their arrivals instead of their departures.

As we walked arm in arm under our umbrellas that Monday morning on our way to work, I enjoyed the moment. The new and improved Elsa had arrived. Did it take an ocean and a country to get me there? Maybe. But it didn't matter. Finally after all these years, it was okay to laugh again. It was okay to love again. And, it was more than okay to live again.

Alexei kissed me good-bye, and I boarded the bus. On the way, I pulled out my notepad and wrote my first letter from London.

July 7, 1997

Dear Laura,

Happy 4th of July! Although now that I'm officially a Brit, I shouldn't say that too loud! Alexei didn't want me to start working yet. He wanted me to get acclimated and have fun. But I've worked my entire life and not having a job would drive me crazy. So when I insisted, he called a few of his connections and within a month, I found a job at an architectural firm. It's a great one, and I'm pinching myself.

Other than the weather, which could be better, I love it here. I've been wondering if that's how you feel about St. Petersburg. That it's all great, except for the weather. It's wonderful to see Alexei every day and to have a home together. I love the flat, and the neighborhood is great. He wants to get something bigger, but it's so cozy. Everything is within walking distance and the Underground is a five-minute walk. To get to work, I hop on the bus and I'm there in twenty minutes. Could it be any better?

I look back and realize if you hadn't talked me into coming for a visit, I would have never met Alexei. So many things in life we plan for or hope for never happen, and then, we're surprised with the unexpected. Remember, it was after Millie died and you encouraged me to come to Russia. At the time, I just really wanted to lie on the beach somewhere, but on a whim, I took your advice. And it so happened he was on the same plane. What were the chances? And what were the chances that it would work out? So thank you. I'll never forget the visit and how we yelled at each other on Red Square. Not one of my finer moments. I was not at all in a good place. You recognized it and weren't shy about giving me advice. Let's just say I'm glad it's behind us. Remember before you left for St. Petersburg, you said you wanted to read Tolstoy in Russian? I'm sure you've done that and more by now.

Say hi to David and, if you can, please come for a visit soon. I'd love to show you around, and Alexei wants to take you to some of the castles and small towns around the city.

Love and kisses,
Mom

I folded the letter and put it in the envelope, holding onto it while watching the stops through the window. With umbrella in tow and my raincoat on, I hopped off the bus a stop early. At the post office, several cards caught my eye for Susan, Matt and Greg, and a few more to Jay and the girls at the office at my old job.

We inched up the line and a young man twirled his keys in front of me. He wore a khaki overcoat and when he turned around, his resemblance to Max surprised me. But the memory didn't take me back to those early days and all the missing years. The man I loved so long ago lived on in Laura—and now his adventurous side lived on in me. I took a chance on London and on Alexei, just like my daughter had asked of me right after the wedding.

When my turn came up in line, I handed the letter and postcards to the attendant and sent them on their way. I walked out and held the door as a woman closed her umbrella and tapped the water from the end. It was a horrible day, the eighth one in a row filled with rain. The weather had been known to put people, especially the tourists, in bad moods for weeks on end, but not me. I dodged a few puddles on my way to the office and, before entering the building, looked up and could tell the sun was about to make its way through.

A Note From the Author

Thank you for reading *The Secret We Lost*. I'm so grateful you picked my novel when there are so many books out there from which to choose. It was a labor of love and an emotional story to tackle. Many parts were hard to write, and I sometimes took breaks to watch cute pet videos. For me, it was important to tell Elsa's story and how it must have felt for someone to be sandwiched between two generations and caring for both—all while dealing with a life-long tragedy that hung over her.

Even though my story is fiction, I, like my character Laura, spent time in Russia teaching English. I left my job—and my home—for an adventure. Yes, it was risky to quit a full-time job, but sometimes in life, we just have to go for it, not knowing what the outcome will be. My experience turned out much differently from Laura's, but we have something in common: It taught us some great life lessons that we'll never forget.

And finally, thank you again for choosing my book and escaping with my words and characters. You probably already know this but, just in case, word of mouth is an author's best friend. If you liked *The Secret We Lost*, please spread the word. And if you have the time, I'd be grateful if you left a review on Amazon. It really helps readers decide what to read next.

All my best,
Linda

Acknowledgments

The Secret We Lost is my second published novel, but it's not the second book I've written. I wrote the first draft years ago, put it in my virtual drawer, and turned my attention to *Among the Branded*, which became my debut novel. Over the years, *The Secret We Lost* persevered through rewrites, revisions, and reimagined scenes. And through it all, the awesome people on these next pages helped me get there.

Evgeny, thank you for being my first reader and reading the book more than once! You always pushed me to work harder to write the best possible story—but you did so with such encouraging words. Thank you for your love and support.

Libby Tripp Cox, Marla Greif, Jennifer Schulman, and Jill Yager: Thank you for sticking it out to read yet another book of mine! You reviewed my early (and not-quite-ready) drafts and gave me invaluable feedback. I'm blessed to have you all in my life.

Collaborating with editor Nicole Tone again was an amazing experience. She had me working overtime on all aspects, from setting to character development. Nicole, you helped me dig deeper than I'd planned—or even thought I could—on an emotional level.

Kate Olson, my critique reader, was priceless in the process and a dream to work with. Kate, you really helped me improve my novel—when I thought it was actually ready! Your keen eye for dialogue, transitions, and the little details I overlooked blew me away. And when it was all said (or actually written) and done, Faith Williams made sure everything looked good during the proofreading stage.

When I published my debut novel, I had the opportunity to connect with several book bloggers and continue to do so. I'm grateful to those who have welcomed me and my work with open arms. There's one in particular, Christina Huber, who runs the Tomes & Tequila blog. Christina, you have been one of my biggest cheerleaders from the start, and I'm happy to call you a friend. A big thank-you also goes out to Anne Cater and Barbara Bos for supporting me and the writing community.

Speaking of cheerleaders, Rosalie A. Lacorazza, Christine Chirichella, Elyse Cooper, and Beth Falk: You ladies have also been part of my cheering section with absolutely no nudging—and it has warmed my heart. I'm so grateful for your support and friendships. Rosalie, thanks also for working "behind the scenes" and hooking me up with Judith McAuley who helped with the German translations. Thank you, Judith! And I can't forget Kimberly Brower, Aimee Ashcraft, and the team at Brower Literary & Management: Thank you so much for all your hard work on my behalf.

Authors Allison Winn Scotch, Rochelle Weinstein, and Edwin Fontánez: As always, your great advice about the publishing business has been a lifesaver! Thanks for letting me bounce ideas off of you when making many decisions. And thank you to family, friends, and colleagues: Your interest and encouragement helped me cross the finish line.

Aleksander, you've got a ton of talent and creativity running through your veins. Thank you for a beautiful cover design and for not rolling your eyes while we worked together—even when I became (a bit) demanding.

Mikhail and Galina: Your love and support for me always shines through. Thanks for always asking when my next book will be ready and when you can read it. I hope I've made you proud like the first time around.

And my parents: I miss hearing your voices, seeing your smiles, and laughing at your silly jokes. My strong will and determination come from you. Without these traits, I would have given up on becoming a published novelist long ago.

About the Author

Linda Smolkin always wanted to be a writer—ever since she saw her first TV commercial and wondered how to pen those clever ads. She got her degree in journalism and became a copywriter. Linda landed a job at an ad agency, where she worked for several years before joining the nonprofit world. For more information, visit her website at lindasmolkin.com.

Also by Linda Smolkin

Among the Branded

Praise for Among the Branded:
"Perhaps the best part of this book is the wonderful friendship between Izzy and Steph, not to mention the rest of her family. While the circumstances that brought them all together are tragic, the resulting relationships are priceless. This is a beautiful and fascinating novel that will keep readers hooked."

- *San Francisco Book Review*

"The plot is highly engaging, and the burgeoning friendship between Stephanie and Izzy is heartwarming and intriguing. The book touches on important themes, such as the bonds of family, the overlooked horrors of history, and the lessons they can still teach us today. Linda Smolkin shows off her storytelling skills in *Among the Branded*, and the power and gravitas of the story make this a successful and enjoyable tale."

- *SPR*

"*Among the Branded* offers something for everyone. The book reads easily and the supporting characters are interesting and believable. The story of Steph and Izzy will keep the reader engaged throughout and, without giving away too much, the story reaches a satisfactory conclusion while delivering a clear message."

- *Awesome Indies*

Also by Linda Smolkin

Among the Branded

Praise for Among the Branded:

"Perhaps the best part of this book is the wonderful friendship between Izzy and Steph, not to mention the rest of her family. While the circumstances that brought them all together are tragic, the resulting relationships are priceless. This is a beautiful and fascinating novel that will keep readers hooked."

- *San Francisco Book Review*

"The plot is highly engaging, and the burgeoning friendship between Stephanie and Izzy is heartwarming and intriguing. The book touches on important themes, such as the bonds of family, the overlooked horrors of history, and the lessons they can still teach us today. Linda Smolkin shows off her storytelling skills in *Among the Branded*, and the power and gravitas of the story make this a successful and enjoyable tale."

- *SPR*

"*Among the Branded* offers something for everyone. The book reads easily and the supporting characters are interesting and believable. The story of Steph and Izzy will keep the reader engaged throughout and, without giving away too much, the story reaches a satisfactory conclusion while delivering a clear message."

- *Awesome Indies*

Made in the USA
Columbia, SC
02 February 2021